SEASHELLS AND WEDDING BELLS

CAROLINA COVE
BOOK 2

KAY LYONS

KINDRED SPIRITS PUBLISHING

CHAPTER ONE

adley Masterson pulled to a stop outside the funeral home and prayed for God to strike her dead.

She didn't *want* to die. But dead would be a whole lot easier than walking in that door alone. And once she was inside? She had little chance at escaping unnoticed.

Truth be told, she'd much rather take her chances with a forgiving Maker than her mother.

Was that bad?

She closed her eyes and shook her head at herself. She was a forty-five-year-old woman who quivered in fear at the thought of facing a woman once crowned the island's Mermaid Queen.

Yeah, well, it didn't have to be like this, did it, Haddie? Why did you wait so long? Lie?

She fisted her hands in frustration and tried to mentally find her bootstraps.

What had seemed like a good idea at the time was now a nightmare, and wishes and wants would get her nowhere. When the time was right, she had to break the news. Somehow.

Hadley got out of the car and fought the urge to dive back in and make a break for it while she could. Squealing away from the funeral home like a NASCAR driver? Her?

But what kind of granddaughter didn't pay her respects? Especially to her namesake?

Hadley inhaled and fussed with the straps of her purse as she slowly approached the entrance.

She'd chosen her funeral clothes with the utmost care and wore a black pencil skirt and a sleeveless black top with a bit of white piping around the half-inch ruffled collar, the strand of pearls and studs she'd received from Nan on her thirteenth birthday, and paired it all with two-inch wedges because, as her mother always said, open-toes and sand just didn't do.

Hadley paused on the sidewalk when her ears picked up the distinct sound of Calypso music.

Surely the music had to be coming from somewhere else?

She turned her head, looking up and down the

street for some sign of an outdoor band or restaurant. Because Calypso music? For a funeral?

For the first time since she'd left Raleigh, Hadley smiled as a huff of a laugh left her.

Oh, Nan, you didn't!

Mrs. Georgia Hadley Benson had died in her sleep at the youthful age of ninety-two, a spitfire of a woman and the last of the Boardwalk Babes' parents.

During the summers of '58 and '59, Georgia, along with three of her prominent Carolina Cove neighbors and friends, had given birth to a baby girl. One even had a set of twins.

The proud mothers had taken the babes for daily strolls in their prams—and the locals had nicknamed them the Boardwalk Babes—a name used to this day by the now sixty-somethings who'd gone on to have their own children.

All in all, Hadley had four pseudo aunts and ten "cousins," seven female—with the twin Babes each having a set of twins of their own—and three male, ranging in age from Hadley's forty-five to the youngest at thirty-two.

The funeral home's ornate door swung open, and sure enough, Mighty Sparrow blasted from within.

Apparently Nan's last act was to go to heaven with a good old-fashioned beach party. Haddie could only imagine her mother's mortification, and despite her own horror at having to go inside, she smiled at her grandmother's moxie.

She really needed to find her own. Fast.

Hadley stopped as an older man surged through the doors, the smell of Old Spice and cheap cigars drifting to her nose. He tipped an imaginary hat, his triple chins bobbing as he hurried along down the stairs.

The door shut once more, and she paused on the steps, hand gripping the white vinyl railing as though that alone would anchor her in the turbulent storm beyond.

Go in. Sign the book. Sneak out as quickly and quietly as possible.

Maybe they wouldn't even notice?

Yeah, what were the odds of that?

She shoved her shoulder-length hair behind her ear and then just as quickly loosened it when her mother's voice sounded in her head telling her it would deform her ears and she'd have to have them surgically pinned or else look like Dumbo.

Amazing what years of fussing could do to a grown woman, no matter her age.

Cheryl Dummit was all about appearances, though, and Hadley couldn't remember a time when her mother hadn't been put together like a perfectly dressed Barbie and expected Hadley be the same.

Even a trip to the beach was expected to be made in full makeup, some kind of flowing coverup that perfectly matched her suit, wedges, floppy hat, and jewelry. All part of portraying the perfect image of a Babe on the beach.

Haddie took another breath and forced herself to climb the remaining steps, heart in her throat as she yanked open the door and forced her foot across the threshold before she could change her mind.

She'd gotten a stress headache on the drive to the coast, and the cloying smell of the many flower arrangements threatened to turn the painful throbbing into a full-blown migraine.

A waiter passed with a tray of champagne, and since she wasn't about to look a gift horse in the mouth, she hastily accepted the offer and turned to face the wall while she gulped it down, all in an attempt to brace herself for the moment her mother and the rest of the Babes realized she'd come alone.

Oh, the horror.

Hadley set the now empty flute aside and lingered in the shadowy corner, taking in the many mourners gathered. Only Nan would or could get by with throwing a party in the very conservative funeral parlor.

But then, Nan and her friends, then the Babes,

had pretty much always gotten away with whatever they wanted.

The ladies believed there wasn't much that couldn't be accomplished with a bright smile, a few compliments, and some well-practiced feminine wiles. And if that didn't work, throwing some money at the problem usually did the trick—though was rarely necessary.

One wouldn't think Carolina Cove fancy enough for such an elite group—it wasn't Wrightsville Beach after all—but the families' longevity and reputations carried a lot of clout on the little island. More so when all five of the Babes wed into well-to-do families and thereby increased the status quo up until the last twenty years or so, when tourists began buying up all of the island real estate and muddying the waters, so to speak.

The original boardwalk homes were now owned by the Babes, with Hadley's generation scattered about, away from the Babes' nosy reach. To spy on their kids, the Babes had to really do some digging more often than not.

Yes, this generation left the Babes shaking their motherly heads. Because of their eleven offspring, only *three* had married so far, much to their complete disgruntlement, disbelief, and matchmaking efforts.

But out of sight didn't equate to out of mind, and

the Babes made a point of nosing into their children's lives as often as humanly possible, distance notwithstanding.

Hadley spotted yet another waiter, this one carrying a cheese tray. She really ought to eat something to absorb the bubbly she'd just chugged, but her nerves wouldn't allow it.

Ever since the phone call informing her of Nan's death, Hadley had run the gamut of emotions due to the required trip back to Carolina Cove and the grief that continuously sucked the air from her lungs at random moments.

Maybe she should've made an excuse? Claimed sickness?

I'm sorry, Nan. You know it's not you. My life won't be the same without you.

Hadley spotted the guestbook and slowly moved that way. Pen in hand, she paused. Lah, why did everything about this have to be so difficult?

Pen poised over the paper, she finally signed her name.

Her name, no one else's.

"Haddie? Is that you?"

The feminine voice belonged to Mary Elizabeth —Allie, Sophia, and Isabel's mother.

Allie was the only other Babe offspring who had married, and Hadley wondered how things were going with them. The last time she'd seen Allie, the poor girl looked stressed, but then, what mother didn't?

Smile pinned to her lips, Hadley turned and faced the striking woman. Mary Elizabeth wore black slacks that showcased her slim figure, kitten heels, and a long-sleeved sweater set that mocked the eighty-seven-degree temperature outside. "MeMe, how are you?"

"Oh, honey, how are *you*? I'm so sorry about your nan. Your mama will be thrilled to see you. She's just heartbroken."

"I'm sure." Nan's relationship with her daughter had been as rocky as Hadley's with her mother, proving generational dysfunction was really a thing. What was it with mothers and daughters? Why did they always butt heads?

Hadley's relationship with her own daughter oftentimes proved difficult, more so than with Hadley and her son.

"Where's that handsome husband of yours? Already at the bar? And where are the kids?" Mary Elizabeth asked, looking all around.

The questions brought Hadley back to awareness, and even though she wanted to laugh at the idea of a bar at a funeral, she inhaled and braced herself for the first of many explanations. "The kids started college a few days ago and are over their heads with that, and...Kyle... He... He's the guest lecturer at a surgical convention," she said.

It wasn't a lie. The kids had told her Kyle had been asked to speak at a prestigious banquet and would be out of town all week.

With *her*.

"Oh, Hadley, you're alone? I'm so sorry, hon."

"I'm fine," Hadley said, wishing she had another glass of champagne if for no other reason than to give her hands something to hold to stop the tremor she was forced to try to hide.

Mary Elizabeth enveloped Hadley in a hug, and she counted backwards in an attempt to maintain her composure. It felt good to be hugged by someone who'd loved her literally her whole life. Too good because the ever-present tears quickly formed and threatened to overflow.

Amazing how such a simple gesture could open up a tidal wave of emotions.

"You're not. But no worries. I'm here for you," Mary Elizabeth said when she finally released Hadley. "Come on. Let's get you something to drink."

Hadley nodded and thanked God for the reprieve even though she knew it would be short-lived. Mary Elizabeth might be satisfied with

Hadley's excuses, but when her mother found out Kyle wasn't there?

More questions were coming. The too probing kind.

Hadley smiled when Mary Elizabeth linked their arms and began the slow, ambling shuffle through the throng of guests. The flutes weren't far from reach, and even though she knew she ought to pass given her empty stomach and the one she'd already had, Hadley gratefully accepted a second glass.

"Your mama is in with Ms. Georgia. Come on, I'll walk you."

"Oh, do we have to?" The words slipped out before she could stop them, and she saw Mary Elizabeth's gaze narrow.

"Hadley? Oh, honey, what's wrong?"

Hadley's expression must have given her away. Or maybe it was that, of all the Babes, including her own mother, Haddie was closest to Mary Elizabeth. "Nothing. Sorry, yes, of course, let's go in."

"Wait. Hadley, what is it? What's going on?"

"Nothing. I'm fine, I'm just... It's Nan. I don't... I don't want to think of her that way, I guess. The image. I-I'm okay, though. Really."

Mary Elizabeth's expression made it clear she saw more than Hadley wanted her to.

Hadley wet her lips and tried again. "MeMe, please just... I can't talk about it. Not here. Definitely not now."

Sadness darkened Mary Elizabeth's gaze, but she nodded and mustered a reassuring smile for Hadley.

"I see. Well, today is about Ms. Georgia, so let's focus on her for the time being and leave that talk for later. Shall we?"

Hadley nodded at the question and took a fortifying sip of the bubbly. "Thank you," she said softly, "even though Mama probably won't agree."

"Oh, Cheryl can be trying but we've got her number after all of these years. You leave it to me."

Mary Elizabeth patted Hadley's arm and turned to lead the way through the throng of mourners once more.

Hadley spied her mother at the end of the long receiving line, looking as regal as ever with her hair swept back in an elegant twist, the skirt of her black suit the perfect length.

Hadley felt older than her mother at this stage. Maybe she should've paid more attention to those lectures on proper skin care.

"Haddie, will you be staying in town tonight after the service?"

Hadley's grip on Mary Elizabeth's arm tightened. "No."

"I see. You're worrying me, sweetheart. I feel you trembling, and while I know you're upset over your grandmother's passing, I'm not convinced that's the reason for your distress."

Hadley closed her eyes for a long second before opening them again, staring at the ugly little dots in the carpet beneath her feet. "It's not. Kyle..."

She couldn't say the words aloud. She just couldn't. Even though Mary Elizabeth was the one person Hadley knew she could trust to be supportive.

"I see. I take it your mama will be upset with whatever it is that brought you here alone?" Mary Elizabeth asked.

Hadley struggled to breathe and shifted her gaze to the woman beside her. "Oh, you know Mama."

"Well, just remember, if you need an escape, my house is always open."

An escape. Yeah, she needed an escape. But the sooner she left Carolina Cove, the better.

MARY ELIZABETH SHIPLEY held tight to Hadley's arm, painfully aware of her goddaughter's quivering form.

Across the room, she locked gazes with her

husband and gave him a slight shake of her head, indicating her suspicions had been right. She'd told Adam for a while now that she just knew something was wrong where Hadley was concerned. And Hadley showing up to Miss Georgia's funeral alone and quaking in her heels was proof positive something was amiss—not that Mary Elizabeth wanted to be right about this.

"Oh," Hadley said, the word a tearful gasp.

"Your grandmother is still the most beautiful woman in the room," Mary Elizabeth said softly, patting Haddie's hand.

"She is, isn't she?"

The raw emotion in Haddie's voice brought fresh tears to Mary Elizabeth's eyes, and she hurried to blink them back. Ms. Georgia had been such a mainstay in her life, but today was about Hadley and Cheryl's loss, not hers. "Georgia is someone we all hope to embody at her age. Do you know she volunteered at the center and then had lunch with her friends up until the day she passed? Georgia lived, right up until the very end. We can only pray to be so blessed."

Hadley nodded and extracted herself to search in her purse for a tissue.

"Here you go," Mary Elizabeth said, pulling one of the many tissues she'd tucked up her sleeve.

A laugh bubbled out of Hadley's chest at the sight, and Mary Elizabeth smiled at the sound, glad she could offer a bit of amusement at such a time.

"Thank you."

Mary Elizabeth watched as Hadley dabbed at her eyes, and once she'd collected herself, they began their trek toward the front of the line once again. The thick crowd made it difficult to move more than a step or two without someone blocking their way.

Finally they made it and Hadley smiled at her mother and stepped forward to hug her. Standing so close, Mary Elizabeth heard Cheryl whisper, "You're late."

Mary Elizabeth frowned at her best friend, but Cheryl purposely ignored the pointed look to back off and not be so critical. "Hadley's here now. That's all that matters."

"Hadley, it's so good to see you," Mr. DeCamp said, standing near Cheryl and the next to make his condolences. "Though I hate that it's under these circumstances."

Hadley nodded and greeted the longtime family friend before she took position beside her mother to receive the mourners.

"I wish someone would turn down that ridiculous music," Cheryl said.

"Oh, that's Georgia's favorite." The older woman

who'd spoken leaned in to give Hadley a hug before moving on to Cheryl. "Georgia *loved* going on those Caribbean cruises. Told us all about them."

The woman was dressed in nurse's scrubs, and Mary Elizabeth watched as Cheryl practically wrinkled her nose right then and there with the woman looking on. No doubt Cheryl expected everyone to be "funeral" dressed no matter the circumstances rather than prioritizing the fact the woman had undoubtedly waited quite a while before heading to work or coming from a long shift just to pay her respects.

"I'm sure. Thank you for coming," Cheryl managed to say to the woman when it was her turn. She extended her hand despite the woman taking a step forward to hug Cheryl like she had Hadley.

An awkward few seconds passed before the woman shook Cheryl's hand and continued on her way.

Hadley's father walked up and kissed his daughter's cheek before placing a supportive hand at his wife's waist. Mary Elizabeth watched Jerry make the gesture with a tug of pity.

Cheryl was a good person, but she was very set in wanting things to be done her way. Today was a difficult day, one Georgia had made more trying due to her individualistic choices and secret last requests, knowing full well the tizzy they'd send her only daughter into. But that was the type of relationship they'd had. One filled with equal shares of love and quarrels.

Leaving the small family to their duties, Mary Elizabeth turned away and made her way over to the back of the funeral home where the other Babes stood talking.

"How's Cheryl holding up?" Tessa asked, her dangly earrings swinging beneath her short-cropped, salt-and-pepper hair.

"As well as expected, I guess," Mary Elizabeth said.

"Oh, I just noticed Haddie finally arrived," Adaline said, peering over her twin's shoulder. "My. She's lost weight since I saw her last."

Rayna Jo shushed her sister and Adaline shrugged.

"It's the truth. Looking downright peaked if you ask me," she said, still staring.

Mary Elizabeth had noticed the change as well. Not because Hadley had ever been heavy but because her average frame had gotten noticeably thinner. "I think she's as beautiful as always."

"No one's arguing that," Rayna Jo said. "Has she been dieting? I heard people lose a lot on that keto one."

"Or maybe she finally decided to test out Kyle's office equipment?" Tessa said. "Where *is* Kyle, anyway? I've been wanting to talk to him."

"Haven't you had enough lifts and tucks for the time being? You and Cheryl are making the rest of us look bad," Adaline said with a lift of her Botox-less eyebrow.

"I beg your pardon, but who made you the cosmetic police?" Tessa's blinged-out earrings flashed despite the dimmed interior of the funeral home. "Besides, if Hadley can use Kyle's little machines to lose weight, why shouldn't I take advantage of his expertise as well?"

"Don't you mean the family discount?" Adaline muttered loud enough for all to hear.

"No one said she's done any such thing," Mary Elizabeth chided in a low voice, more than ready to come to Hadley's defense.

"True. And let's forget Hadley for a moment. You're going after number four, aren't you?" Adaline said to Tessa. "Before every husband, you run off for a 'retreat' and come back looking ten years younger."

Mary Elizabeth watched as the only single Babe shrugged and smiled like the cat who'd swallowed the canary.

Tessa wore a dress twenty years too young for her sixty-two-year-old body, but she pulled it off due to the hours of yoga and running she did on a daily basis. But Tessa and Cheryl were also alike in that they had a whole slew of regimes they performed when it came to skin and hair, not to mention surgical, and would die chasing the fountain of youth.

The tallest and thinnest of the group, Tessa had divorced one husband and buried two, with a child to show for each of them. But after four years as a widow, apparently the tide had turned yet again.

"Look out, Carolina Cove," Rayna Jo said, smiling as she lifted her champagne flute.

"Is there a particular someone you have in mind?" Adaline asked.

"Does this have anything to do with you and Bruce?" Mary Elizabeth asked. Bruce Holloway was Tessa's first husband, and the two had been seen hanging out quite a bit lately after Tessa had had a close call with a con artist.

"Perhaps," Tessa said.

"Really? Why the change of heart?" Mary Elizabeth asked.

"Lord knows why any of us would take on a new man at this age," Adaline added.

"Technically he's not new," Tessa said, earning an eye roll from Adaline. "And I had my doubts as well, but he isn't the stranger who came back from Viet Nam. Thank God."

Mary Elizabeth watched how Tessa glanced toward the front of the room, and her expression softened, her gaze saddened.

"Besides, if you really want to know, Ms. Georgia got me thinking. I realized she's been alone the last *thirty* years. If I have another thirty to go, I'd like to spend them with someone special."

Mary Elizabeth managed a smile at her friend's statement. Tessa had suffered more than her share of heartache.

"Well, I say there are no guarantees. You might feel just as lonely as you do right now," Adaline said. "Maybe you should focus on simply widening your social circle and going out with friends more?"

Mary Elizabeth's gaze landed on Rayna Jo before shifting to Adaline. One night not so long ago, Rayna Jo had confided in Mary Elizabeth, sharing her concern that her twin seemed a little too keen on the attention one of their new male clients was doling out. Was Adaline speaking from experience?

"I'm going to go check on the caterers," Rayna Jo said.

"I need a trip to the ladies' room before I go track down Hugh. I'll come with you," Adaline added.

The sisters walked away and Mary Elizabeth felt Tessa studying her.

"Where's Adam?" Tessa asked.

"Hmm? Oh, he was here but had to step out. He'll be back though."

"Business?" Tessa said.

Mary Elizabeth nodded. It seemed Adam worked longer hours now than he had fresh out of law school. But part of the reason was that their wealthy neighbors knew he worked from home a lot and liked the convenience of an attorney capable of handling their business from the convenience of the beach.

"Hey, are you sure you're okay?" Tessa asked.

Mary Elizabeth nodded, her gaze locked on Hadley's strained features. Her goddaughter was miserably unhappy, and Mary Elizabeth's mind whirled with possibilities, none of them pleasant. "I'm fine. Just tired. It's been a long couple of days, hasn't it?" She linked their arms and gently tugged, ready for a distraction herself. "Let's go get some champagne and talk more about Bruce, shall we?"

CHAPTER TWO

That evening after the service and burial, Hadley sat in Adam Shipley's beautiful home office along the Carolina Cove boardwalk facing the Atlantic in complete shock.

When her mother had insisted they go to see Mary Elizabeth's husband before Hadley returned to Raleigh, she should've known something was up. But this? "You're saying it's... *mine?*"

"Yes. Georgia listed you as the sole heir to everything. Her house, bank accounts. With the economic downturn, the amount isn't what it once was, but the long and short of it is that you are now a wealthy woman," he said, peering through the glasses perched on his nose as he read the papers in front of him and gave her the staggering amount. "Congratulations. And welcome to the neighborhood once again," Adam said, a gentle smile on his craggy features.

Hadley felt as though she was out of her body, floating in the room, watching herself as glanced at her parents and found them looking at her expectantly, pleased smiles on their faces. "You *knew* about this?"

"Of course," Cheryl said. "We have a home we love just a few doors down and are fine financially, so after some discussion, Mama decided to bestow it on you, though I'm not sure why she only listed you. Will Kyle be upset?"

"I-It's fine," Hadley said quickly. "I-I mean, it's not something that has to be addressed right now."

"I suppose that's true. As to your getting the house and money, Mother and I agreed it was the best inheritance she could give us since it would bring you, Kyle, and the kids here more often."

"Time flies," her father said in a sage tone. "Retirement will be here before you know it. And living at the beach is a good way to get your children to come visit, though, truth be told, that hasn't been the case for our own the last couple of years."

Oh, if they only knew. But now wasn't the time to tell them. Not on a day like today. "I-I know, Dad. I'm sorry. Things... Things have been crazy w-with the kids in sports and graduating and going off to college, a-and Kyle's practice." *And his after-hours activities.*

"We completely understand. But *now* you'll have even more reason to come visit since you own the property," her mother added. "Oh, I do wish Kyle could've been here with you to hear the news in person. We should call him right now and—"

Adam cleared his throat and drew everyone's attention back to him.

"We're not finished," Adam said to Cheryl. "Hadley, I'm sorry for your loss," Adam said, "but let me assure you Georgia was thrilled to be able to do this for you. There is quite a bit of paperwork for you to sign for the transfers, but I hope it gives you comfort that you'll be taken care of."

Hadley stared into Adam's kind eyes and realized... He *knew.*

Oh, Lord, have mercy. As an attorney handling the transfer of the estate, he would've... *Really?*

Her stomach knotted up so fast and tight she felt ill.

"Her last request, as it were," Cheryl said, nodding. "Mama was very specific in *all* of her wishes. Which, by the way, did you *have* to tell Mr. Samson to play that awful music at the funeral home, Adam? It was horribly embarrassing."

Adam chuckled as he got to his feet and rounded

his wide desk. He held out a hand for Hadley to take, and when she did, he gently squeezed her fingers and gave her a packet with the blue wrapped deed. "We'll get the paperwork sorted out after dinner," he said quietly. "Or...next week. Whenever you're ready."

"Thank you," she said, watching as she clenched her fingers over the envelope to keep from meeting Adam's knowing gaze. Her godfather was as sweet as Mary Elizabeth, and right now, one wrong glance and she'd be a puddle of blubbery tears.

"As to the music selection," Adam said to her mother, voice rising to a normal level, "Georgia lit up like a Christmas tree when she made those arrangements. She loved to talk about her honeymoon and all her travels with Ed," he added, referring to Hadley's grandfather. "Her choice of music was a delightful surprise to so many and paired perfectly with the photos of their romance. Think of that, Cheryl."

"It was just so *odd*," her mother muttered. "And hardly suitable for a funeral. I can't believe she chose that over the hymns we'd discussed. And a bar? How am I going to face the ladies' group come Saturday?"

Hadley smiled and lifted a hand to hide the fact. No doubt the hymns were discussed by her mother, but as part of the perfect picture of the perfect funeral, if there was such a thing. But Nan had gotten the last say—as she should have.

Hadley stared down at the papers in her hand, trying to come to terms with all the changes the news brought with it. Relief poured through her, but at the same time, panic overwhelmed. What if she couldn't manage things well? If there wasn't enough money to pay the taxes and bills and insurance on the house? Such a huge gift carried a huge weight of responsibility as well.

"Hadley, Georgia also wanted me to give you this, to be read privately," Adam said, turning to retrieve something from the desk.

The smaller white envelope was addressed to Hadley in Nan's beautiful handwriting and sealed tight. The sight of the elegant, looping cursive brought tears to Hadley's eyes and she hurried to blink them back as she glanced at her mother.

Cheryl looked more than a little curious as to what the letter might say, but Hadley had a feeling she already knew. She tucked it and the deed into her bag, though forcing herself to wait rather than rip the letter open wasn't easy.

She stood when her parents did, legs trembling from the news and shock she'd received.

Oh, she'd thought that maybe she'd receive a small sum as an inheritance since she was Nan's only grandchild, but she'd never expected to inherit the oceanfront property—and funds to cover expenses?

Much needed funds.

She could live, *breathe*, and not worry if she'd lose the roof over her head if one day Kyle woke up and just decided he wouldn't pay the spousal support court-ordered by the state.

"Sweetheart? You're awfully quiet. Are you in shock?" her father asked as he slid an arm around her shoulders.

In unison they turned toward the door to follow Adam and her mother, who continued to complain about Nan's musical choices and party atmosphere for the funeral. "Yes. I have to say that I am."

Her father squeezed her shoulder gently and hugged her close.

"I hope it's a happy shock?"

"Of course, but...Dad..."

Her father paused, a frown pinching his thick eyebrows together.

"What is it, honey?"

"Are you coming, Jerry?" her mother asked. "Mary Elizabeth has dinner waiting for us."

Hadley inhaled and backpedaled in her panic to escape. "Nothing. And I'm sorry but I can't stay. I should've planned better," she said to the group, "but I have to get back to Raleigh."

"I suppose you should get on the road while you can make it home before dark, though I'd hoped you'd call Kyle and convince him to drive down for the weekend," Cheryl said. "To celebrate."

"He's...out of town. Guest lecturing," she added hastily. "He...hated to miss the service for Nan."

"Of course. Tell him we understand. You can't back out of such things at the last minute."

Awkward silence followed her statement because good manners dictated that was exactly what you did when a loved one passed.

"Well, reassure him that it won't be an ordeal," her mother said. "We'll hire people to clean out the house, and—"

"*No*," Hadley said, earning a sharp look from her mother. "I-I mean, it's not necessary. I'd like to do that myself," she said, grasping at the excuse to keep control of the situation.

"Oh, Hadley, really?"

Her mother looked appalled by the idea but Hadley nodded. "Yes. I don't want strangers going through Nan's things. She wouldn't have liked that."

"I agree to that statement but are you sure?" her father asked. "That's going to be quite the task. It's gotten crowded in there. You haven't seen it for a while."

"I'm sure. I want to do it," Hadley said again.

"See, Jerry? I knew giving Hadley the house would get them back to town more often."

Hadley smiled weakly and moved through the Shipleys' lovely home to where Mary Elizabeth straightened an already straight napkin on her beautifully set table. "Mary Elizabeth, thank you for the dinner invitation but I'm going to go."

"You're not staying? Are you sure?" Mary Elizabeth asked, giving Hadley a questioning look of concern.

Hadley hugged Mary Elizabeth, the woman's light perfume as familiar as her own because of the many years spent together. Mary Elizabeth wasn't just her godmother but a second mother and friend. "I am. I...need to process things," she said, relating that Nan had given her the house.

"Oh, congratulations!" Mary Elizabeth said, hugging Hadley again.

"It will be nice having at least one of our children as a neighbor, won't it?" Cheryl said to her friend.

"Absolutely. And I understand about dinner. Of course you need time. Drive safely, and let us know when you get there?"

"I will." Hadley gave everyone another round of hugs and left the house, the evening sun blinding her when she stepped outside. She quickly searched for her sunglasses and propped them on her nose, hurrying toward the car so she could crank up the air. There was absolutely nothing as hot as summer in the south. Even along the coast, where the sea breeze lowered the temperature a few degrees but did nothing for the humidity.

She forced herself to focus as she left the tourist-crowded island, but once she made it halfway to Wilmington, she pulled over into a store parking lot, hands gripping tightly to the wheel as the AC blew like the arctic on her hot face.

She owned a home. Not just any home, either, but Nan's.

It was a priceless, precious gift—but no matter how frugal she was, the taxes alone would eat through the money at a rapid rate, and once the money was gone, how would she ever be able to afford it now?

Hadley shoved the car into Park and grabbed her purse to get to the letter and packet beneath it on the seat.

My dearest Hadley,

I hope my gift is a blessing to you in a time of heartbreak. Yes, I know about you and Kyle. When Adam updated my will, he discovered the news.

I can only imagine your upset and think you didn't tell us—me—because you'd hoped to reconcile.

I pray there was never a time when you thought you couldn't tell us anything, but rather wanted to spare us the pain knowing we might never look at Kyle the same way again. Dear girl, you are fearfully and wonderfully made, and don't you forget it!

I hope it gives you peace to know you have a roof over your head, money in the bank, and a life yet to be lived. Don't let the hurt break you, darling. Make the house your home, do with it what you must, and forge ahead knowing, one way or another, it has weathered many storms and will keep you safe.

My love for eternity,

Nan

Hadley wiped away tears and sat there. Only Nan would've been able to keep her mouth shut all this time. Well, Nan and Adam, whose business it was to keep such things confidential.

There had been so many times, so many phone calls when Hadley had wanted to open up and talk, but she hadn't wanted to upset Nan at her age.

Now she hated that she'd missed out on Nan's wisdom and the comfort she would've offered. "I'm so sorry, Nan," she whispered, voice quivering. "You have no idea how sorry."

After a few minutes of sniffling and staring at the traffic flying by, Hadley pulled out her phone to check her messages, seeing several from the kids. Her older, Max, told her he'd dropped a class but signed up for another to maintain his credits, while her baby, Abby, complained about her roommates.

Hadley sent short messages in return of encouragement and love, but when she started to set the phone aside, she found herself telling Abby she was too tired to drive back and had decided to stay on for a few days. She then copied and pasted the same message to Max.

Her parents would be thrilled, though disappointed that she hadn't made her decision earlier and attended dinner.

But it couldn't be helped. Especially when she wasn't in the mood for social pleasantries. She would text later and let them know.

Hadley didn't mention inheriting the property to the kids, knowing full well the news would be relayed to Kyle. She wasn't sure why she didn't want him to be aware of the gift, but considering her shock, she just felt she needed some time to mull things over before everyone bombarded her with their opinions on what she should do. Kyle included.

Their relationship was strained in every possible way. Contact was kept to a minimum and mostly via text these days, and getting through Ab's graduation a few months ago had been a nightmare, with Abby actually telling Hadley not to attend because she wanted Kyle and the mistress there because the girl-friend wasn't welcome at the graduation party Hadley had planned afterwards.

The rejection from her daughter had broken what was left of her shattered heart, and Hadley had spent the time watching the online stream and prepping for a party that no longer held any of the joy it should have.

A horn blared from the road as a truck cut off another vehicle in front of her, jerking Hadley from the dark path her thoughts had taken. She shook her head to clear it and glanced around to get an idea of where she sat.

Since she hadn't planned to stay, she needed to pick up some things. Wearing anything of Nan's might have been comforting but was out of the question considering their body size and height difference.

Hadley gained her bearings and drove to a local discount store. It didn't take her long to find a couple pairs of shorts and T-shirts, tank tops, pj's, and even a pair of comfortable flip-flops.

Her next stop was a grocery store, where she gathered toiletries and makeup. She also picked up a bottle of wine—and a bottle of champagne.

Inheriting a beach house deserved a little cele-bration, right? After a good night's sleep, maybe she'd call and see if any of the cousins would be available to join her for a real celebration. Why not?

"Do you need help finding something?"

Hadley blinked at the question, only then realizing she hadn't moved out of the alcohol section and had garnered the attention of a grocery employee. "Yeah, actually. I'm celebrating."

"Wonderful! What can I do to help?"

The answer came to her in an instant. "Where's your best chocolate?"

By the time Hadley made it back to Nan's home, the sun had gone down and the lights along the boardwalk glowed with warm familiarity. She paused a moment to stare out at the sight of the moon shining on the water, her heart pinching from the pain of being here, now, alone.

She knew she couldn't live a life of regrets, but if only she'd talked to Nan...come to visit instead of staying away to hide the shame she felt at the failure of her marriage...

Shaking her head, Hadley loaded up the many bags and fished through her key ring, looking for the house key as she made her way to the door.

"Can I help you with something?"

The deep male voice startled her, and she gasped, searching the shadowy darkness beside the house. "H-hello?"

"Over here," the voice said.

She tracked the sound and found the man hidden by the shadows and hedges between the homes.

"Can I help you?" he asked again.

"Uh, no. Thank you," she said, wondering if she needed to make a run for the house or dive into the car to lock the doors. All beach towns had crime, and in Carolina Cove, drunkenness and theft were the norm.

Hadley stood between the house and her car, and she shifted uncomfortably, gripping her keys tighter. She wasn't about to be mugged, was she?

A loud clang made Hadley jump after the man tossed something into the back of a truck parked in the driveway next door. It was just bright enough for her to make out the logo on the side.

The house next to Nan's had sold sometime during the year, but since she hadn't been in to visit, she'd never met the new owners. Obviously they were having some work done. She'd vaguely noticed a dumpster as she'd pulled in but hadn't paid it any mind, until now. "Are you the contractor?"

"Yeah," the man said.

The words lifted some of the stress she felt given the dark and the situation. At least now she knew why he was there. "Nice to, uh, meet you. I'm... I'm the new owner," she said, testing out the words. "Um, Nan's—Georgia's—granddaughter."

"My condolences."

So he did know Nan had passed. "Thank you."

"I didn't see you at the service."

He'd gone? She supposed, given Nan's nature, her grandmother would've made friends with the man if he was around enough. That was just Nan's way. "I was a little late."

"For your grandmother's funeral?"

"I-It couldn't be helped," she said, sounding defensive to her own ears. But who was he to comment one way or another? "Besides, I didn't see you at all."

The words came out of nowhere, and the moment she uttered them, she wanted to yank them back. They sounded... "I mean, at the service."

"I had to leave early."

The man folded his arms over his chest and studied her from across the way. It was difficult for her to see much other than a dark tan, red shirt and cargo shorts, and a dark head of hair with a bit of gray along the sides that glinted in the light whenever he turned his head.

"Well, I won't keep you. Have a good evening."

"Y-you as well." Hadley hurried to the porch,

and in her effort to get away from prying eyes, she unlocked the door and stumbled over the threshold.

Inside wasn't any better.

She'd never been there without Nan, and the fact sucked the air from her lungs for a long moment. Nan always knew when someone pulled in, and any time Hadley had been to visit, her grandmother would open the door, smile in place, and more often than not, oatmeal chocolate chip cookies warm from the oven were waiting to be eaten. How many dozens of cookies had been baked in this house?

She and Nan had that in common, too. Their love of oatmeal chocolate chip cookies. To them it was a crime to throw a raisin into something so delicious, and they'd lamented the fact with every baking.

Hadley froze, her back against the door as she took in the room. Nan's TV tray beside her chair, the throw she'd knitted years ago folded neatly and placed on the arm ready for use. Her favorite rag mags on the side table along with a half-empty bottle of water.

Oh, Nan. What am I going to do without you? I wish I'd known. I wish I'd talked to you about this mess I'm in. I'm so sorry.

Hadley closed her eyes, simply breathing in her grandmother's home. The jasmine-scented air mixed with a hint of lemon furniture polish and that indescribable something that made it Nan's.

Packing her grandmother's things and figuring out the house allowed Hadley the perfect excuse to linger in Carolina Cove, but there would come a point when questions would be asked.

Answers demanded.

But maybe in the next few days she could gather her nerve and come up with a plan for the unavoidable breaking of her parents' hearts and the disappointment that was sure to follow.

CHAPTER THREE

Hadley Masterson hadn't recognized him, and even though it was dark and she probably couldn't see him well enough *to* recognize him, a part of Bryson James was still irritated by the fact.

Bryson hauled remodeling debris out of the house next to Hadley's the following morning, carrying it to the dumpster located in the minuscule side yard. He tossed it in with a noisy clang and, on the way back, noticed movement by the kitchen window next door.

His heart pinched when he thought of sweet Georgia being gone. Normally it was her white-haired head he spotted in that window, followed by her wave to come over for coffee.

He was glad he'd taken the time and made the effort to get to know the elderly woman while he'd had the chance. Georgia had been one of a kind. Short as a minute, as genteel in certain settings as any southern lady could be—and just as ornery. She could outwit him at cards and held a particular passion for flavored moonshine.

What a wonderful surprise she'd been.

The memories of their late-night card games and talks brought a sad smile to his lips. He'd never known his grandmother, and he'd lost his mother when he was fourteen. But Georgia had treated him like her own—another of her "kids," as she liked to call everyone.

Hadley had been a topic during some of those conversations, and Georgia had expressed her worry about her only granddaughter, sharing more than she probably should have about the things Hadley didn't say during their brief telephone conversations. He'd wondered at first if Georgia wasn't reading more into things than she should, but it didn't take long to discover Georgia to be a sharp, perceptive woman. And as such, he'd be lying if he said he wasn't suspicious about Hadley's circumstances himself.

What kind of husband would let his grieving wife travel alone? Stay alone? Where was he? Any man worth his salt should've been at his wife's side, comforting her and being there to support her.

Bryson paused and turned toward the old two-story cottage, wondering what would happen to Georgia's home now. Would Hadley keep it? Spend weekends there with the family who wasn't at her side now? Sell it like so many others on the street when the families realized the profit margin?

From what he'd gathered from Georgia, Hadley was living it up as a plastic surgeon's wife in Raleigh in a big house located in an area where all of the city's prominent people lived. Maybe Carolina Cove was too small town for them? Too touristy?

No doubt Georgia's modest home wasn't up to the good doctor's wife's tastes, even though it was one of the originals that had survived hurricanes Fran and Floyd and Hazel.

Georgia's house had great bones and he'd hate to see it destroyed. Maybe he should go ask? Try to make friendly?

He glanced at his watch. It was plenty late enough in the day to pay a call. And he had seen Hadley inside moving around.

Bryson entered the house long enough to pat the Sheetrock dust from his clothes and wash his hands before heading next door. He cut through the over-grown hedges and crossed the driveway to the walk.

"Oh. Hello."

Bryson looked up and found Hadley on the porch, her slender hands wrapped around a large coffee mug. "Morning. Sorry to bother you but I don't suppose you have another one of those?" he asked, lifting his chin toward the cup and grasping at the excuse. "The electric is off in the house while we get a couple things rewired."

"Oh, um, yeah, sure. I'll...be right back."

So the hired help still didn't get invited into the house, huh? Like mother like daughter, he mused.

Bryson tried and failed to tamp down the irritation he felt at being invisible to certain people. The types who demanded he and his crew only use the rear entrance and looked uncomfortable whenever they saw him in public. Some were worse than others and treated him like a second-class citizen because he was a laborer when, truth be told, he probably had more in the bank than they did with their flashy spending habits.

Thirty years ago, he'd worked every summer for his father, learning how to build and repair.

He remembered getting called to Hadley's parents' for a job, and Bryson had seen Hadley and some other girls from school lounging by the pool. Nothing made it clearer that his teenage summer and hers were polar opposites. Or that he wasn't on par with the Dummits, because Hadley's mother was one of those who'd made them enter through the rear of the house rather than through the front door.

Bryson waited impatiently, watching Hadley through the screen door while she poured a second cup.

And even though it wasn't polite, he stared, taking in all the changes the last twenty-seven years had wrought.

Her sandy-brown hair fell a little below her shoulders in gentle waves, and she wore white shorts with a blue tank top that brought out her blue-green eyes. Eyes he'd noticed were heavily shadowed beneath, with a few fine lines at the corners. She still looked like a young woman, though, and nowhere near her age. For a woman pushing fifty, she looked to be in her thirties.

"Would you like cream and sugar?" she asked, the words carrying over her shoulder toward him.

"No, black is fine. Thanks."

She carried both her coffee and his toward him, and Bryson hurried to open the door for her. "Smells great. Thanks, I appreciate it," he said, accepting the steaming mug from her.

"Of course. Caffeine addicts have to stick together, right?"

He let go of the screen door and it closed with a

gentle bang. "Mind if I take a break and sit with you for a bit?"

She blinked at him once again.

"Uh, sure, if you'd like."

Yeah, not the most welcoming of statements. But was it due to her surprise or because, like her mother, she considered him the hired help?

They made themselves comfortable in the cushioned chairs and sipped their coffee, gazes avoiding each other for the most part.

"I keep thinking you look familiar," Hadley said finally. "Have we met? Before last night, I mean."

He took another sip and nodded. Maybe he shouldn't be irked. It had been a while.

His gaze shifted from the ocean waves in the distance to the beautiful woman sitting in the rocking chair beside the love seat she'd left for him. "We went to school together. Middle and high school."

Seven years in all—and while she might think him familiar, until last night, she'd never said a word to him.

"Oh." Color flooded her cheeks. "I apologize. I'm sorry, I-I don't... I'm *horrible* with faces. Please, don't take offense."

"We didn't run in the same crowd." So what was his excuse for remembering her?

He told himself not to go there, because after that fateful trip to her house with his father to repair a door at their pool house, he'd had more than a few teenage fantasies. The kind where she looked at him and actually saw him. Was friendly and flirtatious.

Hadley had been in a league of her own, one of the popular rich kids whose parents owned ocean-front homes and got cars for their sweet sixteens. She'd played lacrosse and was a cheerleader and an all-American girl, while he'd been invisible, working every minute of his spare time, trying to earn enough pocket cash to afford something that could eventually get him off the school bus. "I'm Bryson James."

"Bryson," she said in greeting. "That seems like a lifetime ago. I suppose it *was* a lifetime ago. Wow."

Two sips later, Bryson broached the subject of the house. "Look, Hadley, I don't mean to overstep, especially in light of how recent Ms. Georgia passed, but I was wondering what you plan to do with her home?"

Hadley's beautiful gaze was the color of the Atlantic in front of them, a mixture of blues and greens surrounded by a dark blue rim. She didn't wear makeup at the moment, and he liked her looking fresh-faced. It made her more approachable. Less...hardened?

"Oh. I, uh, haven't really given it much thought. I

wasn't expecting to inherit it, and the shock really hasn't worn off yet since I'd only found out about an hour or so before I saw you last night. Why do you ask?"

"This is a great house," he said simply. "I'd hate to see it bought up and torn down like so many of the older homes here on the island."

"I would, too."

"So you plan to keep it?"

She opened her mouth to speak, but gravel crunched in her driveway and drew her attention.

"Oh, no," she murmured, closing her eyes and sitting forward in her seat.

"Something wrong?" The older woman in the Mercedes sedan didn't exactly look threatening. Though she was giving him the stink-eye now that she'd spotted him. Wait, was that—

"My mother," Hadley said, slowly uncurling her legs from the rocking chair to stand.

Bryson got to his feet, remembering Cheryl Dummit well from that hot summer day way back when.

He waited beside Hadley as the woman exited the car and approached them on the porch, walking as though she wore a book on her head like he'd seen in some movies.

She looked dressed for a ladies' luncheon or something equally pretentious, her long necklace flashing in the sunlight over a dark red blouse and perfectly pressed pants. The kind that should've been wrinkled after sitting but wasn't even though it was a muggy eighty-four already. Wasn't she roasting in that getup?

"Hi, Mom."

The woman greeted her daughter with a stiff hug, never taking her eyes off of Bryson.

"Hadley, you have company?"

"Bryson came over for a cup of coffee. The electric is off next door."

"I see."

"Bryson—I'm sorry, what was your last name again?"

"James," he said, wondering how many times he'd have to introduce himself for Hadley to remember.

"I'm sorry. I'm truly horrible with names. Cheryl Dummit, Bryson James. Bryson, my mother."

"Nice to meet you, ma'am."

The woman's cold smile didn't reach her eyes.

"Mom, would you like some coffee?" Hadley asked.

"No, thank you. I just wanted to check on you. I

was surprised when I woke up to see your text that you'd returned to town but didn't stop back by the house."

"I know. I should've texted earlier, but I had to stop and pick up some things and then get settled here. I was tired, but I texted you before I went to bed."

Bryson listened, intently aware of Cheryl's gaze sizing him up and finding him sorely lacking. "Ladies, if you'll excuse me, I have work to do. Thanks for the coffee," he said to Hadley.

"Take it with you. You can return the cup later."

He lifted the mug with a grateful nod and managed a smile. "Nice to meet you, Mrs. Dummit. Hadley. Enjoy your day, ladies."

Bryson left the porch and was almost to the hedges between the homes when he heard Cheryl speak.

"Hadley, what on earth is going on? Who was that man?"

HADLEY LED the way into the house, every creak of the aged floor reminding her that Nan's house was strong and resilient like she'd stated in the letter.

The boards were worn from years of use and the grit of sand but lovely in their aged patina. So much so, when her mother tried to get Nan to update them several years ago, Hadley had sided with Nan that there was something special about them just like they were.

Maybe she needed to take a few notes from the floorboards, because through hurricanes and king tides, they might have changed, but they'd weathered the storms and turned out even more beautiful because of it. Even the slightly warped, squeaky ones.

"*Hadley?*"

Hadley blinked and forced herself to focus. Especially since her mother's tone made it clear she wasn't giving up. What were they talking about? Oh, yeah. "He's working next door."

"And you just invited him *in?*"

Hadley faced the cabinets in the kitchen and rolled her eyes, because she knew her mother couldn't see her. "I didn't invite him in, he sat on the porch."

"I don't like it, and I'm quite sure Kyle wouldn't like it either. You shouldn't be entertaining men, much less men like that, especially when you're here alone."

A huff left her, and Hadley turned, her hands

gripping the countertop on either side of her hips. "I wasn't *entertaining* him."

"He'll get the wrong idea, Hadley. They think all well-to-do women are lonely and bored and looking for a side piece. It's a game to them."

Taken aback, Hadley stared. "Wow," she said, unable to believe she'd just heard her mother use that expression.

Her mother huffed and shot Hadley a quelling glare.

"You know I'm right. You need to be careful. What if someone said something to Kyle?"

Hadley forced herself to stay calm. *Kyle* couldn't care less since he was too busy chasing someone half his age. "Can we please change the subject?"

"Just remember what I said."

"Okay, Mom, point taken."

"So what are your plans? I dropped by to check on you and ask if you needed help today, but since you said you *weren't* staying in town, I have yet to cancel my plans."

"I'm just going to wander through the house and make a few lists. You go and enjoy your day."

"You're sure?"

That she didn't want her mother hovering over her, lecturing her all day? "Positive."

"Perhaps I'll stop by again later. If not, come to

the house this evening and fill me in on what you accomplished."

"Maybe. We'll see," Hadley said, unwilling to commit just so she could get what would probably be another lecture.

Her mother approached and gave Hadley a hug. The scent of Chanel filled Hadley's nose. The scent was beautiful, but Hadley wished she found it as comforting as Mary Elizabeth's favorite perfume. Or Nan's.

"Keep your door locked. I don't like the idea of you here alone and that man knowing it."

"I'll be fine, Mom. Thanks for stopping by."

"Your father will be thrilled that you're here. Are you staying the weekend?"

"I think I might, yeah."

"Good. I can't wait to see Kyle. Oh, I wish the kids could come."

"Actually, Mom, there's something I need to—"

"Can it wait? I have to run or I'll be late. Do whatever you like with Mom's things. I have what I want to keep already. The rest is all yours."

Hadley blinked at the rapid-fire statements but supposed, given Nan's many years, sentimental items had been handed down over time. For the first time, she noticed her mother wearing one of Nan's necklaces, a gift from her grandfather many years ago.

"Uh, okay. Drive safely," Hadley said as she walked her mother to the door.

Hadley watched as her mother left the house, her head turned in the direction of the home next door.

Hadley stood behind the screen door, waiting to make sure her mother got in her car and actually left the driveway before turning to survey Nan's home.

However inadvertently, she'd gotten a reprieve from telling her mother the truth. At least for now.

And in the meantime...where to begin?

She grabbed a pad of paper and pen from the kitchen and divided the page with several lines, making columns for keep, donate, and undecided.

Nan had beautiful things but she'd stayed true to form with her dark furnishings. They didn't suit Hadley at all. She liked light and bright beach chic, and the dark floors, dark rugs, and dark wood furniture did not say beach house to her.

But was there a market for that type of furniture now? The dark stained wood definitely seemed to be a thing of the past.

The furniture wasn't in bad shape, and some of it held a particular charm with its elegant carvings. In another color, they wouldn't be bad, actually.

Maybe a few coats of paint would make them salvageable and change her mind about keeping them?

The idea appealed and she tucked it back for later. She'd thought at first she needed to get a handle on Nan's personal items, but packing up her clothes and shoes didn't appeal. It was just too soon for that.

Hadley roamed through the house but decided to leave Nan's bedroom to be dealt with last.

Maybe in time she would be able to do what needed done when it came to passing on her grandmother's personal items. For now there was plenty to keep Hadley occupied—like the dark walls that needed painting. Nan had liked jewel tones, and in the nineties, she'd had the house painted from top to bottom in deep burgundies and golds and navy blues. Hadley found the rooms dark and unappealing and definitely not the light and bright style she preferred.

Sorry, Nan, but you said to make it my own.

Unlike Cheryl, Nan wasn't so set in her ways that she'd resent Hadley changing things. In fact, it was easy to imagine Nan sitting in her favorite chair cheering on Hadley's plans.

Hadley moved through the rooms, her lists growing. Hadley planned to get rid of the clutter and knickknacks, keep about a third of the furniture to try her hand at painting the pieces to lighten them up and use in the house. She'd never done anything of the sort before, but the DIY shows on TV made it look easy enough. A few gallons of paint were a lot cheaper than buying new, and she had to make the money Nan had left her last as long as humanly possible.

A knock sounded at the door, and Hadley hurried down the stairs to answer, seeing Adam Shipley on the other side. "Adam, welcome," she said as she opened the door. "This is a surprise. What are you doing here?"

"Good morning, Hadley. I'm afraid we didn't get around to those signatures last night before you left, and I thought I'd stop by on my way home and see if we can't get things in motion so you'll have the funds."

"Of course," she said, accepting the papers he handed her along with the pen he'd come prepared with.

She signed on the highlighted lines and handed the documents back to him one by one.

"You look like you've been busy," he said, nodding toward the pad of paper she'd set aside.

A laugh emerged and she inhaled. "I've never been one to do-it-yourself but I'm thinking of giving it a try."

"I'm sure you'll do great at whatever you set your

mind to," Adam said. "Give me a shout if you need something?"

"Thank you. I will." She walked Adam back to the door and waved goodbye.

A couple of hours had passed since she'd started her tour of the house room by room, and she'd decided painting a small piece of furniture might be easier than an entire room.

She chose a cabinet to start with and moved to empty the drawers to have it ready for her return from the home store.

But the second drawer of the cabinet was filled with photo albums, and in two seconds flat, Hadley found herself on the floor, surrounded by memories.

Black-and-white photos of Nan and Poppy's wedding. Their honeymoon and many trips to the Caribbean. Nan dancing, hands raised above her head as she twirled.

Page after page. So many memories now just images of moments long gone. Of times and places and stories no one else knew. Would know. She thought of how easy it was to get so caught up in her own life and getting through the days that she lost sight of the fact there were *billions* of other people doing the same thing, living their lives, stories, right beside her.

Another flip of the page left Hadley smiling

again. Her mother's baby photos were cute and classic and like something from a time warp. There were pictures of the original Babes all together on the boardwalk in their prams and bonnets, later in short dresses with ruffled socks and patent leather shoes.

Later still, photos of the Babes as teenagers in bathing suits. Long legs, long hair, dressed in the seventies fashions that looked atrocious and cool at the same time. Miniskirts, go-go boots, muscle cars, and...was that a cigarette?

Ah, Tessa. *Such a rebel*, Hadley mused with a smile.

The images were precious. Priceless. Hadley wished she could've witnessed that time firsthand. What would it have been like to know her mother then? She looked happy in the photographs, all smiles and blond curls. The image of the slim, tanned, upper-crust daughter enjoying her ocean-front life.

One by one, Hadley flipped through the yellowed pages of the albums. Her birth photos were next, and then it was as though time repeated as the pictures showed Hadley and her "cousins" over the years.

Another few flips of the pages...and Hadley stared at her own face, at her wedding photo...the sheer joy and happiness she'd felt captured for all to see in heartbreaking detail.

Tears flooded her eyes and her nostrils flared as she sucked in a sharp, choked breath.

How was it possible for so much happiness to turn into so much pain?

____

CHAPTER FOUR

Mary Elizabeth removed the batch of cookies from the oven and placed them atop the cast iron grates to cool. Cheryl had sent out a text to the Babes letting them know Ms. Georgia had left the house to Hadley and that Hadley was staying in town a few days to look things over.

Mary Elizabeth wanted to do all she could to welcome her goddaughter to the neighborhood and hopefully spend as much time with Hadley as she could to get her to open up about the sadness she tried and failed to hide.

Her phone bleeped out yet another notification, and she glanced at the face to see Rayna Jo responding to the news.

Rayna Jo worked at the home decor and gift shop

she co-owned with her twin, Adaline, so Mary Elizabeth told the ladies her plans to put together a welcome basket of goodies.

Texts quickly filled the screen from Rayna Jo, telling Mary Elizabeth to stop by the shop and add whatever she had made to a basket Rayna Jo would put together. Tessa mentioned having a house-warming shower for Hadley, but Cheryl quickly nixed the idea until Kyle and the kids could join Hadley and be part of the fun.

Mary Elizabeth hoped Cheryl would keep her criticism in check where Hadley was concerned. Cheryl had always had high expectations, and while she could be sweet and gentle and generous in many ways, in others she came across as controlling and demanding.

Once, years ago, Cheryl had walked into Mary Elizabeth's home when all three of her girls were home for the summer on school break. The house was a mess of toys and blankets, dog hair and dirty dishes, and Cheryl had turned up her nose and said, "Well, obviously you haven't been cleaning today."

Considering Cheryl had one child *and* a house-keeper, and Mary Elizabeth had three children and no housekeeper, she'd found the statement not only hurtful but spiteful. That side of Cheryl emerged every now and again, and despite Cheryl's intrinsically good qualities, it was that bad side that lingered long after she left and often cast Cheryl in a negative light.

Mary Elizabeth removed her apron and picked up her phone yet again. She sent a note out to her daughters that she'd made cookies and wished they would stop by to enjoy them. She also informed them of Hadley's new home.

Allie stayed busy with her babies on the other side of town, while Sophia tried to conquer the banking world in Charlotte. Isabel...

Isabel was an artist and after a lifetime of ups and downs and wrong turns, she'd recently met and married the love of her life and now split her time between Carolina Cove and New York City.

"SWEETHEART, THOSE SMELL AMAZING."

Mary Elizabeth turned and found Adam striding toward her. Her husband had just turned sixty-five but looked a good ten years younger. "I thought I heard you come in. Still warm from the oven. Have one."

"You're an angel."

"What are you doing home?"

"I forgot to get signatures from Hadley last night before she left. Did you know she's still in town?"

"That's why I'm making her favorite cookies."

He shook his head and winked at her.

"Of course you knew. Well, thankfully Jerry mentioned Hadley had stayed the night, so I stopped by on the way. I'm going to change and get my clubs."

"Ah, Judge Denson?"

Adam nodded.

He and the judge had a standing golf date. "Take sunscreen this time—and a hat."

Adam plopped a cookie in his mouth and chewed before giving her a kiss tasting of everything chocolatey and good.

"I will. Wish me luck. He's been practicing. If he wins, I'll have a heck of a bar tab."

"Just have fun. You work too hard." She worried about him spending his life at that desk, poring over files and cases and books.

Adam hugged her and she welcomed the embrace, leaning on the man she loved with all her heart.

"Give my best to Hadley. See you tonight."

Adam left the room as quickly as he'd entered, and Mary Elizabeth said a prayer of thanks for her life.

Things had worked out well, even though when Adam had proposed all those years ago, she hadn't truly loved him. Oh, she'd cared for him. A lot. But it had taken time, experiences together, to find *love*. Now she wondered how she could ever live without him and hoped to never find out.

While the cookies cooled, she ran over her list of to-dos for the day. She liked being a homemaker and wife, and while some women might think the pleasure she received from her life demeaning or anti-feminist, she felt grateful for the opportunity she'd been given to be home with her girls while they grew up.

Mary Elizabeth moved through her house now, straightening and fluffing and doing general pickup before going back to the kitchen. She arranged the cookies on a pretty plate and covered them, then grabbed her purse.

The ride to Beach Chic didn't take long despite the summer traffic. Rayna Jo and Adaline greeted Mary Elizabeth as soon as she walked in the door of the shop, and she gazed in wonder at all the pretties on display. "I don't know how either of you work here. I'd be broke and out of business with every delivery."

"It gets difficult. I won't lie," Rayna Jo said somewhat ruefully. "So what do you think about this for our newest boardwalk neighbor?"

The large white beach tote had rope handles. It wasn't yet wrapped, but the Babes had added two luxuriously plush blue towels, a bottle of wine, a delicious-smelling candle, black-and-white-striped beach hat, a gorgeous, gauzy coverup, dangly starfish and gem earrings, a book on cocktails, and some other little odds and ends. "It's beautiful. And she will look lovely in that outfit. Maybe she'll take the day and go to the beach to snack on the cookies and wine."

"She did look tired, didn't she?" Rayna Jo said. "I worried about it all night."

"I'm sure she was heartbroken about Georgia. Especially since Hadley hasn't been able to get back to visit for quite some time."

Mary Elizabeth's heart pinched at the thought because she knew it was true. But *why* hadn't Hadley been back? Oh, she had a busy family for sure, but it had never stopped her from making the two-hour drive, if only for an afternoon. What had changed? Had something happened? "Well, let's add these cookies and I'll take it over. Oh, and here's a gift card and mug from London's Lattes so Hadley can get her caffeine fix. I pick up a few things each time I go to have on hand as emergency gifts. Now, can you two come, too, or are you staying here?"

"We have a client coming in. She's redecorating and wants a consult," Rayna Jo said.

"Again." Adaline rolled her eyes. "This is the second time this year that she's redone the same room. Some people have more money than sense."

"So you don't want to take her money?" Rayna Jo asked pointedly.

"I didn't say *that*." Adaline grinned, her diamond earrings twinkling in the sunlight filtering in through the front windows. "Business is business."

Mary Elizabeth shook her head at the twins' antics and laughed softly. "Well, I'll be sure to give credit where credit is due. Hadley will love it all."

Rayna Jo quickly wrapped the tote bag in cellophane and added turquoise satin ribbon that paired well with the blue towels for an ocean-y look. Once done, Mary Elizabeth hugged the basket and carried it out of the shop, pausing long enough to get air kisses from her lifelong friends as they walked her to the door.

Back in the car, Mary Elizabeth made her way to Hadley's new home, taking in the sights and sounds of summer at the beach.

Fall was her favorite time of year in Carolina Cove, but she'd be lying if she said she didn't love the energy of summer. The salt air, the laughter of happy families, the smell of deep-fried goodies from the local restaurants, and the sound of the birds squawking overhead. The worst part was the bumper-to-bumper traffic, but since it was only a few months out of the entire year, she always made sure to give herself plenty of extra time and reminded herself it was the price to pay to live somewhere so beautiful.

Mary Elizabeth finally made it to Hadley's and parked behind Hadley's car. She retrieved the heavy tote and carried it to the porch, every step bringing a crackle of the cellophane.

The door was open, the screen door slightly ajar as it had been since the last big storm. "Knock, knock. Haddie, you home?"

Mary Elizabeth heard a gasping sniffle from within the home and immediately elbowed her way inside. Tears demanded immediate entry, no ifs, ands, or buts about it. "Hadley?"

"Hey, MeMe," Hadley said in a small voice.

Mary Elizabeth turned to find her goddaughter sitting on the floor surrounded by Georgia's photo albums. "Oh, *honey*. Are you okay?"

"No. No, I'm *not* okay," Hadley said, her trembling fingers wiping the tears from her cheeks. "Oh, Mary Elizabeth. What am I going to *do*?"

Mary Elizabeth set the gift on the closest chair and rushed to Hadley's side, kneeling beside the girl who was as much her daughter as her own. She wrapped Hadley in her arms and squeezed her tight. "Do about what, sweetheart? What's going on? Tell me."

HADLEY SHUDDERED at the thought of revealing her secrets. But she and her godmother had always been close, and Hadley knew she could use a friend on the inside, so to speak. Maybe Adam had already told his wife?

"Hadley, honey, whatever it is, you'll be fine. You hear me? Talk."

Mary Elizabeth framed Hadley's face with her palms, forcing Hadley to look at her. After a long moment and fresh tears, she whispered, "It's over. I tried, MeMe. I tried *so hard* but he said he didn't want... He *wouldn't...*"

"What?"

"Kyle's gone." Hadley knew the moment Mary Elizabeth caught on. The woman's eyes widened, and her mouth parted as she sucked in a sharp breath.

"Oh, Haddie. Honey... You've separated?"

"No. *No*, it's *worse*. We're divorced."

"*What?* Honey, in North Carolina you have to

live separate for a year before you can even fi— Oh, my. *That's* why you haven't been around?"

Hadley sniffled and pulled away from Mary Elizabeth, unable to look at her. "I thought maybe Adam had told you."

"Adam knows about this?"

Hadley nodded. "He... Nan left a letter and said he found out when he was doing the paperwork for her will."

Hadley watched as Mary Elizabeth sat back on her heels next to her.

"He didn't tell me," she said softly. "Attorney-client privilege, I'm sure. But Georgia... Oh, Hadley, why have you kept this from us?"

"Because... Because I just kept *hoping*. MeMe, I prayed so hard. I didn't want the divorce. I tried everything. I *begged* Kyle to go to counseling. He wouldn't hear of it. He just wanted... He just wanted *her*."

"You mean he's with some— Oh, that low-down *snake*. There are *so* many words for a man who cheats but none of them suffice. He did that to you? *You?*"

Hadley laughed softly, wondering how Mary Elizabeth thought a forty-five-year-old mother of two adult children could compare to a twenty-six-year-old who told Kyle he walked on water.

Kyle's mistress was the shiny new toy he'd left the old wife behind to play with. After putting him through school, after having his children, building a life and a home together—and for what? "What am I going to do? I can't tell Mama and Daddy now. I *can't*. But they expect Kyle to come visit."

"Oh, Haddie, your parents might be a bit uptight, but if you sit down with them...I'm sure they'll understand."

"No, they won't. Mom *won't*. You know I'm right," Hadley said, completely dejected by the thought of having to put herself in that scenario, even though she knew it would eventually come to pass.

"I know no such thing. Now you listen to me," Mary Elizabeth said, gripping Hadley's hands. "Your parents love you and it's obvious that you did your best to make things work."

"I did. I swear I *did*," Hadley said tearfully.

"Then you have to accept that and move on."

"Mary Elizabeth, I'm almost fifty years *old*. How do I start over now? Kyle didn't want me to work. He said there was no need and that it reflected badly on him, like he couldn't provide for us. And I... I know I'm to blame, too, because I loved being home with the kids, but now I have no training, and even though I worked while he was in medical school, I'm not qualified to work anywhere now."

"Honey, you are a smart, capable woman. You can do whatever you set out to accomplish."

"But you don't get it. A minimum-wage job isn't going to pay the taxes on this place once the money Nan left me runs out. And I can't... I *can't* sell Nan's house. It will kill me if I have to do that, and it will be one more failure in what's turning out to be a long list."

Hadley stood and paced across the room, unable to sit still. Unable to face Mary Elizabeth and see the disappointment on her face.

"Sweetheart, you need to calm down. Why are you worrying about selling the house? You're putting the cart in front of the horse. We'll figure this out. The money Georgia left you will tide you over for a while, right?"

"Yes. But it won't last forever. And all this morning I've been looking around and this place... There's so much that needs done. There's a water leak upstairs in one of the spare bedrooms, and the end of the porch looks like it's rotting. All of the outside fixtures need replaced due to corrosion, the whole house needs painted inside and out, and even the window latches and doorknobs are ruined because of the salt air. And that's just the start."

"Baby, take a breath. Maybe it needs tending to

but it doesn't all have to be done today," Mary Elizabeth said.

"Nan let it slide for too long. The sooner things are fixed, the better."

"Then we'll get it done. One step at a time. But for now, you have to stop worrying about something that isn't going to happen. That we will not *allow* to happen," Mary Elizabeth stressed.

The older woman walked across the room to where Haddie now stood. Mary Elizabeth wrapped an arm around her shoulders and pulled Hadley to the kitchen, gently shoving her down into a chair. "You're letting worry and fear get the best of you when you know good and well God's got this."

"Does He? Because I could've used a little more help in saving my marriage instead of having to end it."

"Honey, like it or not, sometimes God ends things to protect us from worse things further on down the line. He sees and hears all the conversations and goings-on that we don't."

"That's what Nan always said."

"Because it's true. Trust me, He's protected you from something we may never know about, but you should consider it a blessing."

Hadley buried her face in her hands, wondering

how anyone could view divorce and failure as a blessing. "If you say so."

"We need some tea."

"Tea is not going to help," Hadley said with a moan.

"Maybe not. But it's step one of making a plan of what is doable by the many capable members of our families and what isn't. So that's what we'll do. But first... You need to tell your parents about the divorce."

"No," Hadley said with a firm twist of her head. "I can't."

"Hadley..."

"Just shoot me. It'll be easier. Better for all of us."

"*Hadley.*"

"Mama's going to freak. You know I'm right. And Dad... Daddy's going to be so disappointed."

"Your parents love you. And if they're disappointed in anyone, it will be Kyle, not you."

"But I've *lied* to them for over a year."

"Yes, well, that will undoubtedly cause some upset, but in time things will settle down. I do wonder though...why didn't you tell them? Right from the beginning?"

"I don't know," Hadley said as she rubbed at her eyes. "I was embarrassed and humiliated. I just kept hoping Kyle and I could work things out, but then...

more and more time passed and it was too late. I'd kept the secret too long."

"It definitely complicates matters," Mary Elizabeth murmured while filling the teapot. "But your parents are not monsters, Haddie."

"I know. I *know*. I was just...in such a state of shock at first. I couldn't believe it when I found out about the affair, and then Kyle mentioned divorce and... Mary Elizabeth, to be honest, I don't even remember the first six or eight months. Seriously. I can't tell you what I did, where I went. It's all a foggy blur."

"I *knew* something was going on. You've never stayed away so long before."

"I knew I couldn't hide it. That you'd all see and know. For the longest time, I'd break down in tears and it was a struggle just to get out of bed."

"Oh, honey, I hate that you went through all that alone," Mary Elizabeth said. "You're not eating, are you? You're thinner than ever."

"I couldn't keep anything down at first. My appetite had just started to come back when I got the news about Nan."

"Are you sleeping?"

Hadley pressed her forehead into her palms and rubbed her gritty eyes. "Not much this week. The moment I knew Nan was gone and I'd stayed away...

it all got worse again. I can't believe I didn't visit her. That I let a year go by and didn't come see her. I hate myself for that."

"Don't. It'll do you no good to beat yourself up about it now. And you said she knew, so that means she understood what you were going through."

"But I should've told her myself. Confessed! I called every week but...I should've *told her*. I wish she'd have said something to me. Let on that she knew."

"I'm sure she wanted to give you whatever time you needed, hon."

The gas stove clicked until catching fire and Mary Elizabeth put the teapot on the grate.

"Who knows you're divorced? Do the kids?"

Hadley felt a fresh tingling of tears and swallowed hard. Crying would get her nowhere, and heaven knew she'd already done more than her share for a lifetime. "Yes. They're torn. They love us both and were supportive of me in the beginning."

"What do you mean 'in the beginning'?"

"They didn't speak to Kyle when they first found out about the affair, but Kyle has been playing vacation dad and paying for trips all year long, taking the mistress with them so the kids were forced to warm up to her."

"A fool and his money," Mary Elizabeth said.

"Well, it worked, because now Abby talks about how happy her dad is, so it's like the sneaking around and cheating is all okay now and they didn't destroy a twenty-five-year marriage with their behavior. Did I tell you she was born the year Kyle and I started *dating*? She isn't much older than the kids."

"Kyle should feel like a pedophile."

Mary Elizabeth walked back into the living room and dug around in the wrapping of the tote bag she'd arrived with. Hadley knew why when the plate of cookies emerged. "Oh, MeMe. Nan's cookies?"

"I thought they'd be appropriate to welcome you home."

Hadley closed her tear-scalded eyes and shook her head. "I wish she was *here*."

"Me, too, sweetie."

"She'd know what to do."

"Well, in this case, I do, too."

Hadley looked up. "You do?"

"Yes. We're going to have some tea, eat some cookies, and when you're ready, we'll go tell your parents."

"Yeah, no," Hadley said, shaking her head.

"Hadley—"

"I can't, MeMe. I'll do it soon...just...I need more time. Besides, I have to do this on my own. There's no reason for you to get caught in the crossfire."

"You're sure?"

"I'm sure. If Cheryl Dummit goes on the warpath, it should only be me wearing the bullseye."

"Ah, honey, that's where you're wrong. It should be Kyle and the tramp who slept with a married man."

CHAPTER FIVE

Bryson spent the next hour or so installing the bathroom vanity and hooking up the water, but his thoughts kept straying to the woman next door.

His last memory of Hadley was as a starry-eyed senior in cap and gown. They hadn't run in the same crowd, but they had shared a few classes over the years. He remembered her essays and poems and the way she'd looked at life.

But that bright-eyed girl was long gone and he couldn't help but wonder why.

Hadley now carried a wariness and a sadness he couldn't place but recognized, one born of more trials and pain than someone like her usually experienced.

But how bad could things be as a surgeon's wife?

Her car and clothes indicated a life lived well above the average income.

His gaze landed on the coffee mug she'd sent him home with, and he decided to make a second attempt at discovering her plans for the house. His question about whether she planned to keep it had been interrupted by her mother's arrival.

Bryson stood and quickly dusted himself off before grabbing the cup and rinsing it. That done, he headed out of the house and through the hedges, not stopping until he stood outside her screen door. "Hadley? It's me, Bryson."

"Coming."

Hadley appeared on the other side of the door, and he frowned when he noticed her red-rimmed eyes. "Are you all right?"

"I'm fine. It's... It's dusty in here."

She pushed open the screen door, and he took the opportunity to step inside, even though she'd probably just wanted him to hand her the mug. "I came to drop this off. Thanks for the—"

A sharp gasp was followed by the sound of a loud crash and the shattering of dishes. He and Hadley turned toward the kitchen in time to see an older woman's horrified expression as bits of China and cookies and liquid slid across the floor.

"Oh!"

Bryson and Hadley hurried toward the woman as she dropped down and gasped again because she cut her hand picking up one of the many shards.

"Help Mary Elizabeth while I get a towel," Hadley said, rushing into the kitchen.

Bryson bent and prodded the older woman to stand before gently leading her out of the mess. He followed Hadley's path to the kitchen and pulled out a chair, urging the woman to sit.

Hadley returned with a clean cloth and wrapped the woman's hand, and Bryson supported the woman's forearm, holding it up to try to stem the bleeding.

"I'm so sorry," the woman said, upset thick in her voice. "Oh, what a mess I made."

"Don't worry a thing about it. It's fine," Hadley said, her tone reassuring.

"No, I should've been more careful."

"Accidents happen," he said to the woman.

Chin and lips quivering, the older woman stared up at him, more than a little wide-eyed.

"I'll go get the first-aid kit. Keep pressure on it," Hadley said to him on her way out of the room.

Awkward silence filled the air and he felt the need to say something. "My, uh, mother used to say tea was coffee's overrated friend."

Instead of a laugh or look or whatever he'd

expected, the woman's eyes filled with tears, and her shoulders quaked with a silent sob. "Hey, now, was my joke that bad?"

The woman sniffled and shook her head, tears slipping down her gently lined cheeks.

"Found it," Hadley called as she reentered the room. "Oh, Mary Elizabeth, please, don't cry. Truly, it's fine."

The blood hadn't quite stopped but the cut didn't look deep. Hadley asked the woman about blood thinners and nodded when the woman admitted to taking an aspirin a day per her doctor's orders.

"That would explain it. We'll wait a few minutes for it to stop and get you cleaned up and bandaged. It should be fine."

Bryson watched as Hadley knelt on the floor and quickly cared for the woman's injury with practiced expertise. "You're pretty good at that," he said.

"Two kids," Hadley said, her lips quirking up at the corners in a smile. "Max tended to be the clumsiest. Nan always said it was because he was a boy who hadn't grown into his feet, but I tended more scraped knees and palms than I care to remember."

Bryson smiled at the thought, well able to see Hadley as a mom. She had that look about her. Loving and kind but not a total pushover.

"There. All done," Hadley said. "And the bleeding stopped."

"Thank you, sweetheart. I'll get that cleaned up and—"

"You don't move," he said to the woman. "I've got it."

He didn't ask for directions, because he knew the lower part of the house fairly well. The broom was tucked on the first step inside the screened-in back porch, where he and Georgia had sat in the evenings sometimes playing cards, and paper towels were beneath the upper kitchen cabinets—in front of the hard liquor Georgia hid for special occasions.

Bryson used the towels to soak up the tea and then swept up the shards, disposing of them by putting them into an empty coffee can retrieved from the recycle bin on the back porch to keep the shards from splitting the trash bag or someone else getting hurt.

Once he finished, he went back inside to rejoin the ladies only to find Hadley at the door waving goodbye. "She left?"

"Yes. Poor thing. She's so upset about breaking the china even though Nan had enough to serve tea to an army. Thanks for cleaning that up, by the way."

"You're welcome." He took in the photo albums scattered about the floor, chairs, and even the couch and surmised that was the reason for her tears earlier. It made sense considering she was there because of her grandmother's passing. "Hadley, Georgia and I got to be close in the last eight months while I've worked next door. If you need help with anything..."

Hadley nodded her thanks and swept out a fragile-looking hand to indicate the mess.

"Thanks, but right now that's my focus and you can't help with those. I'll box them up and put them somewhere for safekeeping."

Shot down, he struggled to think of a way to try again. "Hadley, look, I don't think there will ever be a good time to say this but..."

"Say what?" A frown pinched her eyebrows together over her nose.

"Well, I just wanted to tell you that if you decide to sell the house for some reason, I'd like to request a chance to make the first offer. They don't build them like this anymore."

"Oh," she said, sounding more than a little surprised. "You do realize the house isn't as sound as it looks."

"What do you mean?"

She ran down a list of issues, including the water leak upstairs.

"Mind if I take a look at it?"

"Now? Shouldn't you get back to the job you're already working on?"

"In a bit. Show me the leak."

Hadley led the way upstairs, and he couldn't help but notice the gentle sway of her hips in those shorts. She wasn't a twenty- or thirtysomething but a woman full-grown, and he appreciated the sight.

"There. That's the room."

Drawn from his thoughts, he slid by Hadley in the narrow hallway and entered the small bedroom. The bay window overlooking the boardwalk below had a window seat, but apparently the angled roof outside had suffered some damage. "Doesn't look too bad, but there's no way of knowing until I get up there to take a look."

"You'd...do that?"

"It is what I do for a living."

"Yeah, but...I'm sure my neighbors won't appreciate it if they've hired you to do a job and you're over here working instead."

He stiffened at her words and then reminded himself life was full of surprises. Maybe it was time Hadley and her family got one. "I'm sure no one would mind me helping out a neighbor."

"Oh, well, that's very nice of you," she said. "Maybe this evening? After you finish over there?"

"Sounds good. Do you know where to access the attic?"

"End of the hall."

"I'll come back tonight to take a look." He found himself following her once again, out of the bedroom, back down the hallway to the stairs. "Will your husband be joining you soon?"

If he hadn't been watching her, Bryson wouldn't have noticed the way her hand tightened on the railing.

"Why do you ask?"

"Just wondered if you were going to have help sorting through all of this. I didn't realize Georgia was such a decorator."

The house wasn't messy. Everything had a place. But every wall from floor to ceiling was covered with furniture, framed pictures, shelves loaded with seashells. Every table had doilies and knickknacks. Every window showcased glass miniatures and more shells.

"It is a bit much, isn't it? I think she got lonely there at the end," Hadley said. "Mom said Nan constantly walked the neighborhood. Stopped at yard sales and the like. It makes me sad to think of her doing that just to have people to talk to."

"Maybe it wasn't loneliness as much as trying to help the people out."

"Hmm. Nan would totally do that. Buy something just to overpay and tell them to keep the change. Thank you. I hadn't thought of that."

Hadley crossed the room toward the front door and Bryson followed. He didn't like thinking of Georgia as lonely, either, and once again, he thanked God he'd made the time to sit with her. "She was a special lady, that's for sure. And the best poker player I know."

A laugh bubbled out of Hadley. "Seriously? Oh, I have to know that story."

Bryson grinned at Hadley's expression and moved to the porch to leave. "I'll tell you...when I come back tonight."

MARY ELIZABETH DROVE HOME but didn't go inside. She left her car in the driveway and started walking, not stopping until she made it down the boardwalk to the swings near the pavilion.

She sank onto one of them with a silent sigh and gripped the edge until her fingers and cut hand ached.

It wasn't possible.

Was it?

"Hey! I thought that was you," Tessa said from

behind her. "I've been calling your name. Didn't you hear me?"

Mary Elizabeth turned and forced a smile, watching her friend walk up with the confidence of a woman who knew herself well. Truth be told, Mary Elizabeth had always envied that about Tessa, how sure of herself she was when it came to life despite all of the difficulties she'd endured. "No, I didn't. Sorry."

Tessa paused and stared at Mary Elizabeth from behind her sunglasses.

"What's wrong?"

"Nothing."

"Yeah, tell me another one. What happened to your hand?"

"What? Oh, I-I cut it on some broken china. It's fine. Shouldn't you be in the salon?" Tessa's salon was the best on the island, a one-stop spa where anyone could be pampered to their heart's content.

"My appointment cancelled last minute so I thought I'd take a walk before my next one. Hey, obviously *something* happened. Did you and Adam have an argument?"

Adam. Dear, sweet Adam. "No. No, he's off playing golf."

"Okay," Tessa said, perching herself on the

boardwalk railing with her back to the ocean so that they were face-to-face. "So it's not Adam. The girls? Are they fighting again? I know it upsets you that they don't get along, but they'll work through it. They always do."

Mary Elizabeth dragged in a breath and wished the salt air could heal what was broken inside of her.

"Okay, you're officially scaring me. Talk or I'm going to call an emergency meeting," Tessa ordered, pulling her cell phone from her pocket and waving it like the threat it was.

"I can't."

"Mary Elizabeth Shipley, you can tell me *any*thing and you know it. Now tell me what's wrong or I call the Babes and get them down here."

She swallowed hard, releasing the bench to cradle her throbbing hand. "I... This would have to stay in the vault. I *mean* it. No one can know, not even the other Babes."

Tessa shoved the phone back into her pocket and shifted until she sat beside Mary Elizabeth on the bench, her pixie face drawn by a frown even Botox couldn't stop.

"MeMe? What's going on?"

"Vault."

"Honey, I swear. It stays in the vault and not

even the Babes will know," Tessa said, her hand shifting to wrap around Mary Elizabeth's wrist. "Nothing you say to me will be repeated."

Mary Elizabeth's gaze flooded with tears and Tessa patted and fussed and fished a tissue from her impossibly tiny purse, pressing it into Mary Elizabeth's hand.

Then Tessa waited, silent. And maybe if she hadn't been content to give Mary Elizabeth whatever time she needed to formulate the words, she could've stayed quiet. But in the silence, memories flooded her and the words began to roll out. "Do you remember that summer when I went away? I stayed at my aunt Dottie's house?"

"Yes. We were all mad because we'd finally gotten old enough to really have some fun and you got shipped off for the entire summer."

"It's because...I had to be."

"What do you mean?"

"I mean," Mary Elizabeth said, her voice shaking, "it was 1973 and young girls were still being sent away when...when they found themselves in the family way."

"The fam— You were *pregnant*?"

"Shhh," Mary Elizabeth said, glancing around them to see if anyone had heard. It was ridiculous, she realized, but it wasn't any easier to acknowledge at sixty-two that she'd gotten pregnant so young than it had been at fifteen.

"I'm sorry. I'm just... *You were pregnant?*" Tessa asked again, though this time in a lower tone.

Mary Elizabeth closed her eyes and nodded.

"I can't believe... All these years and you've never said a *word*. How could we not know this?"

"That was the point," she said softly. "That no one would ever know and I'd take the secret to my grave."

Tessa's expression revealed her shock.

"I'm so sorry," her friend said softly. "I'm sorry you went through that alone and felt that you couldn't tell us. Oh, hon."

Tessa pulled her close and leaned her head against Mary Elizabeth's.

"Who was the father? Did you put the baby up for adoption?"

Mary Elizabeth took a deep breath and focused on the first question. "Do you remember Dean Carpelli? Tall, dark hair? He... He was in our math class."

"Not ringing a bell."

"He worked at the garage and gas station—the one called Ace's now," Mary Elizabeth said. "Frankie

Cohen, one of Andrew and Andrea's daughters, owns it now. The one home from the military."

"Oh, I do remember him. He pumped gas."

Mary Elizabeth pushed herself away from Tessa to ease the ache in her back, saddened at the thought that her friend's only memory of Dean was one of service.

"How did you two...?"

She inhaled and let her mind drift to the days that brought a smile to her lips. "I wasn't allowed to date until I turned sixteen, but we knew my parents wouldn't approve of him regardless, so...we snuck around." Mary Elizabeth smiled again, her mind filled with love and memories. "I could tell he was having trouble in math, so one day I offered to tutor him."

"Sounds like he tutored *you*."

"We fell in love," Mary Elizabeth said, ignoring her friend's comment. "I'd ride my bike to the gas station every day to get a soda and see him. He was amazing. So sweet. Kind. A gentle soul."

"So what happened when you told him?"

Mary Elizabeth wiped a hand beneath her runny nose and shook her head. "I didn't. His draft number came up right before the end of the war. He left before I found out and then he...died three weeks after he got there."

"Oh, MeMe. I remember that now. The town had a funeral for him and some of those hippie idiots protested."

She nodded, tearing up again, remembering it like it was yesterday. "At first I thought I was just upset because of what happened. Sick to my stomach from heartbreak. But then my clothes got tighter and I realized I'd missed my period and...I was so scared."

"I can only imagine your parents' response."

She nodded, remembering the yelling and tears. "I was pretty far along by then. My father threatened to kill Dean, and when I said...when I said he had died in Vietnam, my father said Dean had probably taken a bullet to get out of having to marry me."

Tessa's sharp gasp revealed her thoughts.

"Wow. I can't believe they'd... I mean, you were a kid but... I always knew something had happened between you and your parents that summer. You were different."

"How could I not be? Things like that have a tendency to change people," Mary Elizabeth murmured, focusing on a pelican skimming the ocean in the distance.

"What happened to the baby?" Tessa asked again.

"He died...at least, that's what Aunt Dottie told me when I woke up. You know how they used to put you to sleep in those days and then handed you the baby once the drugs wore off. But today..." She turned toward Tessa and gripped her hand. "I *saw* Dean today."

"What? Honey, that's impossible. Like you said, he died in Vietnam."

"No, I don't mean *Dean* but our baby. It was him, Tessa. I'm telling you it was *him*."

"What? Where?"

"At Hadley's," she said, explaining how she'd dropped by to deliver the basket of goodies and what had happened.

"So the man looked like Dean? Honey, that's easy enough to explain. No doubt Dean has family in the area. Brothers or sisters, cousins who've had children?"

Mary Elizabeth stared out at the waves crashing against the shore and struggled to breathe. "I-I suppose that could be the case. But the resemblance was uncanny."

"Have you ever seen the photo on the internet of Abraham Lincoln's modern-day descendant? It's eerie. I have no doubt it's the same kind of situation with the man at Hadley's. And not to change the subject, but why was he there?"

"I'm not sure. Wait...he brought a coffee cup, I think. To return it? It all happened so fast it's a bit of a blur. I was so surprised to see him that I dropped a loaded tray of tea and cookies. Made a horrible mess."

"Well, I have no doubt it was upsetting for you but realistically you know it wasn't him."

"I know but—"

"What buts?"

"My parents," Mary Elizabeth said, unable to shake her uneasiness about the situation. "What if my parents and Aunt Dottie lied about the baby? About it dying?"

"Honey, no parent could be so cruel."

"The man looked to be the right age."

"Again, perhaps a relative? Mary Elizabeth, do you really think your parents would have done that to you?"

"I think they were mortified that their unwed fifteen-year-old daughter was pregnant and the father... Yes. I think they would have if it meant hiding their shame and keeping it secret. The things Daddy said that day...the way he *looked* at me... It'll haunt me until the day I die."

"Okay, well," Tessa said softly, "if you truly believe there's even a chance the man at Hadley's could be your long-lost son, there's only one thing to do."

"What's that?"

"We need to get a DNA test."

Mary Elizabeth stared at her friend, shaking her head. "How on earth are we going to do that?"

CHAPTER SIX

Hadley poured herself a glass of wine and carried it with her to the kitchen table, where she'd been for the last hour. The laptop screen brightened with a touch of her finger on the mousepad and lit with the job openings for the immediate area. She was set financially for a while, she knew that, but she also knew she couldn't wait until the money was gone before coming up with a plan of action.

She took a sip and savored the tangy white wine as she glared at the screen. *You're not qualified for any of these.*

No way could she pad a resume enough to earn more than minimum wage. And truthfully, none of the job postings appealed anyway.

But that meant coming up with a new idea and way to earn money.

The old house had several bedrooms, and she supposed, once all the repairs were made, she could rent out a few rooms to single professionals wanting to enjoy their downtime by paying a premium for oceanfront living. Did she really want to live with strangers, though? Share a kitchen and living area?

No, but that seemed the most likely opportunity to earn what she'd need to keep things afloat long-term. Maybe a few carefully selected individuals? The kind that were rarely home?

She heard a dog bark somewhere outside and the sound left her sighing again. As much as she disliked the thought of strangers in her home, she hated feeling so alone. Right now she could use a furry cuddle and a friend who loved unconditionally.

Now's not the time to get a dog.

Even if she'd always wanted one. Or two. Dogs were pack animals, after all, and they needed buddies.

Focus.

She took another long sip of her wine and realized the glass was almost empty, so she poured a bit more as she pressed her fingertips to her temple and rubbed, bombarded by memories. Before she'd quit college, she'd considered changing her major and becoming a vet. When she'd mentioned her plans to Kyle, he'd proposed, promising a lifetime together, and then...life had simply taken over.

She'd worked to put Kyle through medical school, gotten pregnant, and they'd moved a few times as he'd done his residency and found employment. Just when she was about to consider part-time work, she'd gotten pregnant again. And after that she'd had her hands full raising her children and being a mom and wife to a doctor.

The desire to return to college this late in life wasn't there, but she tucked back the idea of getting a pet. As for a job, she'd keep looking and hope to find something not only interesting but that paid reasonably well.

Like anything you'd find could cover the taxes alone on this house.

Which cemented the reality of renting some of the rooms as something she really ought to zero in on.

Maybe she could win the lottery?

Muttering to herself in disgust, she went back to perusing the job listings before getting so discouraged she shut the laptop with a gentle slam.

She glanced at the clock. It was past dinnertime. And even though she wasn't all that hungry, cooking proved to be a good way to occupy herself and keep her from focusing on how quiet and empty the house was.

Previous visits had almost always involved Kyle and the kids, the house filled with laughter and bangs of the screen door as the kids enjoyed their time at the beach. Evenings were always the hardest for her to cope with since that was typically the time when the kids had returned from after-school activities, sometimes with friends in tow, and Kyle had come home from his practice.

Hadley set about looking through cabinets and the fridge and discovered Nan had the makings for chicken pasta Alfredo. She also found frozen baby peas and set them out to fix.

A knock sounded at the door, and she hurried through the house, spying Bryson James on the other side of the screen. "Hey. You're back."

"I said I would be."

She pushed the door open, welcoming him inside. He carried a six-foot ladder as well as a bucket full of tools.

"Still okay if I take a look?"

"Absolutely. And thank you for checking it so quickly. Of all the repairs that need done, a leaky roof gets priority."

"Anything that involves water gets priority," he countered.

"Do you need help?"

He smiled at her question and she supposed it was silly. Men like Bryson were hands-on doers whereas she was a hire-it-done kind of woman. But maybe she could learn? Take on more of the work in order to save money?

The interior rooms could all use a fresh coat of paint, and even though she'd never done much DIY work, she'd watched plenty of remodeling shows on HGTV. How hard could it be? "Right. Well, I'll be in the kitchen if you need me."

Hadley watched as he carried the ladder and bucket up the stairs. She listened as he apparently set up the ladder in the bedroom and then moved into the hallway to pull down the folding attic stairs. She tracked his movements through the house with every noise and tried to imagine the cause.

Nervous because she dreaded the outcome and what he might find, she hurried back to the kitchen and took another sip from her glass. Cooking had never been her favorite thing to do, though she had a few go-to meals she could whip up that seemed to easily impress.

Hadley put the pasta on to boil and found a small pot for the peas and a large pan to make the Alfredo sauce. The chicken came last, and she spied a dusty indoor grill on Nan's pantry shelves and decided to resurrect it, liking the balance of grilled chicken on something so delicious but unhealthy.

She was lost in the process of carefully stirring in the fresh grated cheese when Bryson cleared his throat behind her and she whirled. "Oh! Oh, my... I didn't hear you come downstairs."

After a while, she'd started to tune out the bangs and thumps because there were so many of them.

"Sorry. Didn't mean to startle you," he said, flashing her a handsome smile.

She blinked at the thought. Handsome? "I-It's fine. I was lost in my own little world. So? Your expression doesn't look promising," she said, studying him. "How bad is it?"

He grimaced a bit.

"It could be worse," he said as though trying to appease her.

"Meaning?"

"Meaning I'd say you're looking at a minimum of a few thousand dollars or so in repairs, but it doesn't look like it's been leaking long. We had some storms roll through a couple of weeks ago with some wind, and I'd say that's when it happened. I didn't see any signs of infestation, but the area definitely needs to be fixed as soon as possible to prevent it from happening."

A few thousand. Just the beginning of more?

"How soon can you fix it? I mean, you'll fix it. Right?"

Maybe it was presumptuous of her to assume but...

Once again Bryson flashed her the slow, handsome smile she'd come to know as his.

"You don't want to get a couple of estimates? Do some comparison shopping?"

She knew she should but her gut told her she could trust him. The fact that Nan had trusted him gave her the added confidence she needed to move forward. "No. If you rip me off, you're the one who has to live with yourself."

Bryson chuckled at her statement. "Okay, then. I'll, uh, have to get some materials and order the metal to match, but...I can do the repairs once all the supplies are in."

Relief poured through her. The man seemed legitimate, and while she still planned to check with her neighbor regarding his work, only because she knew she'd be stupid not to, she felt as though a weight had been lifted from her. "Thank you. Really, thank you so much. Oh! Have you had dinner? I'm not really hungry but I was nervous at what you'd find, so I cooked. You're more than welcome to stay and have some. It's the least I can do for you coming over here like this."

He looked surprised by the offer but readily nodded. "Ah, yeah. That smells great, actually. If you don't mind."

"Not at all. It's a Nan recipe. She taught me to make it when I was a kid."

"Sure beats grabbing another cold sandwich before going home."

"The, uh, powder room is just through there if you want to wash up while I finish things," she said, turning toward the cabinets to get plates and glasses and utensils.

The sauce was perfect, so she turned it off after another thorough stir and pulled the garlic toast from the oven, then set about filling plates. Bryson reentered the room just as she carried them to the table.

"That looks amazing."

"Thanks. What would you like to drink?"

"Whatever you're having is fine."

She poured another glass of wine and carried his glass and the almost empty bottle to the table, going back once more for the small basket of bread she'd covered with a towel to keep warm.

Bryson waited for her to sit before taking his seat and lifting his glass.

"To Georgia."

Her heart squeezed as she clinked her glass to his. "To Nan."

They sipped, and Bryson waited for her to pick up her fork before he began to eat with the gusto of a hardworking, hungry man.

"Oh, wow. Hadley...this is great."

"Thank you. I'm glad you like it."

She ate a few bites before remembering his comment and latched on in an attempt to break the silence. "So, you mentioned you were going to tell me the story about Nan and poker? How did that come about?"

MARY ELIZABETH WENT HOME after her talk with Tessa, still numb from the shock of meeting Hadley's guest as she set about making dinner.

"Hon? Hey, is something burning?" Adam called from the other room.

She gasped when she saw the smoke curling from the skillet and grabbed the handle, the gauze wrapped around the cut saving her from burning herself. "No. Oh, *no.*"

"I thought I smelled something burning," Adam said, entering the kitchen. "Are you okay?"

She burst into tears yet again and Adam pulled her into his arms.

"Ah, now it's not as bad as all that. Besides, the doc said I needed to cut back on fried foods anyway."

She gripped his shirt and sniffled, clinging to him because she needed his comforting embrace.

"How about we go out to eat? Would you like that?"

She buried her nose into his chest and shook her head. She didn't want to go anywhere. Do anything. She wanted to be right here, in his arms, forever.

"Honey, what's wrong? Why the tears?"

"Just... Just one of those days," she whispered. She'd always been a bit more emotional than the women she knew. She cried at television commercials, songs... Sometimes just a beautiful sunset moved her to tears. She couldn't help it. It came as second nature to her and had always been her way.

Thankfully Adam found the flaw endearing rather than annoying.

Her husband kissed the top of her head and cuddled her closer.

"Let's order in then. We haven't done that in a while. What would you like?"

Sweet. He was so sweet. He had always taken care of her, gone out of his way to check on her whenever she was sick with a cold or laid up with one ailment or another. She couldn't have asked for a better man, a better husband. "I'm not hungry."

"Come on now, you can't let a little burnt fish upset you. Had it caught fire and made us call 911, that'd be different," he teased.

She managed a smile though it felt stiff and painful. "You're right. But I really don't care what we have. You pick something. Anything is fine."

Adam kissed her forehead and started to release her but then paused, the fine lines around his eyes creasing a bit when he narrowed his gaze on her face.

"Are you sure nothing's wrong, sweetheart? What's got you so on edge?"

"I'm fine." She lifted her hand to shove the hair away from her face, and Adam snagged hold of it.

"What's this?"

"Oh. Nothing. I cut myself at Hadley's today. It's just a scrape. She...shared something with me today." Remembering that Adam knew all, she frowned at him. "About her divorce."

Adam inhaled and stroked his thumb over her cheek to dry a tear.

"I would've told you except—"

"Client confidentiality," she said, having heard it more than a few times over their years together.

She cuddled back against his chest and sighed. "She's so broken. Sad. Scared. I took a gift basket to her today from the Babes and found her crying."

"Is that what has you so upset?"

Mary Elizabeth wet her dry lips and forced herself to get a grip on her emotions. "Cheryl and Jerry are not going to like it. Cheryl's always been so hard on Hadley."

"Sweetheart, I know you and Hadley are close, but if this will cause problems between you and Cheryl, maybe you should try to stay out of it as much as possible?"

"I'll try," she said simply. Cheryl was her friend. Always had been. But over the years, when Hadley had reached the age where she could babysit to earn money and she and Cheryl butted heads so often, Hadley had become more than her friend's daughter, more than a babysitter.

"MeMe? Is something else bothering you?"

She stiffened at the query and unlocked her arms from around Adam. "I'm overly tired, I guess. First Georgia and now Hadley..."

The time for tears was long over. She needed to take action, like Tessa said. Find out if the man she'd seen was somehow related to Dean.

"Okay then. So how about we place that order so you can make an early night of it? Maybe Italian? Sound good?"

She nodded, knowing that, regardless of what she ate, it would taste like sawdust. "It sounds perfect. You order while I get this mess cleaned up."

"Will you take a ride with me to go get it?"

She nodded again, finding it amusing that the man had spent the day on a golf course but still loved cruising around Carolina Cove in his golf cart. They could easily walk to the restaurant near the pier, but it wouldn't be nearly as fun for Adam. He'd special ordered the customized cart to resemble an old-fashioned red farm truck like the one his grandfather had used so many years ago.

Adam found the menu he searched for and pulled his cell phone from his pocket. Mary Elizabeth turned back to the mess and dumped the burnt fish into the disposal before cleaning the skillet, listening while Adam ordered her favorite meal.

Adam knew her so well, knew everything there was to know about her.

When she'd gotten pregnant with Allie and had trouble, she'd been forced to reveal her secret pregnancy to the doctor and Adam. It had taken a while for Adam to accept that she'd kept such a thing from him, but he'd forgiven her. They'd moved on and focused on their family.

But now... What if the results of the DNA test changed everything?

HADLEY'S LAUGHTER filled the kitchen, and Bryson liked that he'd been able to draw such a response from her. Her smile transformed her features and brightened her shadowed eyes. "Dinner was outstanding. Thanks again for the invitation."

"I'm glad you enjoyed it. Thank *you* for the stories about Nan. I had no idea she could be such a rebel."

"She was a character, that's for sure."

"She always seemed so...grandmotherly to me. I definitely can't picture her running down the board-walk in her nightgown chasing off a pelican."

"She was bound and determined to get her dinner back because there was plenty of fish for that pelican to eat in the ocean," he said with a shake of his head. "She was a firecracker, that woman."

"I wish I'd known that side of her. I mean, I saw hints of it on the rare occasion, but my mom usually ushered me out of the room and made sure I knew what was proper and what wasn't. I would've loved to have seen *that* side of Nan. It seems the more natural one."

"Maybe your mother stressed the need to set an example." It was more likely that Georgia's fun-loving personality rubbed the uptight Mrs. Dummit the wrong way.

"Maybe," she mused. "I mean, I can certainly see

that as the case. I was the disciplinarian with my kids since Kyle was rarely home, so I've no doubt I came across as militant at times. If you ask Max and Abby, they'd totally say I was the mean mom whereas Kyle was the fun dad."

"When they reach a certain age, they'll understand."

"I hope so. Do you have children?"

He shifted in the chair and shook his head. "No, my wife passed on ten years ago. We were never able to conceive."

"Oh, Bryson, I'm sorry. I didn't know."

"It's fine. It was a long time ago. She had an undiagnosed heart issue," he said since that was usually the next question. "She seemed fine. Then one day she just collapsed."

"I'm sorry. Truly. It... It sounds like you have a fondness for children. I hope you don't think this is too bold of me to say, but if you want children, it's not too late for you. A lot of men our age are just now settling down and having families. I wouldn't be surprised to find out my ex is going to be a new father soon."

Her *ex?* It was the first time Hadley had mentioned her husband—or her marital status. His gaze dropped to the rings she still wore and he frowned. What was going on? "I can't picture myself with a baby on my knee. Not anymore. I don't want to be the doddering old man cheering on my toddler. Some things aren't meant to be. I've accepted it."

"I was an only child, so I always wanted a brother or sister. Instead I have a slew of pseudo-cousins thanks to the Babes."

"Ah, yeah. Georgia told me the story on how the name came about."

"It's great, isn't it? I mean, I can't imagine growing up any other way now. It was nice always having friends and playmates and a built-in family."

"It sounds like a fun way to grow up." Bryson stood and his chair scraped back on the floor. "It's getting late. I should call it a night. I'll help you clean up and go get that order placed for the supplies to fix your roof."

"No, *I'll* clean up while you go do that. I insist."

She downed the last of her wine and got to her feet while he scooted in his chair. "If you insist. I'll get out of here so you can call your husband to give him an update on the roof," he said deliberately, watching her. She'd carried her plate and glass to the sink but froze at the comment before slowly turning, her expression turning guarded. "Did I say something wrong?" he asked.

"It's just... Are you going to have a problem working for me? Because my...my husband isn't going to be the one overseeing the repairs on the house. I am."

Her ex. Her husband. He supposed she could have both. Did she?

He'd been trying to get a bead on Hadley since her arrival. Something seemed off. First showing up for Georgia's funeral alone, now the varied references. "I don't have a problem working for you," he said simply. "You mentioned your ex earlier...but you're wearing rings, so I assumed you'd remarried."

"Ohhh," she said, her tense shoulders slumping a bit. "Nope. I didn't realize I'd slipped. I haven't remarried. It's just me."

"I'm not following."

She lifted her left hand and stared down at the rock that flashed in the light from the ceiling.

"My parents don't know I'm divorced. This," she said, wiggling her fingers, "is a lie. I told Mary Elizabeth today. Now you. You're one of"—she counted off on her fingers—"nine people who now know."

He refused to acknowledge the surge of relief he felt at the news. "I see."

"It's not a secret except...it is. I mean, I want to tell them. I'm going to. I just don't know how. Especially now that it's been so long."

"It'll happen when the time is right. Until then, your secret is safe with me."

"Mmm. My dirty little secret," she said so softly he barely heard her.

Bryson found himself moving toward her. He set his plate beside the sink and noted that she didn't move away from him, even though her shoulder brushed his chest. "We all have them, Hadley."

Her gaze met his and she turned toward him, face lifted.

"If that's true...what's yours?"

CHAPTER SEVEN

The following morning, Hadley awoke with a groan. She pressed a hand over her eyes to block out the sunlight blasting her and tried to unglue her cotton-coated tongue from the roof of her mouth.

How much wine had she drunk?

She painfully pushed herself to a sitting position, only then realizing she'd slept on the couch in her clothes.

But how had she... *Bryson.*

Hadley pressed both palms to her face and collapsed against the cushions behind her, the move banging her brain on the inside of her skull with the force of a sledgehammer.

No, no, no.

What all had she said?

Done?

She remembered dinner...well, feeding him dinner while she'd sipped her wine. She even remembered opening a second bottle. He'd told her about his wife dying and she'd told him... "No," she whispered, shocked at herself.

She didn't even know the man and yet she'd spilled her divorce secret to him? That's when she'd opened the second bottle and they'd kept talking, but things got...fuzzy after that.

A soft knock sounded at the door, and she peeked through her fingers to see a man's broad form on the other side of the leaded glass inset of the door.

She shoved the throw off of her and stumbled to her feet, fighting off the surge of embarrassment bombarding her. "Wh-who is it?"

"Bryson. I brought coffee."

The need for instant gratification and damage control made Hadley's decision for her. She unlocked the dead bolt and squinted at the bright light of day, wondering how he'd managed to lock the door behind himself when he'd left last night.

Bryson's shrewd gaze ran over her face, and she wrinkled her nose and shielded her gritty eyes. "I apologize."

"For?"

"*Everything*."

He grinned and held out a large cup from London's Lattes. "Here."

"God bless you."

"Feeling it this morning, are you?"

"You have no idea," she said with a groan. "Why did you let me open that second bottle of wine?"

"You needed to talk and the wine helped you do it. Be thankful I cut you off before you opened a third."

"I can't believe... I'm so embarrassed. You probably think I'm a complete lush."

"We've all had our moments. After Tish passed, I had more than my share."

"It's still embarrassing. I can't remember the last time I've done that."

"It's all good. Look, I have to get to work, but I wanted to see how you were doing and to bring that...oh, and this," he said, pulling an individual packet of pain reliever from his pocket. "Down those, drink the coffee, and follow it up with lots of water."

She lifted the cup in a salute before she sipped the coffee and welcomed the jolt of clarity. "How much did I say?"

Bryson grinned again and her face flamed with heat. "Oh, *pickles*. Shoot me now," she said, trudging across the floor to the couch. "I'm *sorry*."

"Stop apologizing. You needed to vent, and from

the sounds of it, you've kept an awful lot bottled up for quite some time. I'm sorry your ex is such a jerk."

She could only imagine what she'd told Bryson in her buzzed and drunken state. She remembered bits and pieces, but nothing that made any sense. "Do I have any secrets left?"

He winked at her.

"Possibly a few. You were pretty focused on your ex, the mistress, and your parents' response when they find out. Are you still going to tell them today?"

She blinked. Tell them today? "That was my plan?"

"Uh, no," he said with a wry shake of his head. "The plan was to go to their house and tell them last night, but I managed to keep you from doing that given your...state."

She closed her eyes as though that could somehow block out her embarrassment. "And after all of that, you put me to bed on the couch."

"Nah. You paced yourself into exhaustion, and once you sat down, you conked out. I just covered you up."

A sound emerged from her, a mix of a groan and a whimper. "Bryson, I-I don't know what to say."

"Nothing needs to be said. You got it out of your system. You can move on now."

Move on? Her brain continued to filter through

the murky events of the evening. She could feel Bryson staring at her a long moment but then turning to go. "Wait," she said, her mind finally zeroing in on something. "You told me a secret."

Bryson stilled, his hand on the open door. Wary? "I asked you what your secret was and you said...you said...?"

She looked at him. The words there but still out of reach. "What was it?"

His gaze narrowed on her as he waited for her response, but when she couldn't remember it, he shook his head slowly back and forth.

"Doesn't work that way, sweetheart. Maybe it'll come to you later."

Sweetheart? "What if it doesn't?"

"Well, then I guess it's still a secret."

"Wait...*Bryson.*"

"Hadley, I have to get to work."

"How did you lock the dead bolt?"

Those eyes of his...and the small smile pulling at his lips? Totally made her heart flutter.

Or was it the remnants of the wine?

"Georgia always left a key outside for me to use. I'd bring in cases of water or groceries for her."

"Oh. Right. I forgot there was one out there."

"Mmm. It's been a rough few days for you."

"You can say that again."

He chuckled at her statement and the sound warmed her insides.

"Hadley, can I give you some advice?"

"After what I've put you through? Have at it."

"Take the meds, get a shower, and go talk to your parents. Rip the Band-Aid off and move forward. From what you told me, you did everything you could, and you're torturing yourself for nothing. They can't fault you."

"That's what Mary Elizabeth said, too."

"See? So what are you afraid of? Get it over with so you can stop worrying and get on with your life."

"I-I will. Today," she said. Because he was right. It needed to be done just so she could breathe again and stop stressing over something she couldn't change.

Bryson lifted his hand in a wave and let himself out the door, and she watched him walk away before closing and locking it behind him.

Hadley opened the package of pain relief pills and downed them, sitting and sipping the coffee to give them both time to kick in.

Once she'd finished, she went upstairs to shower, staying beneath the hot spray so long it cooled and forced her out.

She didn't want to continue lying or deceiving her family and friends, and the only way to do that was to do what Bryson advised. Rip the Band-Aid off and brace herself for the fallout.

But he was wrong about torturing herself for nothing. He didn't know her parents—namely her mother. Nor how they would react to such news.

Hadley got dressed and put on a bit of makeup to cover the shadows beneath her eyes. Prepped for battle, she texted her parents to let them know she was on her way. Her father had retired several years ago from the hotel industry and now acted as a consultant, working from home, and her mother rarely left the house before ten.

Hadley used the short walk and salt air to clear her head and practice what she'd say, but all too soon, she stood on their porch. She took one last fortifying breath before knocking.

"Hadley," her mother greeted as she opened the door. "I just saw your text." Cheryl's gaze narrowed. "Are you all right?"

Hadley took in her mother's perfect appearance. As always Cheryl Dummit looked dressed to impress.

Hadley shoved her dark sunglasses atop her head and entered, walking into the living room, where she spotted her father reading. "I have something I need to tell you both."

"About the house? Is something wrong?" her mother asked.

"It's not the house." She inhaled and fisted her hands until her nails dug into her palms. "Mom, Dad...Kyle and I are divorced."

Her mother gasped. Her father simply lowered his head and stared at her from atop his reading glasses.

"Hadley, that's not... I can't believe you've separated," Cheryl said. "Surely you can work things out."

"Not separated, Mom. *Divorced*," Hadley said. "I didn't want it, and I didn't tell you because I'd hoped to work it out with him and stay together with no one the wiser, but...it didn't. The divorce was final a little over a month ago."

Her father stood while her mother sank onto the edge of the couch as though her knees went weak.

"You kept this from us for...for over a *year?*" Cheryl asked.

More like several years given the problems they'd hidden from prying eyes, but... "I'm sorry."

Her father silently left the room, and seconds later, Hadley heard a door open and close somewhere in the house just as quietly.

Hadley stood there, feeling very much like the wayward child in the principal's office due to bad behavior. Her mother sniffled and wiped a tear from her cheek but another fell. Then another.

"I don't know what to say. How you could've done this...kept this from us..."

"It wasn't intentional. Not at first."

"Of course it was! You should've told us."

"I'd hoped it would work out, Mom."

"But when you filed and *knew* that it wasn't going to?" her mother asked.

"By then I'd kept it secret so long... Mom, I was devastated. It took *me* a-a while to come to terms and accept it. To be able to take a breath without wanting to... I'm sorry, okay? I'm the one who was betrayed, but it's over and done and everyone needs to just...accept it."

Her mother shoved herself to her feet and glared at Hadley.

"Well, I don't accept it. You don't give up on a *twenty-five*-year marriage. How could you?"

How could she? A huff left her chest and Hadley shook her head. "Do you really think I had a choice? Believe I gave up *that* easily?"

"Hadley, he's a surgeon. A doctor. Under pressures and stresses we can't begin to imagine. Did you go to counseling? Talk to your pastor? Seek help?"

Hadley lifted her hands in disgust and turned on

her heel. "Yes, Mom, I did. But he didn't. He *wouldn't*."

"You should've waited. Given him more time and simply stayed separated for a while longer. You're the one who filed, aren't you?"

Hadley closed her eyes and fisted her hands. "Yes, I did."

"You should've waited," her mother said again.

"Yeah, well, I'm sorry I didn't torture myself long enough for you, but when he kept sneaking around to be with his mistress, I got a little upset."

"Hadley—"

"One person can't make a marriage work! My life fell apart, Mom, and there was *nothing* I could do to hold it together no matter how hard I tried."

"If you'd told us, we could've helped you."

"How? What could you have possibly done? Forget it. I have to go."

"Hadley. Hadley, come back here."

Hadley stalked back through the house to the door and yanked it open. She hurried outside, reveling in the slam of the obnoxiously heavy panel behind her that shook the front of the house with the force of her anger.

Hadley walked for a while, every step faster than the last. Eventually her upset faded, and she found herself on the sand, sitting and watching the waves until the sun got so high and hot she knew she'd burn if she didn't go home.

She headed back up the beach and over one of the dune bridges, meandering along the boardwalk toward Nan's.

"Haddie! Haddie, wait up!"

Hadley turned at the sound of the voice and spotted Isabel Drake jogging toward her, her growing baby belly looking like a small pumpkin beneath her shirt. Hadley managed a smile and welcomed her friend with open arms. "Izzy, it's so good to see you! You look fantastic!" she said. "I love the new look."

Isabel's short platinum hair had a dramatic flair perfect for the up-and-coming artist.

"Thanks, I just had Tessa chop it. Mom hates it, by the way, but Everett thinks it's sexy," the woman said with a grin. "And with it growing so fast from the baby vitamins, it won't be long before it grows out again."

"I can't wait to meet your little one," Hadley said to the expectant mother. "How's married life?"

"Better than I ever thought possible."

Izzy looked happy. Not only happy but glowing with health and love. The sight shot a tug of envy through Hadley.

"I'm glad I saw you. Mom said you're now a homeowner? Congrats.

"Thank you. I hope you'll stop by sometime? I could really use the company." And maybe with Izzy around she wouldn't be so compelled to share secrets with a certain handsome contractor next door?

"Of course! But won't Kyle and kids be joining you?"

Now that the dam had broken, Hadley shook her head. "Kyle and I aren't together anymore. Today's the day I spread the news," she said, sounding more than a little flippant. "Feel free to tell whomever you like so I don't have to."

"Oh, boy. I'm guessing your parents didn't take it well?"

Hadley rolled her eyes and hated the way her hungover brain flinched in the doing. "What gave me away?"

BRYSON TOOK a lunch break around one that afternoon. He'd seen Hadley leave an hour or so after he'd dropped off coffee, and he hoped by now that she'd set the record straight with her parents.

The news of her situation had come as welcome surprise, and ever since last night's dinner and her many confessions—everything from being divorced to secretly loving pickled corn—he'd found himself thinking of her more and more. Even though he warned himself off. Women like Hadley tended to go for the doctor/lawyer/white-collar type and that wasn't him. Never had been.

"Yo! Boss man, you up there?"

Bryson called back and continued chewing, listening as the man made his way up the stairs.

Zack didn't have a head for business, but he was a hard worker with a knack for building and design, which made him a really good foreman.

"Hey," Zack said, joining Bryson on the second-floor oceanfront balcony.

"Hey, yourself. You bring that tarp I asked for?"

"Yeah, I got it." Zack braced his hands on the balcony and stared out at the view. "Still can't believe you managed to snag this one."

"I wouldn't have been able to had it not been tied up in estate court and in such bad shape after the last hurricane. The judge made the family sell it just to make peace."

"Yeah, well, lucky you. Once it's all fixed up, you're gonna kill it."

"That's the plan." At least it had been the plan. Now, he wasn't so sure. He found himself wanting to hold on to this one rather than sell it as he'd intended.

But was his reasoning the house or because it put him closer to his beautiful neighbor?

Zack whistled long and low. "Man, no wonder you've been hanging out here so much. Who's she?"

Bryson instinctively knew who Zack referenced before he turned his head and saw Hadley walking toward her house. "New owner."

"I need to win the lottery or something. Move up in the world so I could get a piece of—"

"Watch it," Bryson all but growled. "I know her, and even if I didn't, no one on my crew is going to disrespect women. We don't need to catch any flack for that should someone ever overhear you."

Zack's eyebrows shot high above his sunglasses but he didn't comment further. "It's a compliment. There's just a certain look when it comes to women like that, you know?"

Yeah, he did. The look was called money and it reinforced his thoughts from earlier.

Expensive clothes, designer hair, perfect makeup. There were normal women and then there were women who wore their money. Some did it better than others, but it all boiled down to the same thing.

Bryson finished the sandwich and washed it down with water. "Come on. You can help me get the tarp up over there before you go to the jobsite on Sixth."

Bryson got to his feet and led the way through the house. They got the tarp and a ladder off the company truck, carrying the items between the hedges separating the properties.

By the time they'd climbed up and spread and secured the tarp, Hadley stood in the yard, a hand shading her eyes as she gazed up at them.

"Is it supposed to rain?" she asked.

"Showers possible tonight," Bryson told her. "Better safe than sorry." Right now the damage inside the bedroom ceiling could be fixed fairly easily, but a downpour and fresh leak could lead to more serious problems requiring a lot more work.

Zack climbed down first and stood there like a lump on a log, staring at Hadley.

Once his feet hit the ground, Bryson introduced them.

"Pleasure, ma'am."

"Oh, please don't ma'am me. It makes me feel old."

"You're hardly that."

"Zack," Bryson said, tilting his head to indicate the man should get going.

"Yeah, right. I gotta git. Nice to meet you, ma'a— uh, Ms. Hadley."

Bryson focused on Hadley and noticed she looked much better than she had this morning. "How are you feeling?"

"Good, actually. Thanks for the caffeine and tablets. They did the trick. Well, that and...confession."

"So you told them."

She shoved her hands into the back pockets of her shorts, and he couldn't help but admire the gifts God had given her.

Hadley had always been pretty. As a teenager he didn't remember her ever having an awkward stage. But he'd take the woman over the girl any day.

"Yup. Ripped the Band-Aid off like you suggested."

Impressive. She'd looked so scared at the thought, he'd wondered if she'd actually go through with it. "How'd they take it?"

"About as expected. My dad got up and left the house, and my mom sat there crying in between yelling at me. So I left. Now I'm here."

She untucked her hands and stared down at the rings she still wore.

"I suppose I can take these off now."

He didn't comment. The set was beautiful. Big and sparkly and the kind he supposed women got all excited about. But they represented her belonging to someone else. Someone who hadn't appreciated her. In that sense, to him they weren't worth the money spent on them, and he'd much rather she not wear them.

"You should've heard my mom. I mean, it's not like I wanted the divorce or planned it. I never thought I'd be this age and starting over. I know it happens, but usually it happens early on, you know? When you make it as long as we did and *then* it happens, it really blindsides you."

"I'll bet." As hard as Tish's death was to handle, he knew she hadn't chosen to leave him or their marriage. In that sense he imagined divorce was worse than a spouse's death. Vows weren't meant to be broken. Lives torn apart. Hadley mourned a man who was very much alive and a life no longer hers. Question was...did she want to go back to that?

"Yeah, well, now it's time to come up with a plan so...that's the goal for today."

"A plan?"

"Yeah. My parents know, so that pressure is off, but I still have a life in Raleigh, and this house needs a lot of TLC. And once that's done, I have to find a way to fund the cost of it."

"You don't get support from your doctor ex? A good attorney should've gotten you that given how long you were married." He realized how personal of a topic it was and shifted uncomfortably. "Sorry. That's none of my business."

"No, it's fine. After seeing me less than my best, it's safe to say this topic isn't as embarrassing," she said with a wry grin. "I get spousal but the child support ended when Abby graduated high school. The agreement was that I could stay in the house until the kids graduated college, but then one of us would have to buy the other out, or else we sell the house and split the proceeds. Now that I have Nan's, I have another option. But I'm not sure how the kids will feel. It's a lot to consider."

"What's your gut tell you to do?" he asked.

"My gut says to never drink so much again," she said wryly. "But other than that, it's not much help."

"You'll figure it out. You just need to think on it some more."

"I suppose. But regardless of what I get in spousal, I still have to do something. I can't sit on the beach here or do lunches with the ladies in Raleigh every day. I'll go stir-crazy without a purpose, not to mention the fact I need to be earning."

Some women would do just what she'd said, but he was glad to know Hadley wasn't one of them. He also had a feeling there was more to it than the story she shared, but he negated the urge to ask. Hadley would tell him what she wanted him to know in her own time...or during her next vent. "So your goal is to figure out what to do now that you own two houses," he said.

"Well, a house and a half," she said dryly. "But it's definitely easier to think about now that I'm not worrying about telling my parents."

"Confession has done you good."

She grinned. "It has, hasn't it? It is a relief, even though things are going to be tense for a while." She took a step back. "I've talked your ear off. Sorry about that. Thanks for the tarp. And the advice. I appreciate it, Bryson."

Bryson dipped his head and smiled at her. "You're welcome, Haddie. Thanks for the laughs."

"Laughs?" she said.

When she realized he teased her about her tipsiness last night, her cheeks colored a rosy hue and he chuckled. "Have a good day."

"Wait...one more question. How hard would it be to fence the backyard?"

He shook his head and shrugged. "Not hard at all. Why do you ask?"

"I'm thinking about getting a dog."

"A dog? Are you sure now's the best time to get one?"

"I'm sure it's *not* but...I'm thinking about it.

Whether it happens now or later, I'd still like to get the yard fenced, to prepare."

He liked that she was making plans. Changes. For herself and her future. "I can work up an estimate for you if you like."

"Yes, please." Hadley grinned. "This is exciting."

"You're a special woman if you think a fenced yard is exciting."

"Well, it is," she said. "Thanks to Nan, this is my home, and in her letter, she told me to make it my own, so that's just what I'm going to do."

They chatted for a few more minutes about the type of fence she might like before Bryson got back to work. On the way into the house, he couldn't help but ponder her words.

Making the house her own. Getting a fence, a dog...

Did that mean Hadley considered moving to Carolina Cove permanently?

CHAPTER EIGHT

Mary Elizabeth entered Cheryl's home without knocking. Whenever the Babes were called together for an emergency meeting, doors were unlocked, husbands made themselves scarce, and there were drinks aplenty.

And since she knew exactly what this meeting was about, Mary Elizabeth brought a tray of finger sandwiches to help soak up the alcohol.

"I just don't understand it," Cheryl said to Adaline as Mary Elizabeth walked into the living room. "They were the *perfect* couple. And how can she already be divorced? How could she not have told us? All this time and she couldn't *mention* it?"

"Hey, sorry I'm late. Cheryl, I'm so sorry," Mary Elizabeth said, knowing the only thing they could do for their friend at the moment was lend sympathetic ears.

"Did you know?" Cheryl asked Mary Elizabeth, her gaze zeroing on her like a laser beam. "Before I texted everyone and told you, did you *know*?"

Faltering because she'd never been comfortable lying, she said, "Hadley confided in me yesterday when I stopped by, but *only* because I caught her crying. She was terribly upset about not telling you."

Cheryl's fingers shredded the damp tissue in her hand.

"Well, no wonder. She should've told us *before* it ever happened. To have gone all this time and keep us in the dark. And the children! Max and Abby must be devastated. Why didn't *they* tell me?"

Mary Elizabeth uncovered the tray of goodies and set about topping off everyone's glasses to keep herself busy.

"And I don't care if she *is* divorced, she shouldn't be inviting strange men into her house."

"Strange men?" Tessa asked, choosing a sandwich to nibble. "What men?"

"Some blue-collar worker from next door," Cheryl said in a snide tone. "He was in her house and her all alone."

"I hardly think she would've invited him inside if

she'd felt threatened in any way," Mary Elizabeth said.

"That's not the point. That man used to check on Mama, pretending he cared."

"Maybe he did actually care?" Mary Elizabeth said.

"Or maybe he was just after whatever he thought he could get."

"Getting a little judge-y there, aren't we?" Tessa said, sliding a glance in Mary Elizabeth's direction before turning her attention back to Cheryl.

"Well, it's one thing to be kind to an old woman, but Hadley is a woman alone now, *with* an ocean-front home. Men like that...they *prey* on women like her. I'm sure he probably thinks the worst. He sees the house and no husband and... She still wears her rings. Doesn't that mean *any*thing to people these days?"

"I think it means she didn't want you to notice she didn't wear them and ask before she was ready to tell you," Mary Elizabeth said, trying and failing not to take offense at Cheryl's comments.

Cheryl had always been a bit entitled, and that attitude of hers was coming out in spades. It was Cheryl's greatest flaw. Not that they didn't all have them, but...it didn't show her friend in her best light.

Cheryl didn't keep up with the Joneses, she *was* the Joneses.

"I was going to call Kyle and demand answers, but Jerry *ordered* me not to. Ordered me!" Cheryl said, downing her drink before holding up her glass for someone—anyone—to refill.

"Well, Kyle is probably with his patients," Rayna Jo said. "And a calmer head when you do eventually talk to him wouldn't be a bad idea, either."

"Calm. Who can be calm?"

Certainly not Cheryl Dummit, Mary Elizabeth mused, exchanging another secret, silent look with Tessa. "I'll get another bottle," Mary Elizabeth said to the room when Rayna Jo poured the last of the wine into Cheryl's upheld glass.

Mary Elizabeth left the Babes and entered the kitchen, struggling to keep her nerves in check.

"Don't think you're escaping that easily," Tessa said.

Mary Elizabeth turned and watched as her friend gave her a stern look.

"Ignore her," Tessa said. "She's in shock."

"She's always like that."

"Yeah, well, we love her anyway," Tessa said, giving Mary Elizabeth a pointed look. "Have you given any more thought to what I said about getting a you-know-what done?"

Mary Elizabeth shook her head, not having a single clue how she could manage to snag a sample of Bryson James's DNA. "No. And please don't talk about it here," she whispered.

"Fine. But don't let anything she says bother you. Especially when you don't know what you don't know."

Mary Elizabeth opened the floor-to-ceiling wine cooler and removed a bottle from the middle, knowing the upper shelf selection was for special occasions and the lower to be served to people Cheryl didn't particularly like but was sometimes forced to entertain. "Poor Hadley is a mess. I know my girls and I don't get along sometimes, but I don't ever want them to think they can't tell me something. Especially something as important as getting a divorce."

"My girls tell me everything, but Jack...he's another story. Getting information out of him is like pulling teeth," Tessa said in reference to her only son.

"Do they know about Hadley and Kyle?" Tessa asked.

"After Cheryl sent the text, I let my girls know so they'd check on Hadley. She babysat them for so many years they love her like a sister."

"They don't fight with her like one, though,"

Tessa teased. "I haven't said anything to Jack and the girls, but I will. Hadley needs all the support she can get, even if it's long distance with most of the kids scattered about as they are. I can't imagine how she felt going through the divorce alone."

"It proves how strong she is. And at least she's here now," Mary Elizabeth said. "We can coddle her and make sure she's okay."

"Girls, wine emergency!" Rayna Jo called.

"Coming!" Mary Elizabeth found the button-press opener and went to work. "Guess we'd better get back in there."

"Just remember this is a shock for Cheryl and Jerry. I know you and Hadley are especially close, but imagine if one of your girls showed up a year plus after the fact with this kind of news," Tessa said.

Mary Elizabeth nodded because truth was truth. "I'd be livid. And hurt."

"Heartbroken," Tessa added with a pointed look. "And that's exactly why we're here today. Now let's get in there and commiserate, even if we have to grit our teeth sometimes while doing it."

***

HADLEY PULLED into the driveway later that afternoon and parked close to the walkway. Buckets of paint and bags of supplies with drop cloths, putty, brushes, stir sticks, and more filled the rear of her car and intimidated her, but she was excited at the thought of digging in and doing some work.

It felt good to be busy and keep her mind occupied on making progress with her new life. Selecting the perfect color for the walls had taken her hours, but she'd gone with a creamy white-gray that made her think of aged driftwood. She hadn't been able to find the colors for the furniture she'd like to try, so that remained on the list to track down.

On her trip to the box store, she'd also stopped by the rescue center. She had planned to only look, but after meeting one dog in particular, she'd filled out an application for a nine-month-old chocolate Labradoodle named Hershey.

Hershey was a big girl, ninety-five pounds of energy and fluff. But her sad brown eyes had broken Hadley's heart, especially after Hadley found out Hershey's owners had abandoned her after they'd had a baby and decided the dog was just too much on top of parenthood.

Hadley knew exactly what abandonment felt like, and in that instant, she'd known what she had to do.

It would take a day or so for the application to be processed and for Hershey to get her vet check, but the woman had told Hadley the odds were in her favor since Hershey's size and lack of obedience training had scared off the only other person who'd inquired about her.

Hadley grabbed the notebook from the seat beside her and flipped to the page she'd created on items she wanted in her new life.

*Make Nan's home my own

*Get a dog?

*Purpose/income

She checked off dog, because she'd said enough prayers and He would make it happen if it was meant to. She'd taken the first step. Now it was time to be patient.

She tossed the notebook into her purse and got out to unload and carry her purchases inside. She knew she should've gotten rid of some of Nan's furniture first to give herself more room to work, but right now? All she could think of was painting the dark interior and brightening up the place. And after much consideration, painting walls seemed easier than sanding furniture, even if that meant stacking things up room by room to be dealt with later.

She wanted the house to have that cozy cottage chic feel, and painting furniture she already owned just made sense.

"Looks like you're going to be busy," Bryson said from behind her.

She turned and saw him eyeing the contents of her open trunk. "I am, aren't I?"

He reached inside and grabbed the two five-gallon buckets of paint, carrying both of them with ease.

Okay then. She'd wondered how she was going to get those into the house, but apparently that was no longer a problem. "Just set them inside the door. Thank you."

"No problem."

She made one more trip for the last two bags and spotted the tarp on the roof. Given the dark clouds rolling in and the rain they'd gotten overnight, she welcomed Bryson's forethought.

"The supplies should be here in the next day or so. I'll work on the repairs in the evenings."

"Thank you. Be sure to get me an invoice. Oh, and I'm going to need that fence sooner rather than later."

His gaze narrowed on her.

"What did you do?"

Hadley shrugged casually but couldn't contain her grin. One, she noted, Bryson matched with ease. The fluttering in her stomach returned at the sight.

"I couldn't help myself. It's not a done deal but...a definite possibility."

His chuckle warmed her insides because he was so dang cute when he smiled.

"I see. I suppose I can make it a priority."

"After the roof," she said.

"Yeah, after the roof. So you really got a dog?"

A laugh bubbled out of her, and she pulled her phone from her purse, unlocking the screen and flashing Hershey's sweet face. "Could you have resisted this? Look at her."

Hershey had stared up at the camera with her big brown eyes, very much the sad puppy she was.

Bryson smiled and shook his head.

"Ah, probably not. What's his name?"

"Her name is Hershey. If my application is approved, I should hear something tomorrow or maybe the next day."

"I'll see what I can do tonight then since the roof is on hold anyway."

"You don't mind?" she asked. "I don't want you to get into trouble with your boss."

Hadley watched as Bryson opened his mouth to say something but then closed it and shook his head.

"It'll be fine. Are you going to start painting now?"

She looked at the bags and the walls of furniture

and frames and shook her head. She wanted to do this right, and that meant watching some more videos online and making sure she had a solid grasp of the dos and don'ts. "No. This can wait until morning. I'm hungry and some of my cousins said they'd drop by. They should be here any minute."

"I'll leave you to it then," Bryson said. "Enjoy your evening."

"Thanks again. For everything."

She walked him to the door and watched as he left, his broad shoulders and muscular form drawing her notice even though she warned herself not to ruin what was turning out to be a surprising friendship. And a comfortable one. There was just something about Bryson that left her feeling...safe. Not in a boring way but...it was hard to explain.

Bryson had no sooner walked between the hedges dividing the properties when gravel crunched and Hadley turned to find Izzy's pulling into the driveway.

She made her way onto the porch and waved at the woman. "I'm so glad you're here!"

"Of course you are," Izzy said, smiling as she climbed out of the vehicle and retrieved a gift bag from the backseat before heading toward Hadley. "A couple of the other girls are on their way. The rest send you hugs, say Kyle is a louse, and will be sure to visit on their next trip to town. Oh, and Michael can't make it, but he said if he sees Kyle, he'll give him a beatdown—his words. In the meantime, happy housewarming!"

As Izzy made her way to the porch, Hadley watched as Izzy's eldest sister, Allie, pulled in and parked behind Izzy. Lily and Zoey, Tessa's daughters, arrived next. "You guys, thank you so much! I wanted you to come visit but I didn't expect this! You're wonderful, all of you."

Her "cousins" each carried in bags of food and bottles of some sort, and within minutes, the house rocked with laughter. Izzy and her sister, notorious for fighting, even managed to get along for the most part.

Zoey excused herself to take a call and went outside to better hear. The screen door slammed gently behind her when she returned, but it was her expression that drew everyone's attention.

"What's up?" Hadley asked.

Zoey remained silent for a long moment.

"Zo?" Izzy asked. "Come on, you're freaking us out here. Did you get bad news?"

"N-no. It's not bad. I'm just...confused?" Zoey said.

"Who called?" Izzy asked.

"Logan," Zoey said, referring to one of Adaline's

twin sons. "He's in town and, um...he asked to meet me."

"What?"

"Like a date?"

"What did you say?"

"Are you going to go?"

Hadley listened while the girls bombarded Zoey with questions, but she remained quiet, not wanting to pressure Zoey or coerce her in any way.

"Zo," Lily said. "Do you want to go out with him? Date him?"

Despite the Babes' many attempts to matchmake and set their children up, all of the pseudo-cousins had made a pact not to date amongst themselves in order to keep things from getting awkward. The pact came after Michael's best friend, Oz, and Devon dated and were engaged to be married—until Devon chose a job in New York City over settling down with her fiancé.

The news had rocked not only their families but the entire community, who inevitably chose a side while sharing the latest gossip. But that was back when they were young, with their whole lives ahead of them.

Now?

Zoey was thirty-three. Logan thirty-eight, a twenty-year military man in the process of retiring from service to join the public sector as a doctor. They were adults with established careers and life experience, not two kids still living at home.

"I said I'd have to get back to him," Zoey said, searching their gazes before landing on Hadley. "I mean, he's probably just wanting information on working at the hospital, right? He didn't mean an actual date. I just misunderstood. I'm sure of it. Right?"

CHAPTER NINE

Hadley rolled over in bed and stared at the ceiling. It was early yet, the sun just starting to make an appearance, but thanks to limiting herself to two glasses of wine and then water the rest of the night, she wasn't suffering a repeat of yesterday morning.

Thoughts of Zoey's dilemma filled her head and Hadley frowned. She understood Zoey's hesitation in dating Logan—if that's what he wanted—because one misstep could cause major friction. They were family by choice, but it worked because they weren't romantically involved. Things tended to get messy when that happened, as Oz and Devon would attest. Ever since their breakup, things had never quite been the same, even though Oz was Michael's best friend and not an actual "cousin."

Would Zoey say yes? As of last night when she'd left, she hadn't decided what her response was going to be.

Hadley stretched and rolled to the edge of the bed, excited to get started on her day.

Izzy had given her some great tips last night on the best way to prep for painting, and along with what the guy had said at the box store, Hadley felt she had a good handle on how to begin.

She changed into the same shorts she'd worn yesterday since she was sure to get messy and added a simple tank top before making her way downstairs. If she planned to stay much longer, she really needed a trip to Raleigh to pack up her clothes and the items she wanted brought to Carolina Cove. But that also meant dealing with Kyle, and she wasn't quite ready to face him just yet.

After learning of his cheating, she'd discovered it took a certain mindset for her to speak to him and keep a civil head about her because the hurt and betrayal ran so, so deep. Forgiving was one thing, forgetting another. Being in the same room, hearing his voice, smelling his cologne—it took shoring up her defenses to cope.

Coffee first, breakfast. Then thinking serious thoughts.

She shoved her wonderings away and forced herself to focus.

While the coffee perked in Nan's old-fashioned machine, Hadley moved through the lower level of the house. She knew to start small and that whatever room she chose to tackle first needed to be easy since it was her first try at DIY.

She knew how privileged she'd been in that she'd never had to worry about such things until now, but that fact was also a motivating one. She felt the urge —*need*—to create her new home with her own two hands.

She finally chose the downstairs powder room because it was tiny and the gloomiest of all since it had no window.

After a breakfast of peanut butter and banana toast and two coffees, she set to work removing everything she could from the bathroom walls. Nan had a three-tiered shelf stacked with knickknacks above the toilet along with various pictures that were too large for the space with their thick gold frames.

She couldn't wait for the bathroom to be light and bright with only a simple seascape and maybe some shells for decoration.

She found a screwdriver and removed the towel holder and then wiped down the dusty walls before getting the hole filler and the thingamabob that scraped the gunk flat. It didn't take long for the patched holes to dry, and she opened the packet of sandpaper next, remembering the comment to make sure the walls were as smooth as possible or else the flaws would show beneath the paint.

She might've overdone the sanding because that took her the longest since she was OCD about the patches being smooth to the touch. Finally finished, she realized she needed to wipe down the walls *after* sanding rather than before.

Groaning, she cleaned the walls again, vowing as she sneezed that she wouldn't forget next time. She was also thankful she'd started in the smallest room since it didn't take long to redo the step.

She put down the painter's plastic and taped it in place, then stood back to survey her handiwork.

That was everything, right?

Hadley managed to pry open one of the five-gallon paint buckets, but since she couldn't lift it, she found an old plastic ladle and managed to scoop it into her paint pan without making too much of a mess. She turned on music, grabbed her newly purchased roller, and was about to make her first dip into uncharted paint territory when she heard a car door slam.

A peek out the front window left her gasping and she hurried out of the house. "Hershey!"

The dog's tail began wagging, and a goofy smile broke across the Labradoodle's face at her greeting.

"I thought you might like this surprise," Amie, the rescue manager, said. "Everything was approved and she passed her vet check with flying colors."

Hadley knelt on the ground and cuddled Hershey, rubbing the dog's big, fluffy ears and head while staring into her soulful eyes. "Oh, you *are* a surprise. A wonderful surprise!"

"You have a beautiful home. And that view!"

"Thanks. It'll be nice to have someone to share it with."

"You're a lucky dog, Hershey. I hope it's a good time to drop her off? I could tell you had your heart set on her, and I hated to take her back to the kennel when she'd been given the all clear."

"Oh, you're sweet. Both of you," Hadley said, smiling at the younger woman. "Thank you for bringing her. I'm so happy to get her."

"No problem. She comes with a small bag of food that should last several days, a few toys, and the bed the family left her with."

Hadley kissed Hershey's soft head one last time and got to her feet. "I'll be sure to pick up more food right away. We'll get some new toys and treats, too."

"I can tell she will be well loved," Amie said, handing over the leash.

Amie helped carry Hershey's belongings to the porch, and Hadley waved as the woman got back in her car.

Once Amie had left, Hadley looked down and found Hershey watching with a wary, uncertain expression in her eyes. "Hey, I know I'm new at this but I am really glad you're here. We've got each other now."

Hadley held out her hand and laughed softly when Hershey lifted a paw as though to shake. "*Good girl*. Let's shake on it."

Hershey blinked at Hadley and Hadley remembered the dog had yet to be trained. She held out her hand again. "Hershey, shake."

More hesitant this time, Hershey lifted her paw and almost placed it in Hadley's but lowered it before she followed through. "Aww, sweet girl, it's okay. Hershey, shake."

This time the dog followed through with the move, and Hadley practically jumped up and down in her excitement, petting and praising and loving on the dog. "Oh, you're a smart girl! Yes, so smart! Okay, come on. Let's get you settled inside. You can supervise and tell me if I'm doing it wrong," Hadley said, opening the door.

Hershey entered but stopped a few steps into the living room. Hadley removed the leash and watched as Hershey roamed, sniffing and checking things out. "What do you think? Not bad for your new home and way better than the kennel, yeah?"

Hershey moved to the kitchen tile and slowly sank down, sprawling out on her belly.

"I guess you are a little hot wearing fur, huh?" Hadley found an old plastic bowl and filled it with water before tossing in some ice cubes. "We'll just put this right here for you," she said, placing it on the floor near the dog.

Hershey lowered her head with a deep, seemingly dejected sigh that broke Hadley's heart. "Oh, Hershey. I know I'm not your family yet but we're gonna be friends soon." She stroked her hand down the dog's head and back. "And I promise I won't give up on you if you don't give up on me, okay? We'll figure out how to do this."

Hershey didn't move.

"Okay. Well, you think about it while I get back to work."

Hadley kept an eye on Hershey and returned to the paint pan. The paint had set up a bit in the time she'd been away, and she used the roller to mix it all up again. It was a little gloppy but she made her first roll on the bathroom wall and grinned. She so had this.

Hadley lost herself to the process. She focused

on her task and managed to get an entire wall done in no time. Then again, the bathroom was small and the wall she'd chosen the easiest to paint, with no obstacles.

Now she had to work around the vanity and toilet and light fixtures and switches.

Little by little, Hadley rolled the area before switching over to a brush. She scooted the paint pan into the hallway out of her way and was on her hands and knees painting behind the toilet when she heard the screen door slam.

When she didn't hear a greeting, she poked her head out of the bathroom. "Hello?"

She didn't spot anyone—or Hershey in the kitchen.

She turned toward the door again and looked down, her gaze flaring wide at the trail of suspiciously large paw prints across the floor. "No, no, *no.*"

Hadley tossed the brush aside and scrambled to her feet so fast she got a head rush, but she had sense enough to grab the leash on her way out of the house. "Hershey? *Hershey!*"

"This who you're looking for?"

Hadley turned to find Bryson leading Hershey by her collar. Hadley gasped. The chocolate Labradoodle now had a white muzzle and face, four white "socks," and random spots along her dark, furry body. "Oh, wow."

Bryson chuckled and paused at the base of the steps, looking up at her.

"You can say that again. I think you're wearing almost as much paint as the dog."

She looked down at her paint-spattered legs and arms and shrugged. "It's a learning process," she said to Bryson. "Oh, Hershey, what did you do?" she asked, hurrying down the steps.

"Your paint roller is history. Hope you bought several."

"I did. Thank you for catching her."

"She came up to me carrying her prize like she'd won the lottery."

"I'll keep the door closed from now on. She hadn't moved from her spot for over an hour, so I wasn't expecting her to just take off like that."

Hadley leashed the dog and made sure to keep a firm grip.

"Just too much temptation, eh, girl?" he said to Hershey. "Want some help cleaning her up?"

Hadley stared down at Hershey and the momentous task that loomed. "You don't have time for that."

Bryson chuckled. "I have time. It'll be worth it to see what happens next," he said with a teasing wink.

"Come on. Let's go round the back and put the water hose on both of you."

Hadley shook her head at Bryson's teasing and gave him Hershey's leash so she could run back inside and get dish soap and towels. She ached to clean the paint off the floor but first things first. Hershey had to be bathed before the paint dried completely.

She exited the back door and discovered Bryson had tied Hershey to a tree in the shade and was already gently rinsing what paint he could from the dog. "Here," she said, squirting a line of soap down Hershey's long body.

Bryson soaped his hands and used them to gently scrub Hershey's face and muzzle.

"Beautiful dog."

"I think so, too," she said, working on one of Hershey's paint-coated legs. "The rescue worker said Hershey's owners abandoned her when they had a baby."

"Ah, well, they didn't deserve you then," Bryson said to the dog. "No one should be abandoned."

The words melted Hadley's heart.

It took quite a bit of time and repeated washes to get the paint out of Hershey's fur. Hadley was soaked with sweat by the time they'd finished, and she longed for a shower herself. "You've saved the day. Again," Hadley said to Bryson.

"Happy to help." He lifted the spray nozzle and aimed it at her.

"Don't you dare."

"Hershey's clean. It's your turn," he stated with a grin.

She held up her hands, laughing. "I'll shower—after I clean up the mess she made in the house."

Bryson grimaced. "In there, too?"

"Yup," she said, wrinkling her nose. "It's undoubtedly dried now but maybe I can scrape it off the floors."

"Let me take a look."

"Aren't you tired of helping me?"

"Just being friendly."

She stared at him, a little suspicious of his motives now that her mother had planted the seed. Bryson must have sensed her thoughts.

"Hey, no pressure. Just offering."

Hadley shook off her hesitation, because even if his motive wasn't sincere, she wasn't ready for any kind of entanglement. Not after what she'd been through. "Hey, if you want to, have at it."

"Okay, I will. I also have some good news. I was on my way to your house to tell you I have the materials to start on that fence when Hershey came running up. I can start tonight."

"That's wonderful!"

"I thought you might like that."

Bryson smiled at her and Hadley felt her stomach clench and flutter.

He really was a handsome man.

The kind of man her mother had always warned her about.

BRYSON SPENT way too much time at Hadley's. First with the dog, then helping her clean the paint off the old wood floors.

His typical workday was almost over so he called it a wash. Once the last of the paint drips were cleaned up and Hadley had excused herself to shower, he left to retrieve the supplies to start on the fence.

Zack stopped to help and dusk was setting by the time they called it a day. Zack left while Bryson gathered up his tools and locked them up for the night.

He'd made a second trip when a car pulled into Hadley's driveway, and he turned to find Hadley's mother glaring at him. Bryson dipped his head in greeting and waited for the woman to emerge. "Ma'am," he said once she did.

"You're here again?"

"Yes, ma'am. I'm installing a fence," he said, even though it was none of her business.

"I see," she said with a lift of her pointy chin. "Well, you can get back to it."

Yeah, because that's all he'd ever be to people like Cheryl Dummit. The hired help. "You have a good evening, ma'am."

Bryson started to make his way through the hedges once more but paused to watch as Cheryl's knock went unanswered. She tried to open the locked door, then used one of her keys to let herself in.

Bryson had just taken a step to continue on when Cheryl's shrill screams filled the air. He dropped his tools and ran for the house, entering the same time Hadley came running down the stairs clutching a towel to her wet body.

Hershey barked nonstop in the kitchen, the dog's fear and panic tangible.

"Hadley! Hadley, *help*!"

"Mom?"

"Get this creature away from me!"

Bryson tried and failed not to take in every aspect of Hadley's damp towel as he followed her into the kitchen, where Cheryl Dummit cowered in a corner, shooing the dog away with a kitchen chair.

"Mom! Put that down. Hershey isn't going to hurt you."

"Get that mongrel away from me!"

Hershey let out another bark that changed into a whining growl as she looked to Hadley as though for instruction.

Bryson silently praised the dog while stepping toward her. "Hey, Hershey. Come here, girl. Come."

Hershey turned her head toward him and Hadley and, after a last glance at Cheryl, moved to sit by Hadley's bare feet.

"What on earth is that thing doing here?" Cheryl asked. "And why are you naked?"

Bryson watched as Hadley blinked and drew back at the barrage.

"Hershey is my dog—and I was taking a shower behind a locked door. What are *you* doing here?"

Hadley slid Bryson a glance over her shoulder and hitched the towel higher on her chest.

"Do you mind?" Cheryl said to him. "You can leave."

Dismissed, Bryson ran a hand over Hershey's head, patting her. *Good girl.*

"Mom, why are you here?" Hadley asked in a measured tone.

"I came to finish our discussion about Kyle. I'm glad I did, too, so I can put a stop to this nonsense. A dog, Hadley? You think you're going to replace your husband with a dog?"

"Well, at least she's loyal and isn't going to screw around on me," Bryson heard Hadley say.

"You're being ridiculous. I demand you get rid of it."

"Absolutely not."

"Hadley Jo—"

"Hershey is staying, but *you* can go if you don't like it, and from now on, I'll visit at your house without bringing Hershey."

"How dare you! I get scared within an inch of my life and you stand there and take up for a dog?"

"Mom, if you hadn't barged in, she wouldn't have barked at you. Hershey is just settling in, but she knows this is *her* home now and I am her person. You can't blame her for being protective of it *and* me."

"If that's the case, then why didn't she growl at that man? Hmm? Why didn't she bark at *him*?"

Bryson grinned, and even though he knew he'd outstayed his welcome, he lingered, wanting to hear what happened next.

"Because Bryson is our friend."

"Oh, Hadley, you can't be that naive."

"Mom—"

"Go put some clothes on so we can talk. And take that thing with you so I don't have to worry about it biting me."

Hadley whirled around and stomped into the living room with Hershey faster than he could get out the door. Caught in the act of eavesdropping, Bryson met her surprised gaze.

Hadley opened her mouth as though to speak but then shook her head, giving him a silent expression filled with apology.

Bryson dipped his head in an understanding nod and quietly let himself out of the house, pulling the door firmly shut behind him so Hershey wouldn't get any ideas.

The streetlights had come on while he'd been inside, and he used them to find the tools he'd dropped in his mad rush to get to the screaming woman.

Once everything was locked up, he found himself at a loss because he was in no mood to go home.

Drawn by the sound of the crashing waves, he headed toward the sand and spent the next hour walking along the shore. The salt air helped clear his head along with the surf, and soon he headed back to his truck.

Along the way, he passed by Hadley's house and

noted that her mother's car was no longer parked in the driveway.

Bryson continued on by the hedges and into his yard.

"Hey."

He lifted his head and found Hadley sitting in the shadows of the stairs, Hershey lying on the ground at her feet. The dog stood the moment Hadley spoke. "Hey, yourself."

"I owe you an apology."

"For what?"

"My mom can be amazingly..."

A low chuckle emerged and he shook his head several times. "Yeah, she can be. But there's no need to apologize. That is, unless you feel the same way."

"I do not," she said firmly. "You've been nothing but kind and helpful and...a wonderful friend, not only to me but to Nan."

Bryson stared at her, the knife sliding deep.

A friend. Okay then.

"Bryson?"

"Good night, Hadley."

"Wait... Did I say something wrong?"

He told himself to walk away. But like earlier, he couldn't. "Yeah, you did."

"I'm sorry, I'm not following."

Of course she wasn't. Because he was so far off

her radar she didn't see even him. Same as in the old days. "Forget it."

"Tell me. What did I say wrong? *Bryson?*"

"What if she's right?"

"Who? My mom? Right about what?"

"What if I am interested in more? In you?"

He'd shocked her with the question but no more than he'd shocked himself with saying the revealing words aloud. Thinking it was one thing, but actually telling a woman like Hadley that he was interested? Attracted to her?

"I-I... Bryson—"

"Go home, Hadley."

"No. I-I'm flattered. Truly. It's just... I don't know what I'm doing. You know that, right? I don't know how to *be* this person. Not yet."

Her choice of words left him wanting more insight. "What person?"

She stood and moved several steps toward him. "Single. *Divorced.* Alone. It's all so new," she said softly. "The kids *just* left to go to college before I came here, and I've hidden the truth from my parents for so long it's like...it feels like a lot of it's just now sinking in. I'm only now processing some of the emotions because I haven't had time to figure them out so if... I wonder who it is you're interested in, because right now I don't even know who I am."

The truth in her words resounded with him, and even though she didn't see herself as a whole, he did. And he liked what he saw. "You might not. But I do. And for now I suppose I can accept that."

He remembered his state of mind after Tish had passed. The fog and grief and finding his way through the days and weeks and years that followed.

"Do you mean that?"

"Yeah. I get it, Haddie. I do."

"So...we're okay?" she asked, the tentative question a reflection of the lack of confidence she felt in herself.

"We're fine," he said with more conviction than he felt. "All good."

She took another step closer.

"And you'll ignore my mom?"

He watched Hadley smile at the face he made. "I'll have to get back to you on that one."

Hadley slowly held out her hand, and Bryson eyed it before he took her soft palm in his, unsure of how he was going to keep his thoughts and interest in her in check but determined all the same.

She stepped toward him and brushed her lips over his cheek, quickly moving away before it could turn into anything more.

"Thank you," she whispered. "Good night, Bryson."

CHAPTER TEN

Mary Elizabeth sipped her coffee and waited for Tessa to join her at London's Lattes, a little coffee shop set several streets back from the pier but within easy walking distance.

Tessa had promised to be on time, but as yet she was ten minutes late, and Mary Elizabeth was losing patience.

She went back to looking at the laptop in front of her, frowning at the screen. From the Google search she'd just typed in, it would be impossible to get a DNA test without Bryson knowing.

"I'm sorry, I'm sorry, I'm so sorry," Tessa said as she hurried toward the table where Mary Elizabeth sat.

"I locked my keys in the car and had to wait on

Allie to come with a key to the house so that I could get the spare. I would've walked but Allie said she had to come right now because of picking the girls up in a bit from their swim class."

"It's fine," Mary Elizabeth said as she always did whenever Tessa gave her excuses. "You're here now."

"Let me get an iced latte and we'll figure this out. I've got an idea."

Mary Elizabeth fought off her nerves and took another sip, glad she'd chosen decaf.

She kept the computer screen turned toward the wall so there was no chance a passerby or customer sitting nearby could see.

Finally Tessa returned after placing her order, the owner herself promising to bring her drink to the table when it was ready. Mary Elizabeth looked at her somewhat desperately. "I don't know why you insisted on meeting. This is impossible."

"Nothing is impossible," Tessa argued.

"It is. We can't very well walk up to him and ask for a cheek swab or blood sample," she said, careful to keep her voice to a low whisper.

Tessa tilted her head to one side, her mouth twisted as though she bit the inside of her cheek.

"Maybe not. But we can get a hair sample," Tessa said.

"What?"

"You know how much I love crime stories. Bruce and I watched one last night where they did a DNA test on someone's *hair*. I asked Bruce if that actually worked and he said it's accurate."

Mary Elizabeth blinked at her friend. "Okay, but how do you propose we get a sample of his hair when we don't even know the man?"

"Easy. I'll offer to give him a free haircut."

Mary Elizabeth blinked and sat forward in her chair. "You can do that without making it totally obvious?"

"Here you go."

They both turned toward London, the owner, and stared.

"Whoa. You two look like you're plotting to take over the world," London said with a teasing smile.

Mary Elizabeth forced a smile at the coffee shop owner and firmly shut the lid of the laptop. "Just girl talk."

"Must be serious. Let me know if I can bring you anything else. Enjoy, ladies," the woman said as she walked away.

"Seriously, can you do that?" Mary Elizabeth asked the moment London moved out of earshot.

"Of course. There's always a chance he'll say no, but I'll do my best to convince him to accept my offer, and when he comes in, I'll get what you need."

Mary Elizabeth palmed the cup in front of her and stared at her friend, unable to express the level of her gratitude.

Tessa reached over and placed her hand on Mary Elizabeth's, squeezing gently.

"It'll be okay, MeMe. Breathe."

Breathe? She didn't think she'd taken a deep breath since the moment she'd set eyes on Bryson James.

Once they'd finished their coffees, they decided to change clothes and stop by Hadley's to pitch in on her painting projects.

They'd heard all about Cheryl's visit the day before and somehow managed to keep their amusement in check. Cheryl had never been dog friendly, and Hadley's rescue had obviously sensed it.

The two picked up sandwiches for lunch, grabbing an extra just in case, and arrived a few minutes after noon.

"Here we go," Tessa said, winking at Mary Elizabeth.

A knock at the door led to a loud round of barking from within and the sound of hurried footsteps. Hadley opened the door, looking a bit frazzled.

"Oh! Hi!" Hadley pushed open the screen door. "Come in. Sorry about the noise."

After hugs and greetings, they followed Hadley

to the kitchen, where she'd rigged up a barrier to keep Hershey contained.

"Oh, she is a big one," Tessa said.

"Beautiful, though," Mary Elizabeth hastened to add, knowing how quickly pet owners became defensive of their animals. Hadley had such a huge heart and the big, fluffy dog had the kindest eyes. No doubt Hadley had fallen in love instantly. "And so soft."

"We brought lunch," Tessa said.

"And came ready to work." Mary Elizabeth made friends with the dog, fascinated with the texture of Hershey's velvety fur. "You really are beautiful, aren't you?"

"She's so smart," Hadley said. "I've been teaching her a few commands and she picks them up right away. She's protective of me, too. I think we're going to be good friends once we work out the kinks."

"Kinks?" Tessa asked.

Hadley laughed wryly.

"Let's just say she stole a paint roller and made quite the mess—and a pretty epic escape. Thankfully the guy working next door caught her before she got lost."

Tessa met Mary Elizabeth's gaze and began digging through the bag of food. "Oh, would you look at that. We have an extra sandwich. Hadley, you should invite your new friend over and share. To thank him for helping out."

Hadley turned and leaned her slim hips against the countertop behind her, eyeing Tessa with a pointed look.

"Okay, what's up with you two? Did Mom send you over here to check him out?"

"What? No," Tessa said. "Don't be ridiculous. Mary Elizabeth mentioned he was cute, though, and I thought maybe he might be into older women. You never know. I could be a cougar."

Hadley and Mary Elizabeth laughed at Tessa's comment because it was so true.

"Well, how about we take this out onto the porch, and if he makes an appearance, I'll invite him over so you can test your flirting," Hadley said.

"Sounds like a plan to me." Tessa sent Mary Elizabeth a pointed, eyebrow-waggling look.

Within minutes they'd carried their lunch to the porch facing the Atlantic and settled in with large glasses of sweet tea. The surf crashed against the beach in the distance, and the sounds of summer were present, with the breeze carrying the unbridled laughter of children screeching as they ran from the waves.

"So did you really come to paint? Because if so, I'll totally put you to work," Hadley said.

"You have us for the whole afternoon," Mary Elizabeth said.

"Mondays are my day off," Tessa added. "The salon is closed and I am free."

"And you want to spend your free time painting?" Hadley asked, sounding doubtful.

"You should know by now that if you need anything, we're here for you," Tessa told Hadley. "We thought you could use a hand is all."

A loud bang sounded next door, and Mary Elizabeth noted all three of them turned toward the sound.

"Is that him?" Tessa asked, getting up to peer over the railing with her head turned in Bryson's direction.

Oh, yes, it was, Mary Elizabeth thought. Her heart stopped in her chest, then picked up speed, just like it had the first time she'd seen him. The man was so *Dean-like* in his appearance.

Tall and handsome. Dark haired. This man carried a bit more weight and muscle than Dean had at eighteen, but even the way Bryson moved reminded her of her long-lost love.

"Girl, did you ever hit the jackpot," Tessa told Hadley. "He's a cutie."

"Yes, well, he's not *my* anything," Hadley corrected. "I told him I'm not ready for... more."

Tessa and Mary Elizabeth turned toward Hadley, and the younger woman's face heated up like she'd spent the day in the sun.

"He asked you out?" Tessa asked.

"He...indicated that he might be interested in me but..." Hadley avoided their gazes. "All this is so new to me. Dating? My last first date was twenty-seven *years* ago."

"Well, there is nothing as fun and exciting as a first date," Tessa said. "You should reconsider."

"Tess," Mary Elizabeth chided. "Don't rush her. She'll know when she's ready."

"Exactly," Hadley said. "And right now I'm not. I went from my parents' home to a dorm with other girls to being married with kids—the last of whom just left for college, I might add. I've literally never been alone."

"Well, with that cutie inside, you're not now, either," Tessa said.

"Humans and canines are not the same," Hadley murmured.

Mary Elizabeth nodded in agreement. "No, they're not. And I think it's good that you know yourself well enough to know you need time."

"Ladies," a deep male voice said from nearby.

"Invite him to lunch," Tessa ordered under her breath. "Before he leaves!"

Hadley shook her head at Tessa's excited whisper but called out to Bryson and asked him to join them.

An invitation, Mary Elizabeth noted, that was quickly accepted by a man who couldn't seem to take his eyes off of Hadley.

Tessa hurried to get him a plate and drink while Hadley and Mary Elizabeth welcomed him to the porch and made small talk.

"You're working hard over there," Tessa said. "And looking a little scruffy."

"Tessa!" Hadley said, laughing and shaking her head. "Please don't insult my guest."

"Let me finish," Tessa said, smiling and batting her eyes at Bryson. "I was just going to offer a hard-working man a free haircut. My salon is just a few blocks away."

"Thanks, ma'am, but—"

"I *insist*. It's the least I can do for you since you've helped Hadley out so much with the house. I simply won't take no for an answer."

Mary Elizabeth's breath stalled in her lungs while she waited for Bryson's response.

He glanced at Hadley, looking at bit embarrassed as he conceded.

"If you insist, I'd like that. I could use a good trim. Thanks."

Mary Elizabeth released the breath she held and ignored Tessa's triumphant wink, hoping, if Hadley saw it, she'd take it as Tessa's happiness that her flirtatious gesture had been well received.

But getting Bryson to accept an invitation when put on the spot was one thing. Would he actually follow through and show up?

HADLEY and her aunts worked on painting the living room that afternoon, and by evening, when they'd gone, Hadley collapsed into an exhausted heap on the floor and stared, appreciating a job well done.

The three of them had shared a lot of laughs while working, and she was glad to note that, despite her mother's instant dislike of Hershey, Mary Elizabeth and Tessa had no problems bonding with the gentle dog.

Hershey had lapped up the attention with nonstop tail wags and had been on her best behavior so long as she was able to see what was happening from her confinement in the kitchen. Once they'd moved to an area out of Hershey's sight, the dog had whined and gotten stressed.

Hadley supposed it was only natural for Hershey

to worry that her new owner would abandon her like her old one, but the sounds had broken Hadley's heart. She decided she needed to make a point of leaving Hershey home alone for short periods at a time at first, and then longer ones, to teach the dog that she would return.

After a quick shower, Hadley walked downstairs, and a low grumble sounded from behind the barrier of baby gates Hadley had erected to keep Hershey in the kitchen and out of trouble.

She met Hershey's gaze through the gates she'd purchased from a moving sale down the street. "I hear you complaining but see? I came back," she said, opening the gate. "You were just fine. Nice and safe."

Hershey stared up at Hadley with her big sad eyes, and Hadley had to hold back a grin. "You were a good girl today, Hershey. Yes, you were," she said, petting the dog. "So do you want to go take a walk now?"

Hershey barked and hurried toward the door. Hadley grabbed Hershey's leash, and when the dog saw it, she immediately sat on her haunches so Hadley could fasten it to her harness. Whomever Hershey's original owners had been, they'd given up a wonderful dog.

Hershey picked up her commands almost instantly and was smart enough to know not to give

Hadley trouble fastening the leash because it would delay going outside.

Hadley locked the door behind them and they headed across the yard. Due to the time of year, Hershey wasn't allowed on the beach, so Hadley stuck to the road and boardwalk area and gave Hershey free rein to sniff and sprinkle to her heart's content.

The setting sun had turned the sky bright pink by the time Hadley walked Hershey back to the house.

Hershey growled and Hadley had one foot on the porch step before she realized she wasn't alone. *"Dad...hi.* What are you doing here?"

Hershey was strangely silent, tail low but cautiously wagging as she stared at their visitor.

Her father stood and held out his hand for the dog to sniff. Hershey gave her father a wary stare before moving closer. After a moment, her tail lifted and began to wag in earnest, and Hadley took it as a good sign of her father's mood. "Would you like to come in and see the progress we made today? Mary Elizabeth and Tessa came over and helped me paint the living room."

"You painted it?" he asked, following her into the house.

Hadley lifted her chin as she turned. "I painted

the bathroom, and they helped me paint the living room."

"You could hire someone. You have the funds to do it."

"I know but...why spend the money when I can do it myself? I think we did a great job and it was a lot of fun to spend time with them. Besides, I need something to focus on. To keep busy."

She glanced at him and broached the subject they'd avoided thus far. "Dad, look, I know I owe you an apology. And I *am* sorry. I handled things badly but...all I can say is that I was so overwhelmed, I wasn't sure what to do. When my head finally cleared some, so much time had passed that I couldn't tell you."

Her father knelt and filled his hands with Hershey's soft fur.

"Some things are too painful to share," he said finally. "I don't imagine any divorce is easy."

"It wasn't. I hated every moment of it. I thought... Some days were very dark," she said simply, truthfully. "And I know, if you'd known, you'd have been there for me but... I needed time to process things on my own. To get through them and come out the other side. The kids were there for me, at least until Kyle began playing Disney dad."

Hershey nuzzled her father's chest and gave him

what Google had told her was a "Doodle hug," something the dogs were prone to do to show affection.

"Aren't the kids a little old for Disney?"

"One would think but...a dozen trips in a year would indicate otherwise," she said with a wry twist of her lips.

Her father shook his head in disgust and stared into Hershey's big brown eyes.

"I've always wanted a dog."

"Really?" The news shocked her. "You always told me I wasn't allowed to have one."

"Your mother doesn't like them. She's scared of them, and since I traveled so much, she would've been the one home with it."

"You're retired now. Maybe you can soften Mom up?"

A low chuckle sounded from her father's chest.

"Highly unlikely. Besides, they're a lot of work and mess, and your mother wouldn't put up with it. She likes things to be neat."

That she did. Cheryl Dummit was anything if not image conscious. "Well, you're welcome to walk Hershey or come play with her any time. She likes you, I can tell."

"She's a sweetheart. When your mother came home claiming you'd rescued a 'monster beast dog,' I wasn't quite sure what to think."

Leave it to her mother to make the sweet Doodle out to be a monster. "I was taking a shower when Mom arrived and she scared Hershey when she let herself in. Hershey's still adjusting to her new home."

"Well, it certainly looks as though she's adjusting well. Huh? Are you settled?" he asked Hershey.

The Doodle lifted her paw and placed it over her father's wrist, holding it while looking at him with her big brown eyes.

"I suppose you are. It's not every day a dog gets to move to the beach," he said, slowly straightening. "I'll take you up on that offer as often as I can," he said to Hadley. "I know of a few good dog parks in the area we can go visit."

"She'd love that, Dad." And it might also help with Hershey's separation anxiety. To know if she wasn't with Hadley that Hershey would be safe with select others.

"So how about you give me a tour and tell me what you have planned for the house?"

"You really want to know?" she asked, surprised by his question since her father had never been one to care about such things. That was always her mother's thing.

"Hadley, I want to know about anything that's

brought you back home and keeps you here. Show me—and tell me about this new friend of yours."

"Oh, geez. Mom is overreacting. Bryson's working on the house next door, and when I mentioned the roof leak here, and he said he'd fix it and do some other work I need done. He's just a friend."

"Mmm. That's some friend if he's doing all of that."

"I'm paying him to do it. He's a professional contractor."

"Bryson James," her father murmured. "Now that you mention it, I think we hired his father once or twice over the years."

"See? Now stop worrying."

"A parent never stops worrying. Just...don't let the man take advantage of you."

"If anything, I'm taking advantage of him. His company has other jobs yet he's made my requests a priority."

Her father frowned at the news.

"And why is that?"

"Uh, what?" Why had she said that? Told her father Bryson was giving her special attention?

"If you're just friends, why is he making you a priority?"

"I-I don't know." *Liar,* she thought, her mind

flashing back to Bryson verbalizing his interest in her.

"Don't you?"

Hadley stared at her father for a long moment before changing the subject and starting the house tour, asking his opinion on a couple of things just to get him off the subject for good.

Still, her father's words stayed with her long after he'd departed. Hadley turned on some music and poured herself a glass of wine, carrying it with her to the porch.

The full moon glistened off the water in the distance, and the busyness of the day had settled into the quiet reserve of evening.

A few people walked the boardwalk, voices low. Some held hands; others walked side by side but distant, their body language familiar in a way she recognized all too well.

They were the ones struggling to reconnect. To find that special something that had brought them together in the first place.

A noise sounded from next door and she turned her head toward the house. Lights were on in the interior, Bryson's truck in the driveway.

And even though she'd only known him a short time, the sight and sounds brought comfort and that...that made her groan and take another sip and remind herself of the pain she'd been through in the last several years.

Who was to say a relationship with Bryson would be any different?

Who was to say she was even ready to tread those waters at all?

But having been alone the last year—basically alone the last three years of her marriage due to Kyle's interests being elsewhere—it wasn't like she hadn't spent an appropriate amount of time mourning the inevitable end.

After tucking Hershey safely inside the house, she carried her glass and descended the steps, slowly making her way through the hedges. The full moon lit the way as she left the bright lights of the board-walk and street and moved into the shadows of the taller house.

The door was open and Bryson worked on laying flooring. He looked up when he saw her and smiled.

"Hey, you. Come in."

"The, uh, owners probably don't want strangers wandering around."

"You're fine. You can't hurt anything."

HADLEY DIDN'T COMMENT. She just stared at Bryson and watched his approach and wondered if the same could be said of himself. She certainly didn't want to hurt him—nor did she want to get hurt.

But wouldn't that be the case if she allowed her curiosity to get the best of her?

"Hadley?" His gaze narrowed on her. "You okay? What's going on in that head of yours?"

She lifted her chin, flicked her tongue over her lips, and saw the way his gaze dropped, distracted by the movement. She told herself to stop, to not go where her thoughts were leading her, but then she thought of his advice and applied it this moment. "Kiss me."

"What?"

"Are you really going to make me ask twice?" She wanted to blame the wine for her behavior but she'd only had a few sips.

Bryson closed the last two steps separating them and lifted his palms to her stroke her hair away from her face. His thumb brushed just under her lower lip, and she parted her mouth to drag in a much needed breath, her pulse racing so fast the rush of blood in her ears drowned out the sound of the waves crashing behind them.

Still, he didn't kiss her.

Bryson looked as though he fought a silent battle with himself as he gazed down at her, but he didn't take the next step.

So she did.

She placed her hand on his forearm and gripped the wineglass tight as she rose onto her tiptoes, gaze lowering as she nuzzled his mouth with hers.

"Hadley..." he growled.

"Bryson," she murmured, the word a breath of sound.

Then she kissed him softly. Once. Again.

"What are you doing, sweetheart?"

"Ripping the Band-Aid off."

CHAPTER ELEVEN

Several days later, Bryson slowed his truck as he drove along Southport's busiest street, his gaze zeroing in on the brunette woman walking along the sidewalk.

He'd recognize Hadley anywhere, especially now.

Hadley had avoided him ever since that night when she'd appeared and asked him to kiss her. And even though things hadn't progressed beyond kissing, there had been a lot of it—until Hershey's incessant barking carried over from next door.

Hadley had used the excuse to escape and bolted, and she'd remained elusive ever since.

He drove a half block and then whipped the truck into a parking spot. It was lunchtime and his stomach growled from hunger, but he decided to take the opportunity that had presented itself.

He'd driven to Southport to pick up some faucets and other supplies he needed. The store in Wilmington had been out of the ones he wanted, but the Southport location had them in stock. The order now waited for him but it could wait a while longer.

Bryson called Hadley's name as he jogged across the street to where she stood gazing into a window. "Hey, I thought that was you."

"Oh, uh, hey, yourself," she said, her beautiful gaze hidden behind dark sunglasses.

He took in her outfit, admiring her long legs revealed by the bright shorts she wore with a white top. "Shopping?"

"Browsing. I've always loved the store down on the corner, and the internet said it carries the paint I'm looking for, so I decided to take some time to explore."

"I know that store. Mind if I join you? That's a great place to treasure hunt, and I need a mirror for the powder room downstairs." He'd planned on getting one at the box store, but it was as good an excuse as any to spend time with her.

"Oh, sure," she said, taking a step in the store's direction. "I thought the owner usually picked out such things?"

"The owner is."

It took a moment for his words to sink in but he could tell by the drop of her jaw when they did.

"You own the house?"

"Is it that surprising to you?"

"No, but—Why haven't you mentioned it before now?"

"If someone only finds me socially acceptable because I own an oceanfront house, they're not someone I care to get close to. You kissed me thinking I'm just a working man. That proved you understand the difference."

He held the door for her to enter and watched as she shoved her sunglasses atop her head. Bryson tucked his into his shirt collar and followed her inside.

"Welcome! Oh, what a lovely couple," a woman said as she approached. "How are you today? Are you looking for something in particular?"

"Oh, we're—"

"Just looking," he told the lady, interrupting Hadley before she could specify their friendship status.

"Well, it's a beautiful day to be out and about. Let me know if you need any help."

Bryson noted the rosy color of Hadley's cheeks and wondered if her embarrassment was due to him referencing their kiss or the woman assuming they were a couple.

"The, uh, the fence looks great," Hadley said, pausing at a display of beach-themed signs. "Thank you for getting it done so quickly."

"You're welcome. Is Hershey home alone?"

"Yeah," she said, wincing. "She has a lot of separation anxiety. The recommendation is to leave her alone a bit longer every day just so she knows I always come back. I, um, called your office and paid for the fence this morning."

Was that why she thought he'd stopped to talk to her? "Yeah, I know. My assistant told me. You could've just come over, you know." He lowered his voice. "But then you would've had to see me again and you've avoided me after what happened the last time..."

Hadley bolted once again, face reddening to the point of looking painful. What *was* she so embarrassed about?

Since she'd made a point to steer clear of him the last several days, he'd shifted his attention to getting the fence done as soon as possible, on the off chance Hadley would emerge from her house to check on the progress.

She hadn't. Even though they'd finished up the job late last night.

When he'd gotten the rundown for the day, his office manager had informed him she'd received payment in full for a job—one she wasn't aware he was even doing. "There was no rush on payment, you know."

"I do believe you'd be the first contractor ever to complain about getting his money."

Her words brought out a chuckle and he smiled at her. "Yeah, I suppose you're right. I just meant you could've...made payments if you needed to."

"It's fine but thank you. For offering. That's sweet."

Sweet. Okay then.

Awkward seconds ticked by as they continued through the store. She paused again, looking at a selection of furniture paints. "Find what you were looking for?"

"Hmm. Yeah. I saw these online." She chose one and then scanned the rest and chose three others.

"More projects?" he asked.

"I hope so," she said. "Do you know anything about paint guns?"

"Do you mean sprayers?"

"Yes, sprayers."

He crossed his arms over his chest and looked his fill of her, clutching the small containers to her chest like she'd scored gold. "I do."

"I don't suppose you could recommend a good one?" She turned and lowered her selection to a table so that she could pull out her phone. "One like this?"

He looked at the screen and then fought off his own embarrassment when he had to put on his prescription sunglasses to get a better look. "Yeah, they have those at the building supply. I'm heading there to pick up an order. How about we grab lunch together and then you go with me? They have a few different ones you'll need to look at."

"Oh, that seems like a lot of hassle. You wouldn't mind?"

"No—so long as you let me buy you lunch first. I'm a hungry man."

She looked hesitant about the lunch, and he knew why, understood, but he didn't give her an out.

"I'd love to—if we go dutch," she said.

He nodded, letting her have the compromise since it meant they'd spend time together. "Deal."

Hadley gave him a small smile and gathered up her paints once more.

"Let me pay for these and we'll go feed you."

She rushed toward the checkout, and Bryson carried her phone with him since she'd taken off without it.

Curiosity got the best of him and he touched the now dark screen. A picture of Hadley and her kids appeared. All were smiling, but even he could see the strain on their faces, and he figured the picture had been taken sometime during the divorce. Her daughter looked like her, whereas her son had darker hair and more masculine features most likely from his dad.

The women chatted quietly and he heard Hadley ask about the furniture on display.

"That's the last of it if you're interested. The person I got it from retired and moved closer to her family."

"I see. I was more interested in watching them work," he heard Hadley say.

"I've watched videos online but it's never the same as learning something in person."

"I can help you," Bryson said, earning glances from both women.

"I've already taken enough of your time, Bryson," Hadley said as she handed her card to the woman.

"We can talk about it over lunch."

Bryson caught the older woman's curious smile and winked at her, but Hadley seemed oblivious to his reasons for offering.

Hadley gathered her bag of goods and said her goodbyes to the woman.

"Have fun," the woman said, adding softly, "And good luck to you," to Bryson.

"Thanks," he said, still holding the door after Hadley had exited. "I think I'm going to need it."

He followed Hadley outside, and she accepted his offer to store the paints in his truck and walk with him to the restaurant.

The lunch crowd had come and gone so they were seated right away.

"I love this place," she said, sunglasses on her nose as she stared out at the water on the other side of the railing. "It's always been one of my favorites to visit."

"I like it, too. Casual and fun."

Their order came quickly. Bang bang shrimp tacos for her and a portabello mushroom melt for him. "So tell me about you wanting a paint sprayer. What's that about?"

"Just something I saw when I was looking online. Nan has so much furniture packed into that house, and I'd like to try to salvage what I can so that I don't have to replace it. It's beautiful but it's all so dark."

"It would be easy to set up a painting studio in that little shed out back."

"Oh, I hadn't thought of that. I suppose I'd have to since I don't want to risk another Hershey disaster inside."

The mention brought a smile to both their lips, and they talked about what she'd need to do to set up a painting area. As they finished up lunch, she went on to share some of Hershey's latest antics.

"I'm just amazed at how quickly she's learning commands and tricks. She's very smart."

"She knows a good thing when she has it," he said.

Lunch finished, they declined dessert and paid their separate checks, then agreed to meet at the building supply store a few miles down the road.

It didn't take long to get there, and he liked the act of walking into the store with Hadley at his side. It felt normal, like something a couple would do as they worked on a home together.

He also noticed the male heads that turned their way as Hadley walked by. She paid no attention to the stares she received, and he wondered if she was even aware of them. Or simply so used to them she didn't notice them anymore.

While Hadley mulled over the differences in the sprayers he recommended, he watched her. The way she worried her lower lip between her teeth as she pondered the pros and cons of each one, the gentle curve of her cheek still flushed from the heat of the day and their walk inside.

She made her decision and went to the small handheld sanders next. Once she'd also found one she liked, she moved on to the paint colors on display while he picked up his order before meeting her at the front of the store. As he approached, he noted she browsed through a book on refinishing furniture.

Everything about Hadley had come as a surprise. Having met her mother, Bryson really wouldn't have thought Hadley the type to do manual labor, but Hadley seemed very excited at the thought of being hands-on with her DIY projects. He liked that about her, that she obviously didn't consider herself too good for such things.

On the way out of the building, Bryson found himself thinking about the last ten years. He'd dated a few times after Tish's death, but he'd never been one of those men who went from woman to woman. It just wasn't in him. He'd had real love for a time, and having had it, he wanted it again.

He'd never found a woman he liked enough to consider dating long-term, but in the short time since seeing Hadley, she not only held his interest but distracted him from his work.

He wondered at her thoughts, if she wanted company to combat the quiet, lonely evenings alone. He also wondered what her reaction would be if he showed up at her door and ordered her to kiss him the way she had him.

Bryson tossed a roll of plastic into her cart and

she looked up at him in surprise. "For your painting booth."

"Ah. Perfect. Thank you so much for your help. I can't wait to get started. Are you finished here? I should probably be heading back."

"Are you taking the ferry or driving around?"

"The ferry. You?"

He typically made the drive as it was sometimes faster during the tourist season, but knowing her answer... "Ferry. We can go over some refinishing tricks on the ride if you like."

"That would be great."

The smile she gave him shifted his attention to her lips once more before he forced himself to look away. Hadley had made it clear she wasn't looking for more than friendship. She didn't consider herself ready. And yet...something about that kiss told him she was more ready than she thought, just too afraid to take the next step.

Which meant either she really wasn't ready...or she knew her family wouldn't deem him suitable for more. He knew why. Because even though he was a successful business owner and good man, he would never be someone her mother would accept as an equal. He'd googled her ex last night and read up on the man. Looked at photos of Hadley's life on his arm at various hospital events where black tie and big checks were the norm.

He could flirt all he wanted, but how could a contractor and carpenter compare to a wealthy plastic surgeon? Would he only be a flirtation on the rebound as Hadley started her new life?

***

HERSHEY'S exuberant response to Hadley's return left Hadley laughing and feeling loved. The dog repeatedly jumped high into the air, her big doggie smile in place, before finally calming down enough to simply rub against Hadley's legs to be close.

Hadley left her purchases on the floor by the door and knelt to cuddle the lovable dog. "I missed you, too," she said, kissing Hershey's fuzzy head. "Were you a good girl? Hmm?"

She took a look around the kitchen, where she'd contained Hershey, but didn't notice any messes or destruction. "Did you sleep while I was gone?"

Hadley had brought down Hershey's bed and some toys and set up the gates blocking off the kitchen before she'd left, and even though the large dog could probably take them down with a simple bump, she hadn't. "Oh, you *have* been a good girl, haven't you? That deserves a cookie."

She got Hershey a treat from the cabinet and the dog immediately sat on her haunches. "Good girl. Easy," she said, having felt the brush of sharp teeth a time or two in the past in Hershey's excitement for the snack. "Good girl, Hershey," she said again when the dog carefully took the bone from Hadley's fingers.

While Hershey munched, Hadley moved through the house to the powder room, her thoughts on the man next door and the time they'd spent together in Southport.

Running into Bryson had been a gut-clenching surprise but a pleasant one. She felt awkward after their kissing encounter, even though she wasn't sure why. She had instigated the kiss, after all. And she didn't regret it. Bryson was the first—the only—man she'd kissed since her divorce and as such, it had been a good one.

Finding out Bryson actually owned the house next door had been another surprise, but his words as to why he hadn't told her tugged at her heartstrings in more ways than one. Seeing how her mother treated him, Hadley didn't doubt Bryson walked a fine line at times when it came to his profession versus the majority of people he found himself working for. She could see where some would treat him differently despite the fact his name was on the business.

It had been nice to wander the stores and sit across the table from him. To share a meal and have someone's full attention.

He didn't keep his phone on the table or constantly check it. He kept the conversation going whenever it lagged, asking about Hershey or the kids and her plans for the house.

The sun had sparkled in the dusting of gray at his temples, and Bryson's tanned good looks had drawn her in. She'd always found salt and pepper attractive on a man, and despite his work clothes of cargo shorts and a logo-ed company shirt, Bryson was no exception.

He looked strong and masculine, in *really* good shape for a man his age, which she'd learned was forty-nine as of August second.

Hadley let Hershey out to play in the newly fenced yard and made her way to the shed discussed at some length over lunch.

Nan had used it to store beach chairs and umbrellas, flowerpots, and the like, so it was a bit cluttered, but if she got rid of some junk and organized it, there should be more than enough space to make it a paint room.

The plastic could be attached to the beams above

her head to keep it from damaging anything stored on the other side, and she could easily envision using the area as a workstation.

While Hershey ran off her energy and piddled, Hadley began sorting through the shed's contents.

Hershey kept a close watch on Hadley, returning every little bit to sniff and make sure Hadley was where she'd left her.

Hadley worked in silence, enjoying the sounds of the ocean in the distance and the squawk of seagulls outside paired with the jingling of Hershey's tags as she ran.

Hadley knew she had more than enough rooms to paint inside the house to keep her busy, but now that she had the bathroom and living room finished, she really wanted to try her hand at a piece of furniture.

Who knows—maybe if she got good enough, she could sell some of the pieces like in that shop in Southport? Could that actually be a business idea? And if so, would it be enough to keep her afloat if she were very, very careful? Was that possible if she marketed to the high-end crowd, whether locals or visitors?

The thought intrigued her. Enough to speed up her organizing efforts and make her give herself a little more room than originally planned. She wasn't talking about simply smearing a coat of paint on old furniture and calling it done. No, she wanted to create art.

She'd watched videos that

made turning the old brown furniture into an absolute art form. They used glazes and shading and multiple colors of paint to highlight the elegant carvings and details that were simply painted over in the other videos.

But that level of turning a piece of wood into a showpiece? That was something she really hoped to achieve. Something she could envision being lucrative if done right and well.

On the ferry ride to Southport, she'd gone over the numbers in the car. The spousal support she received from Kyle would *almost* cover the taxes on the property, but it left nothing to live on. If she could find an income stream that would cover the basics, she could make ends meet and save the money from Nan for emergencies. Living at the beach, there were lots of free things to do on any given day, but there was still the matter of health insurance and utilities on top of the property taxes and maintenance. Was it going to be a struggle in vain? Would she limp along for a few years but have to sell in the end because she simply couldn't maintain the upkeep?

Cross that bridge when—if—it happens. Until then work your butt off to see that it doesn't.

Work. Getting a job would be the "easy" way, but at her age, she found herself intimidated at the thought of interviewing and putting her empty resume out there to be mocked by people who cared nothing for the fact she'd thought being a stay-at-home mom and wife was the thing to do. Something that had nothing to do with being Kyle's wife but everything to do with loving her family and wanting to be there for them when they needed her.

She forced her thoughts away and focused on the task at hand. All she could do was try, give it her all and see what happened. The creative outlet appealed to her. That and the fact she had quite a bit of inventory in Nan's over-furnished house to get her started before she'd ever have to invest in purchasing pieces to work on.

In short order, she had emptied the shed of trash that would be picked up tomorrow. The building was piled full of beach chairs that had rusted to the point of being unusable and old umbrellas stained beyond repair. Bins of Christmas decorations smelling of mold and mice were quickly shut and carried out as well.

Once all of that was gone, she had plenty of floor space to work. She found a ladder and hammer and nails and pondered the best way of establishing a curtain to protect the few items she'd decided to keep.

She spread the plastic and tacked up a corner, moving slowly across the floor toward the opposite wall. She was halfway there when Hershey came barreling into the shed. The dog saw her and immediately began jumping up and down, bumping Hadley's feet and the ladder hard enough to send her scrambling for balance when the ladder tilted sideways.

Hadley shrieked and grabbed the beam she'd been tacking the plastic to, holding on for dear life as the ladder crashed against the items stacked on the other side of the plastic.

"Hang on, I got you," Bryson said as he wrapped his arms around her legs above her knees.

Hadley was so glad he couldn't see her mortified face. "The ladder!"

"Let go."

"What? No!"

"Put your hand on my shoulder," he said, his tone sounding amused. "Come on, I won't let you fall. Hadley, I've got you."

Hadley kept a firm grip on the beam with one hand while searching blindly for his shoulder, smacking him in the head and feeling the rough rasp of his five-o'clock shadow on the tender skin of her inner wrist in the process.

A tingle shot up her arm, and she blamed the sensation on getting the feeling back into her nerves after her death grip on the beam.

"Sweetheart, let go. I won't let you fall."

Her hand found his shoulder, and he loosened his hold until she slid down because she didn't have the upper body strength to swing by one hand, his arms catching beneath her rear. That was when her mind zeroed in on being called *sweetheart* in that husky, gravelly voice of his and the way it made butterflies appear in her stomach seconds after the fact.

Bryson continued to let her slide down, *slowly*, and her heart raced from the scare of the near fall and the fact Bryson was...

Bryson.

Strong, hard, muscled, sexy Bryson.

Her toes touched the floor but Bryson didn't release her. He stared down at her with such a look she could've sworn he wanted to kiss her and ached for him to hurry it up.

But when his gaze shifted from her mouth to her eyes, his jaw locked into a hard line. He inhaled and lowered his hands, took a step back, and she felt the loss all the way to the depths of her soul...

"You shouldn't be on a ladder with the dog running around."

She blinked at him and the angry tone he'd used, stared down at her hands, rubbing them together.

"Are you hurt?"

"N-no. No, I'm fine."

"Let me see," he said, taking her hands in his.

"I... I think I might have a few splinters is all."

Bryson muttered something under his breath that she couldn't make out and wasn't sure she wanted to.

Bryson gently turned her and ushered her out of the building toward the house, Hershey following at a slower pace, head hanging as she stared up at Hadley with sorrowful eyes. "It's okay, Hershey. You didn't mean to."

Inside the kitchen, Hershey crossed to her bed still on the floor, tail tucked, and settled down into a tight circle, obviously sensing the tension she'd caused and reacting to it.

"Here."

Bryson had gone to the sink and now held a damp dishtowel. He gently cleaned her hands and winced when she did.

"You scraped them up some and I see at least four, maybe five, splinters. Want me to get them out?"

Since most of them were in her right hand and she was right-handed, she nodded. "Please. Sorry to be such a fuss."

"You're not fussing. Do you have tweezers or do you want me to use a knife?"

A knife? She quickly moved to the downstairs bathroom and found tweezers in one of the drawers and alcohol swabs in the first-aid kit she'd tucked beneath the kitchen sink after treating Mary Elizabeth's injury.

Supplies gathered, Bryson donned his sunglasses, tilting his head a certain way as he stared down at her hand. She realized then they were prescription, and even though it was silly, she liked that visible sign of his age. It drew her like so many other things about him. Scary things like the way his eyes crinkled when he smiled and the little hint of a cleft in his chin. The fact that his voice revealed his frustration with her, and it was starting to dawn on her as to why.

Bryson had Hadley sit on the kitchen table, her hand propped palm up on her knee. He went to work on retrieving the first splinter while she studied him, liking that she could observe him so closely without him being aware. "You keep coming to my rescue. Thank you."

"No problem," he murmured, focused entirely

on his task. "Ah," he said, holding up the tiny prize. "One down."

He went to work on splinter number two, and she noted the laugh lines on each side of his mouth. The sight reminded her of her crush on Tom Selleck as a girl. "Tell me about your wife."

The words appeared out of nowhere, and Bryson stilled for a moment, shooting her a quick glance over the glasses on his nose, but after a moment, he went back to what he was doing.

"What do you want to know?"

"Anything. I'm sure she was pretty."

A smile crossed his handsome features and she felt a niggle of envy—or was it jealousy? She had no right to that, but the fact that she was reeked of something she wasn't quite able to accept just yet.

She'd love to be loved by someone that way, all the way until the end. That's how marriage was supposed to be. *Till death do us part.* That was the struggle she had. The fact that she had initiated the divorce because she'd been left no other choice, but didn't want to give up on her marriage after so many years. It was that spot between the rock and hard place, where to stay meant accepting Kyle's infidelities and overlooking them but to go meant destroying the only thread left holding them together.

"She was. Tish had bright blue eyes, jet-black

hair. A laugh that was just... No one could hear it without laughing, too."

"What did she like to do? Did she work?"

"Yeah," he said. "She was a preschool teacher. Her kids loved her."

His gaze flashed to hers momentarily once more before moving back to her hand.

"You know those old black-and-white movies? The classics? She'd pop some corn and settle in and binge on them for hours."

"That sounds like a lovely way to spend an evening."

"It was," he said softly. After a few seconds he cleared his throat. "So how about you? Tell me about your ex."

"Ah, well," she said, wondering what she should share. "He's handsome. Charming when he wants to be," she added. "Arrogant, which seems to be a given in his profession. I don't know what he likes at this point, nor do I care. The last two years we were together were very different from the others."

"And your kids?"

As always, a proud smile came to her lips. "Incredible. Smart, beautiful. Determined to conquer the world while taking selfies."

He laughed at her joke and gently rubbed his thumb over the spot he worked on after she flinched.

"Sorry."

"Not your fault."

"How about some ice to numb it?"

He didn't wait for her to respond but moved to help himself to the ice dispenser in the fridge, carrying the pieces back to the table where she sat. "Thanks."

It was awkward sitting there, just looking at one another, and she racked her brain for something to talk about other than exes or past loves. "How did you do it? Go back to dating? I mean, I'm assuming you've dated since your wife passed so many years ago—"

"I have," he said simply.

"And? Every time I think about it, it...seems so stressful and awkward."

"Not when you meet someone you're interested in and form a friendship. Then it's...natural." He held out his hand for hers and began pressing on her skin with the tweezers.

"That sounds nice. But I'm not sixteen anymore, and there are more people in my life now who factor in."

"It's still your life, Hadley. You set the pace, the boundaries. It falls into the same category as telling your parents about the divorce," he murmured.

"When the time comes and you're ready, you'll step up."

Step up. What did he mean by that? Her family had approved of Kyle but she knew a man like Bryson... Her mother's feelings for him were clear, and it was sad that she judged so harshly, but realistically, how could she date someone knowing full well it meant catching the brunt of her mother's disapproval? Wasn't that the same as setting herself up to fail? "How do you meet people?"

He pulled the second splinter out, and she quickly placed the ice over the ache to soothe it. When she looked up, she saw the way he gazed down at her, and she faltered.

"That's a little harder. But...I doubt you'll have any difficulties. Any man would be lucky to date you."

She swallowed hard and flicked her tongue over her lips. Boundaries. Her mother wasn't living *her* life. Nor would she. A heartbeat passed and Hadley decided to...step up. "Does that include you?"

Bryson stilled, his gaze meeting hers. "It does."

His words touched a place in her she didn't know existed, and when she thought of taking that big first step into the dating world, she wouldn't mind having a friend at her side. "Well, um... I was thinking...er, wondering if... Would you like to accompany me to an art show this weekend? Be my plus-one? It's okay if it's not your thing but I thought—"

"I'd like that," he said.

She clamped her lips to stop the rambling. Okay then. She bit her lower lip and managed a smile he returned with that oh-so-gorgeous grin, increasing the fluttering in her body. "I guess we...have a date then."

Bryson winked at her, upping the sensations even more.

"I guess we do."

CHAPTER TWELVE

I got it," Tessa said the moment Mary Elizabeth said hello on the phone.

"What?" Mary Elizabeth sank down on the edge of the tub she'd just finished cleaning.

"Our *friend* came in today for his free haircut, and I made an excuse to pull a few for a DNA sample. I did just what the instructions said to do and now we wait for the results."

The air left Mary Elizabeth's lungs in a rush of relief mixed with fear. Because what if the test came back positive? "Did you put a rush on it?"

"You know I did. And since I paid for it all and sent it out, no one will ever know unless you tell them."

Tears filled her eyes and Mary Elizabeth blinked hard. "Oh, Tessa. You have no idea..."

"Of course I do. Now stop worrying. Whatever will be will be. Right?"

"Right." But she wouldn't stop worrying until the test results came back and she knew, one way or another.

But if Bryson was her son...what then?

"That's not all the news I have," Tessa said in a gleeful tone.

"Oh? What else?"

"Our Haddie has a *date* with the very handsome Bryson this evening. That's why he stopped in. He wanted to get spruced up for it."

"*Oh?*" The thought pleased her and brought a smile to her lips. She loved Hadley, and after all that her goddaughter had been through, she deserved happiness. Dating a seemingly kind, handsome man was a good start. "Did he say anything else?"

"He asked me about her. What I could tell him that might help him along."

"And you said?"

"To keep it low-key. Go slow. I said she's much more about being in the moment with someone rather than how much they spend on her, and since they're going to Isabel's gallery show this weekend, to let Hadley set the pace."

Mary Elizabeth winced. She'd forgotten all about her youngest daughter's show in the turmoil of the last few days. "That's good advice. I'm glad you told him that."

"I did mention that flowers might be a nice touch, though, or a walk on the beach after they get back. Something to prolong the evening rather than it just being the show and back home."

A thrill raced through Mary Elizabeth, and she was excited at the thought of Hadley experiencing new love. *Romance.* Because every woman deserved that. But if Bryson turned out to be her son...how would that make them feel?

What did she plan to do if he was? Would she tell him?

Tell Adam?

Her children?

The rest of the Babes?

Her stomach lurched with unease and nausea rolled over her.

"I've got to run. My next appointment just walked in the door. I had to call you and tell you, though. Oh, and just so you know, since I wouldn't let him pay for the haircut, he tipped big and wouldn't take no for an answer. He's a good man."

She closed her eyes and pressed a hand to her tight chest, over her heart. "Thank you. I mean it, Tessa. Thank you so much. Let me know the moment you hear something?"

"You know I will."

Tessa said goodbye and Mary Elizabeth heard the phone click in her ear. She stared down at the cell in her hand, her family smiling back at her from the photo taken last Easter Sunday.

Isabel looked stunningly beautiful as always. Her wild child and free spirit was as beautiful as she was talented and determined to do things her own way. Thank God her husband was the understanding type and Everett seemed to have good insight on handling her daughter's artistic ways.

Sophia's petite frame and baby face deceived those who didn't know her well enough to see her tough-as-nails backbone and take-charge attitude.

And Allie... Her eldest held her youngest babe, a tired motherly smile on her face with her oldest and middle child in front of her, husband beside of her.

Mary Elizabeth and Adam were on either side of them all, ever the proud parents smiling for the camera while waiting for the timer to go off.

But now Mary Elizabeth looked at the image and wondered how much would change if her belief about Bryson's identity was true.

Not only with her family but between her and the stranger who would be her son.

If Bryson was hers, could they ever recover from

the forty-eight years and the lies that had kept them apart?

BRYSON HAD AGREED to be Hadley's date for Isabel's upcoming gallery show. And since she needed more than the shorts and tank tops she'd picked up on a whim the evening of the funeral, Hadley packed Hershey in her car and made the two-hour drive to Raleigh.

She hoped that seeing the house would confirm her thoughts and feelings about her decision to move home to Carolina Cove permanently and finally give her closure on a painful past.

Hadley let Hershey into the fenced backyard to potty and explore while she gathered and checked the stack of mail that had come through the slot at the door.

There were a few condolence cards, a few bills, catalogs, but nothing urgent. Hershey scratched at the glass door beyond the kitchen, and Hadley smiled at the dog's nose art left behind. The moment she opened the door, the dog scrambled inside and made herself at home, checking things out with periodic sniffs and quiet investigation. "So? What do you think?"

Hershey's tags *clinked* as she padded across the floor and sat on her haunches, lifting one paw toward Hadley. "Aww, sweet girl. I love you, too. Let's get this done, shall we?"

Hershey followed Hadley up the wide staircase to the master bedroom. Hadley dug out her suitcases and overnight bags and began filling them up. She'd take the clothing today and call to get some estimates for movers to do the rest?

Frowning, she paused halfway between the closet and bed where she'd started packing.

Reality set in. Why bother moving anything more than her personal belongings? Where would she put it?

Nan's home was packed to the gills with furniture. Furniture that better suited the house once it was painted and thinned out.

She looked at the massive king-size bed, the oversized wardrobe, and nightstands too modern for the house at the beach.

Hadley dumped the clothes on the bed and left the master, moving through the large house and looking at the furniture purchased with such care and at great expense.

The kids might want their bedroom furniture, but as she moved room to room, she realized there was absolutely nothing she desperately wanted to keep or couldn't live without.

Every piece held memories, and she realized... she was ready to let them be just that. Apparently *this* was a step toward closure as well.

The furnishings were beautiful, but she wanted a fresh start with things that didn't remind her of her life here with Kyle. While her heart had been true, his actions had tainted the beautiful things that made up their home.

By the time she went through the entire house and made her way back to the bedroom with Hershey following her every step, Hadley felt as though a weight had lifted from her.

She'd gathered a few framed photos of the kids, the scrapbook albums she'd made of each of them from birth to now, and packed those in one of the suitcases along with the shoebox full of kid-made Christmas ornaments spanning the years. Those she'd pulled from the storage closet on the landing, leaving the rest of the Christmas items behind, even though Christmas had always been her favorite, and she normally decorated the house top to bottom.

She now stared at the bins and baubles, wondering how something she'd once thought so necessary and special could turn into something that now felt shallow and distant.

Once Hadley filled two small suitcases, she carried them down and left them at the foot of the stairs before going back to load up more.

Hershey ran up and down the stairs ahead of her, keeping track of Hadley as she packed her shoes and purses and clothing. She'd just walked into the kitchen for a bottle of water and a brief rest from the many trips when Hershey tipped her head and released a low growl. The dog took off so fast she skidded into the wall during her race across the tile floor toward the front door.

Hadley hurried after the dog, grasping her harness and stepping in front of Hershey as she peeked out to see Kyle on her doorstep—his mistress in the passenger seat of his car parked behind him.

Hadley braced herself and opened the door just wide enough to speak.

"Uh, hey. You're home," he said.

Hershey issued a low, dangerous-sounding growl unlike any Hadley had ever heard the dog make. Hershey tried to nudge her way past Hadley, and she struggled to control the large dog. "You act surprised."

He held up a key. "Abby told me where the emergency key was. She forgot to take her noise-cancelling headphones and wanted me to get them and bring them to her when we go to see her this weekend at school. She said you were in Carolina Cove."

"I was. I'm... Come in," she said reluctantly because it was getting harder and harder to hold Hershey. "Just give me a minute to put her out in the yard."

She didn't wait for Kyle's response but shut the door in his face and coerced Hershey to follow her by talking and dragging the dog down the hallway and out the back door. Thankfully the tile made it easier since Hershey couldn't get a good grip despite her locked legs and resistance.

She'd always heard that dogs had a sixth sense about humans. That they could actually smell bad people. "Where were you when I met him?" she muttered to Hershey.

Hadley gently but firmly shoved Hershey outside and quickly shut the patio door behind the dog, who had no interest in exploring things again when her human had a visitor.

Hershey pawed at the door to get back inside, yipping and whining at being kicked out.

The front door opened with a squeak of the hinge, and after a moment's hesitation, Kyle's footsteps echoed in the quiet house.

"When did you get a dog?"

Hadley struggled with her emotions in the face

of Kyle's sudden appearance and took a steadying breath. "Recently," she said simply, turning to face her ex.

Kyle had always been a good-looking man, and dressed as he was in his suit and tie, now was no exception. He was an older, more handsome version of the man she'd fallen so hard for twenty-seven years ago. "I'll go get Abby's headset."

"What's with all the suitcases?" he asked, watching her as she moved toward him once more.

"I'm...moving."

"To Carolina Cove?"

He sounded surprised. Score one for the wifey. *Ex-wifey*, her mind countered. "Yes. I was going to call you or email. To let you know I'm ready to sell my half of the house to you, or we can put it on the market."

"I told you I'd take care of the mortgage for as long as the kids were in school."

"I know but they're going to spend so little time here. It makes no sense to wander around in this huge house alone while they're away at school." And she didn't like the thought of it giving Kyle control when she was dependent on him making those payments. "When they're on break, they'll be doing their own thing or visiting me in Carolina Cove anyway so... If you don't want it, let's just sell it. That way we'll be done, once and for all."

"Baby—"

"*Don't* call me that," she said, her gaze meeting his briefly before she looked away.

The endearment pierced her heart and left her floundering for control over her emotions. Hurt, anger. So much anger. Not because she still loved him but because of how he'd handled things. How he'd torn their family apart. "I'm not your... Not anymore. You lost that right when you chose her," she said, waving a hand toward the door and his child-girlfriend beyond.

Kyle had the grace to wince at the reminder, and she turned and hurried up the stairs, her tired muscles screaming from the many previous trips.

She found the headset placed over the top of Abby's headboard and grabbed it, taking an extra few precious seconds to wipe the moisture from the corners of her eyes before rushing back down as fast as she could so he could be gone. "Tell Abby I love her and miss her," she said.

"I take it you finally told your mother?" Kyle asked when she stood in front of him once more.

"Why do you say it like that?"

"Cheryl's left multiple messages with my receptionist the last two days. I haven't called her back. I wanted to check with you and ask what she knew."

"You don't have to call her back," Hadley said. "I'll take care of Mom, but, yes, I told her."

Kyle gripped the headset in his soft surgical hands. How had she never noticed how feminine they looked?

Unlike Bryson's calloused, hardworking hands.

Sexy, raspy-rough hands that sent shockwaves through her when he lightly touched her face or arms when they'd kissed.

"Look, Hadley, I'm sorry about Georgia. I sent flowers. And I put both our names on the card."

Such a grand gesture, that. Was it supposed to make things better? "Is that everything Abby needed?" she asked.

"Haddie... Have you lost weight? You look good, babe."

She faltered, unsure of what to say when he obviously didn't get the point. She swallowed hard and forced herself to take the two steps toward the door and open it. "You should go."

"Come on, Haddie. We have kids together," he murmured. "We need to be able to speak without it being tense."

"That will take time," she said tersely.

"Fine. I get that. But let's try, okay?" He placed

his hand on her shoulder and then moved it toward her neck. "You're still my—"

"You should *go*, Kyle. *She's* waiting for you like the good little girl she is."

Kyle scowled and lowered his hand, the fingers of his other hand tightening over the headphones until the plastic cracked in complaint.

"I screwed up. I should've told you instead of hiding it."

The admission was probably as close to an apology as she'd ever get, but it was little comfort now. Him not telling her meant the entire hospital and their friends all knew while she'd remained the clueless wife whispered about in hushed tones. But what he should have done was honor their vows in the first place. "Tell Abby I love her. Goodbye."

The moment his feet crossed the threshold, she shut the door with a soft click that revealed none of the rage boiling inside of her.

Twenty-five years of marriage. Two years of dating. Memories and lives intertwined and meshed together for eternity by vows before God and the children they shared—all gone because of a wandering eye and a flirtatious piece of fluff who'd set her eyes on a prize and managed to lure it away.

Good riddance.

In the end, she needed to look at things a

different way—as a blessing, like Mary Elizabeth had said. Even if the thought was a hard pill to swallow.

But truthfully a good man *couldn't* be lured away. Mary Elizabeth was right. The fluff had actually done her a favor.

CHAPTER THIRTEEN

Bryson couldn't believe how nervous he was. It wasn't like he hadn't dated his fair share before he'd married Tish and a few ladies in the years since her death, but this—Hadley—was different.

He stared at himself in the mirror and fussed with the button on his shirt. Should he wear a tie? Considering it was summer at the beach, he told himself no, but doubts still reared and made him second-guess his attire.

Hadley was used to a white-collar man, and they wore ties and jackets, knew which fork to use. Not that he didn't. But only because he'd made a point of googling the question just in case. *Outside in,* he reminded himself, or wait and watch what others used if he wasn't certain.

He'd also never been to an art gallery show before and he wasn't sure of the protocol. Maybe he should've googled that instead?

Why had he agreed to this?

When Hadley had asked him to escort her to her friend's show, he'd automatically agreed, happy to do pretty much anything so long as it meant spending time with her. But now he felt like that country song about wearing boots to a black-tie affair.

Muttering to himself, Bryson pulled out his phone and googled what was probably the silliest question of all. No doubt Google would be laughing, whomever Google was.

He quickly scanned the results of his query and felt a little better about his choice of dress. According to the big G, business casual was fine, especially for such a setting as the beach.

Maybe he should've consulted with Hadley first, though?

Bryson shook his head at himself. He was pushing fifty, not a teenage boy about to go on his first date. Enough already.

He left the bedroom carrying his lightweight sports coat and made his way to the kitchen, where he'd placed the hydrangeas he'd picked up on his way home.

The drive from his home along the Intercoastal

to Carolina Cove didn't take long despite the heavy summer traffic, and he was two minutes early when he knocked on Hadley's door.

Hershey barked like always, but Bryson heard her take a few sniffs from the other side and then settle down. He liked that the dog knew him and seemingly approved.

Hadley opened the door and Bryson caught his breath. She wore a strapless blue dress that hugged her figure to perfection. Short in the front, it fell several inches above her knees. The skirt was longer in the back, and she wore the kind of flat-soled heels that didn't sink into the sand and showcased her long legs to perfection. "Wow," he said softly. "You look amazing."

Hadley blushed and smiled at the compliment.

"Thank you. You cleaned up pretty good yourself," she said.

"I brought a jacket and tie. I wasn't sure how fancy this is."

"You're perfect just as you are," Hadley said.

Hershey sat on her haunches and stared up at them, head cocked as she listened to the conversation. "Hey, you," Bryson said. "Are you going to behave while we're gone?"

"Of course she will," Hadley said. "She has proven to be a smart, wonderful dog. I can't believe how blessed I am to have gotten her. Hershey, come."

The dog immediately followed Hadley into the kitchen, where Hadley gave the dog a treat and a pat on the head before shutting the gates behind her.

"You be a good girl and watch TV until we get back," Hadley said.

For the first time since his arrival, Bryson noticed Hadley had the television on a cartoon station for kids. He chuckled softly, wondering if Hershey knew how blessed *she* was to have a mama like Hadley. Hershey had won the dog lottery in his opinion.

"I'm ready," Hadley said. "And I think you're fine without the jacket and tie."

"Works for me."

"Did you get a haircut?"

"Yeah. Your friend Tessa did a good job."

"She's fantastic."

Bryson held the screen door while Hadley locked up. He walked her to his personal truck, glad he'd made the effort to drop it off and get it detailed earlier in the day.

He opened the door for her and wondered what she would've done had he shown up in his logo-ed work truck. Would she have insisted on driving her car? Made an excuse and refused to go? He wouldn't mind knowing the answer. Just to satisfy his curiosity.

His mood darkened at the thought, and he told himself to shake it off as he climbed behind the wheel. "Downtown, right?"

"Yes. The arts district near the Cotton Exchange building."

Bryson backed out of the drive and struggled to find a topic of conversation that would get Hadley talking. With this being an official date, he felt more pressure to try to entertain.

"I love the island at night," Hadley said, staring out her window. "It's busy but quiet, and the sunsets are always amazing."

He inhaled and forced his nervous energy away. "Have you had dinner? We didn't discuss that. We could stop somewhere along the way if you like."

"They'll have hors d'oeuvres at the gallery, and I promised Izzy we wouldn't be late. She's really nervous about this one, since it's her first since her big splash in New York."

Izzy wasn't the only nervous one. "No problem. So your friends know we're coming? That I'm coming?"

Hadley smiled at him from across the interior of the car.

"Yes, and they're all very excited to meet you."

Great. No pressure there. "And they know what I do?"

The moment the question emerged from his mouth, he mentally kicked himself. Way to keep his insecurity low-key. "I mean... I'm sorry. That sounded bad, didn't it?"

"Yes, it did."

"I get it. It's just after your mother's response to seeing me at your house, I'll admit I've wondered how much their approval matters to you."

He stared straight ahead, foot heavy on the gas while he waited for her to respond.

"Bryson, what do you see when you look at me?" she asked softly.

He turned his head, surprised by the counter question. "I see a beautiful woman. Smart, kind," he added, remembering her with her friends Mary Elizabeth and Tessa. Both women had sung Hadley's praises, not that he needed to hear them.

"Want to know what I see when I look at you?" she asked him.

His hands tightened on the steering wheel. "If you want to tell me."

"I see a handsome, hardworking man who is also kind and smart and sweet. A friend I'd like to get to know better."

His hand loosened its death grip at her words.

"Guess I'm a little nervous meeting your friends. I know I'm not your usual type."

Hadley laughed softly.

"What?" he asked, smiling because he couldn't help it.

"Do I *have* a type?"

"You know what I'm saying."

"No, I don't."

"Hadley... You grew up in an oceanfront home. Married rich—"

"I married a college student I then put through medical school," she countered dryly.

"And now you've inherited an oceanfront home," he continued. "I'm just saying, I get it that people are going to see us together and...wonder why."

"Who's to say they're not wondering why you'd choose to date such a shallow-sounding woman?"

"You're not shallow."

"And you're not less than because of what you do," she stated matter-of-factly. "Don't you *own* the business, or am I mistaken about your name being on the side of your work truck?"

Caught in a trap of his own making, he nodded. "I do, but—"

"But nothing. Look, how about we just have fun tonight and let whoever wants to talk, talk? Hmm? Because if you're okay with me, and I'm okay with you, anything else is their problem. Right?"

TWO HOURS LATER, Bryson watched Hadley peruse one of Izzy's paintings. It was an oil painting of the ocean done in dark, stormy colors, a hint of sunlight breaking through the clouds far in the distance. A lone figure walked the beach, dark hair blowing in the wind. He found the painting as fascinating as Hadley, probably because the woman could have easily been her. White shorts, gray-blue top, long legs. Stark beauty braving the storm and staring at the light from above.

"Here you go," he said, handing her the glass of wine she'd requested.

He sipped the club soda in his hand and asked about the painting.

"Izzy titled it *The Return*," Hadley said, sliding him a look over her shoulder. "The colors and tone are dark but...hopeful?"

"I can see that," he said, meaning it. There was just something about the light in the sky and the way the woman was focused on it.

"Sooo, what do you think?" Isabel asked from behind them.

Noting the way the younger woman looked at Hadley, Bryson figured the question held more weight than the obvious.

"It's lovely," Hadley said. "The storm looks intense but your subject looks...unafraid. Strong."

"Mmm," Isabel said, smiling at the description. "I'm glad you think so. I saw you walking the beach when you first got here, right as a storm rolled in, and I knew I had to paint it. It amazed me how fast it came flooding out of me onto the canvas."

"You mean it's...*me*?" Hadley asked, her attention shifting from the artist to the painting.

"Yup. I almost titled it *Hadley's Return* but I figured you wouldn't approve."

A low huff of a laugh escaped Hadley and she shook her head.

"No, definitely not. I-I don't know what to say. I'm flattered. It's beautiful, Izzy."

It was, so much so he made a mental note to inquire as to the price of it.

Someone called Hadley's name, and they turned in unison to find a wall of people watching them. Hadley's mother and the man Bryson remembered from years ago as her father, Tessa, Mary Elizabeth, and others.

"Oh, wow," Hadley said with a nervous expression.

She glanced at him and pinned a smile to her lips as she faced them once more.

"Hello, everyone."

"Hadley, don't you look beautiful," Mary Elizabeth said. "That color is gorgeous on you."

"Thank you. I think we're all looking particularly nice for Izzy's showcase."

"Aren't you going to introduce us?" the man standing by Cheryl asked.

"Of course. Dad, this is Bryson James. Bryson, Jerry Dummit."

"Nice to meet you, sir."

"Likewise," her father said, drawing Hadley close for a kiss on her cheek before shaking Bryson's hand.

Hadley went on to introduce the others and Bryson shook hands and greeted everyone. That done, Bryson watched Hadley glance uncomfortably toward her mother while the other woman eyed him like roadkill.

"Have you had a chance to look around? Izzy's work is *a-mazing*. I always knew she was talented, but I had no idea how far she's grown as an artist in the last couple of years. You must be so proud," Hadley said to Izzy's parents and husband, hugging Izzy close to her side.

"We haven't made the rounds yet," Mary Elizabeth said.

Awkward silence filled the air.

"Bryson," said Adam Shipley, "I hear you're working on that house next to Hadley's. Do you know the owner well? I'd like to speak to him sometime and ask what he plans do to with it. You wouldn't happen to know, would you?"

"Actually--"

"I'm not sure of the plans," Bryson said, cutting Hadley off before she could tell them he owned it. He caught Hadley's surprised glance but was glad when she didn't continue.

"Why do you ask?" Mary Elizabeth said to her husband.

"Adam and I have discussed the difficulties of sharing Isabel's tiny apartment," Everett said with a chuckle.

"Indeed. Bryson, can you give us a name?" Adam asked.

Considering public records would reveal him to be the owner, Bryson reluctantly owned up to it. "Uh, actually, you're looking at him." And just like that their expressions changed from interest to surprise.

"Ladies and gentlemen, if I could have your

attention, please," a voice said over a microphone, ending the conversation, much to Bryson's relief.

"I'd like everyone to welcome our featured artist this evening, Ms. Isabel Drake."

The crowd applauded and they all watched as Isabel moved toward the podium to say a few words.

"Oh, she's beaming. Look at her," Hadley said quietly so only he could hear.

Bryson couldn't take his gaze off of Hadley because she glowed with pride for her friend. It was more proof of Hadley's kind heart and something he liked about her. She wasn't the type of woman who felt there was only so much success in the world to go round. No, she cheered on her friends and celebrated with them and that told him a lot.

Sensing someone staring at him, Bryson reluctantly shifted his gaze until it locked with Cheryl Dummit's. The woman stared at Bryson, and he knew at some point in the near future they would have words. He dreaded it, only because he knew it would make Hadley feel bad.

Izzy made a short speech about being an artist in such a beautiful and inspirational area before she thanked her husband, family, and guests for attending. Speech done, the gallery owner took over once more and reminded the attendees that the artwork would remain on display for two weeks, but purchases could be made tonight until the end of the showcase.

Music began and waiters once again circulated with drinks and snacks, and

Bryson found himself separated from Hadley for a moment while she congratulated Isabel once more and chatted with one of Isabel's sisters he'd met earlier.

Taking advantage of the moment, he made his way over to the gallery owner and asked to purchase the painting of Hadley.

He'd never spent so much on an image before, but he relished the sight of the tiny *sold* sign that was placed on the painting moments later.

He finished the transaction in the rear of the gallery with the assistant, hoping to get back before Hadley noticed his disappearance, but turned to find Cheryl Dummit approaching.

"I know what you're up to."

"Ma'am?"

"Stay away from my daughter."

Bryson frowned and fought back the urge to tell the woman what she could do with her threats. "I believe your daughter is old enough to make her own decisions. Besides, she invited me to be her date tonight."

"Yes, I did," Hadley said from behind them.

"And I'm grateful Bryson graciously accepted my invitation. Mom, Dad is looking for you," she said to her mother. "I think he's picked something to buy."

Her mother was visibly frustrated at the interruption, or maybe it was that Jerry had dared select something without her approval, but either way, Bryson relished the woman's quick departure, though it came with one last glare.

"I'm sorry. My mother can be very trying."

"She's protective of you," he said.

"That's one way of putting a good spin on it," Hadley said wryly. "What are you doing back here? Oh, Bryson, did my mother drag you here to lecture you?"

"It's all good," he said, falling back on a favorite saying. "But I'm getting hungry for more than the nibbles they have here," he said, hoping to change the subject without her noticing. "Shall we make our way to the door and go get some dinner since we're downtown? I know a great rooftop restaurant not far from here."

"Oh, I'd love that."

Bryson offered her his arm and noted that Hadley didn't so much as blink before sliding her hand into the crook for the walk through the gallery toward the door. Cheryl might not approve, but Hadley apparently didn't have an issue with him not being a white-collar professional like her father and his friends.

They said goodbye to a few people on the way toward the door, but Hadley didn't go out of her way to say goodbye to her parents.

But he wondered—was it her taking a stand or merely avoiding the fight?

HADLEY WALKED across the porch to her door later that night and paused. She stared up at Bryson in the light of the moon shining down on them, the salt air thick with moisture and the hint of an overnight shower to come. "I had fun tonight. Dinner was delicious and I can't remember the last time I danced. Thank you. For going with me to Izzy's show and putting up with my mother."

"You're welcome. It was fun."

She had a feeling it wasn't as much fun for him but was glad he was willing to play along. The rooftop restaurant had a person playing ballads on guitar, and after dinner they'd danced to several songs. She'd relished being held close, Bryson's whisker-rough chin at her temple as they swayed back and forth.

The city lights reflected along the Cape Fear

waterfront below, and from their vantage point above, it'd looked and felt like something from a dream. *A romantic dream.*

Hadley fished her keys from her purse and bit her lower lip, wondering if Bryson would end their first official date with a handshake or...

She sucked in a sharp breath as Bryson stepped toward her and lowered his head, his mouth brushing against hers. Like the night when she'd asked him to kiss her, the caress was full of heady tension, intrigue, butterflies, and the sweet chocolate cake and wine they'd shared for dessert.

She slid her arms up his chest, around his neck, tucked her fingertips into his newly shorn hair, and held him close while he kissed her like a man starving for more.

Her heart pounded in her chest when he backed her up, his thickly muscled arm behind her protecting her bare shoulders from the hardness of the door as one kiss blended into many, *many* more.

After a long while, Bryson ended the kissing and dragged his lips along her jawline to her neck, every nibble making her arch deeper into his embrace. His free hand roamed to her waist, where he gently squeezed.

"Hadley."

The gruff sound of her name on his lips sent her

blood pulsing through her veins, and she tugged his mouth back to hers, kissing him again.

Finally Bryson tore his mouth away, his breath hot on her lips.

"Sweetheart, we either have to stop or you have to invite me in," he murmured. "And since I don't think you're ready to invite me in, I'm going to go."

He brushed his lips over hers once more, this kiss soft, tempered. Nothing like the ones before but every bit as seductive because he'd chosen her well-being over his own.

She gripped his arms, lashes lowered as she nodded her agreement. Kissing him was one thing. One wonderful, tantalizing thing...but she *wasn't* ready for more and she appreciated his insight.

"Good night, Hadley. Sweet dreams."

"Night." Bryson released her and Hadley trembled as she shakily unlocked the door and let herself inside. She shut the door behind her and realized Bryson waited to hear the dead bolt slide into place before his footsteps retreated across the porch.

Hershey whined from behind her barrier, jumping up and down like a puppet on a string in her excitement that Hadley had returned.

Bryson's truck engine starting up sounded loud along the quiet street, and his lights flashed through the windows as he backed out of the drive.

She made her way across the room on trembling legs, fingers fumbling to unlatch the tall gates and make her way to the kitchen door to let Hershey outside to potty in the fenced yard.

While Hershey sprinkled her usual spots, Hadley watched from the screened porch, trembling fingertips covering her tingling lips as her mind relived every moment.

A smile formed, and she felt a little silly standing there in the darkened porch blushing like a school-girl. But after the last few years, Bryson's kiss, the intensity and passion they'd shared... It went a long way to lift her mood and brighten her outlook like nothing had in a very long time.

Her confidence had been shattered by Kyle's behavior. She'd wondered if she'd lost her sex appeal, her looks. Her ability to attract a man. If anyone would ever want her again.

Maybe the thinking was negative in nature, but she couldn't help herself. Life had dealt her some devastating blows...but tonight had shown her the truth.

And for the first time in a long time...she felt like a woman again.

THE FOLLOWING MONDAY, Mary Elizabeth lifted her hand to knock on Tessa's door, but before she could make contact, the door swung open.

"Get in here," Tessa ordered. "The suspense is killing me."

Killing *her?* Mary Elizabeth thought as she hurried into Tessa's home. The house was the farthest down the row of Babe homes, with Rayna Jo's next door. Thankfully she had already left for work and her husband, Richard, was never home.

"What took you so long?"

"Adam decided to work from home this morning, and I couldn't think of a good excuse to leave."

"You couldn't just tell him I wanted some girl time?" Tessa asked. "It is my day off. He knows that."

Had she been thinking clearly, that might have worked, but instead she'd waited for him to finally leave for an errand before rushing out the door. "I'm here now. Where is it?"

"Kitchen table."

Mary Elizabeth hurried through the house with Tessa hot on her heels, but after setting her keys on the table and picking up the large envelope, all she could do was stare at it.

"*Seriously?*" Tessa asked, eyes wide.

"I'm just... I need a minute. Once I open this, everything could change." Mary Elizabeth could feel

Tessa's impatience, but she needed a moment to breathe.

Finally she grasped the tab between her finger and thumb and yanked, opening it up and removing the papers within.

The ink blurred in front of her eyes and she blinked, struggling to focus. Tessa's voice sounded like it came from a tunnel, and the room swirled a bit as Tessa's arms wrapped around her and her friend shoved her into a chair.

"MeMe? MeMe!"

Mary Elizabeth shook her head and lifted trembling fingers to her temple. "Dizzy."

"So I gathered," Tessa said, concern heavy in her tone. "Just breathe. Nice and easy. Slow breaths. In and out. Oh, honey, you've gotta calm down. It'll be okay. Whatever that paper says, it'll work out. You'll see. Just breathe and sit tight while I get a cool cloth."

It took several minutes and a baggie of ice placed on the back of her neck before Mary Elizabeth felt like herself again.

She unclenched her fist and attempted to smooth the now wrinkled sheets. "What does it say? You read it," she said, handing it off to Tessa.

Tessa took the paper and gasped softly.

"*Well?*" Mary Elizabeth asked.

"It says...it's a boy." Tessa knelt down beside

Mary Elizabeth's chair, her hand covering Mary Elizabeth's and squeezing tight. "You were right, MeMe. You have a son."

HOURS LATER MARY ELIZABETH returned home, her legs feeling every bit as quivery and numb as when Tessa had shoved her into the chair.

Tessa had broken out the tequila and found some margarita mix, and then the two of them had alternated between talking and sipping for hours.

It hadn't worked. Mostly because the shock was thick as pea soup, and even though a part of her had *known* the truth all along because of Bryson's uncanny resemblance to Dean, it was still a doozy of a revelation.

One she wasn't sure how to handle now that she *knew*.

Had she hoped it wasn't true? Why hadn't she come to a decision before now? Decided one way or the other what she would do if the results had been...well, accurate with her thinking.

"There you are," Adam said from the living room. "I was about to put a call out to the Babes to ask if they'd seen you."

She turned to look at him, the envelope clutched in her hand.

"I thought we could fire up the grill tonight. I picked up some steaks on the way home and— Hon? Are you okay?"

She shook her head, at a loss. Unable to speak due to the sheer weight of it all.

Adam moved toward her and gently prodded her toward the couch, his expression changing to a worried frown. She knew she had to say something, prepare him, but she wasn't sure how.

"What's this? May I?"

She let him take the envelope from her, but she wasn't able to look at him as he read the results.

"A DNA..." he said. "Mary Elizabeth, what is this?"

Mary Elizabeth swallowed the lump in her throat and forced herself to lift her chin, to meet his gaze through the sheen of shattered tears she couldn't control. "I'm sorry."

"What?"

"I didn't know. I swear *I didn't know*. I thought... I thought he was dead."

Adam drew back in shock and turned to pace across the floor. He stopped short of the window and stared out, no doubt trying to collect his raging emotions before speaking. It was such an Adam thing to do.

"How did this come about?" he finally asked. "Who is he? How long has this been going on?"

She flinched at the barrage of questions, trembling from her very core from the devastating news. "I wasn't sure. How could I be when I thought... I saw him at Hadley's and the resemblance was just..."

"You saw whom?"

"Bryson James," she whispered. "The day I cut my hand? That's...that's why. He walked in and I was so shocked I-I dropped a tea tray. The mess... Oh, Adam, I thought he was dead. They told me my baby was *dead!*"

Adam ran a hand over his hair, and she recognized the gesture as one of frustration and anger. Because she knew him so well. They'd shared everything over the years since she'd told him about the baby she'd carried but lost. Now... "I didn't lie to you. I swear I didn't. I didn't know."

"This test proves otherwise. You suspected."

"I did but... How could I mention it when it wasn't supposed to be possible? I didn't want to needlessly upset you when it might not have been true."

"You wouldn't have done the test unless you believed there was a chance that it was. How many people know about this? Did you keep this from me but tell them?"

She shook her head, silent tears streaming down her cheeks. "Tessa. Just Tessa. No one else, I swear."

"And Bryson?"

"No, he doesn't know."

Adam ran his fingers through his hair once again, yanking hard.

"How on earth did you manage to get his DNA?"

She explained the process and watched as her husband paced and muttered words she couldn't hear. "Adam, I'm sorry. I am so very sorry."

"What do you intend to do?"

"Do?"

He stopped in his tracks and looked at her, waving the paper still in his hand.

"You did this test for a reason and now you know he's your son. What do you intend to do next?"

When she simply stared at him, Adam released a rare curse.

"You didn't think it through, did you?"

"I-I..."

"Did you think discovering he's yours wouldn't change things? Wouldn't change *everything*?"

"I didn't believe it could be true. I didn't think it was possible!"

Adam leveled a stare at her, one that stole her breath and broke her heart at the same time.

"You should've known you can't undo the past. You should've thought of our girls and how this will impact them knowing that all of their lives you never told them they had a half brother. You should've thought about *us*. Mary Elizabeth, you...you should've talked to me first."

"Why? So you could talk me out of it? I had to know. I had to know if my parents *lied* to me about my baby."

"Well, now you know," he said with a hard twist of his lips. "I hope hurting the people who haven't lied to you was worth it," he added before he turned on his heel and stalked out of the room.

Worth it?

Tears flooded her eyes. She might have gained a son, but had she lost her family in the process?

<h1 style="text-align:center">CHAPTER FOURTEEN</h1>

S o, you and Bryson, huh?" Izzy asked as she helped Hadley carry a small fold-down side table down the stairs.

"Yeah, me and Bryson." They took a rest at the bottom before picking it up and continuing on through the kitchen and out toward the shed.

"Can't say he isn't pretty to look at with all that muscle," Izzy said. "I can't believe I haven't seen him around."

"You would've snapped him up pre-Everett, huh?" Hadley asked. Izzy's gorgeousness allowed her pretty much her pick of men, and Hadley couldn't help but feel a bit of unease at the thought of Izzy pursuing Bryson. Thirteen years younger at thirty-two, Izzy represented all the women still young enough to have the family Bryson had missed out on.

Which meant what? That she was jealous? Afraid Bryson wanted a family more than he let on?

"Maybe," Izzy teased, winking. "You two look perfect together, though. Really. Quite the stunning couple."

"Thanks," she said, thoughts dark as she backed her way along the grass toward the shed.

Hadley and Bryson had spent the weekend emptying the shed of the rest of the items she wasn't sure what to do with, adding them to the dumpster next door because Bryson insisted it was okay.

Then they'd turned the entire shed into a painting area, and he'd shown her the basics of sanding and prepping and using the sander and paint sprayer she'd purchased.

She'd followed those lessons up by bingeing an online class from someone creating remarkable painted furniture that earned top dollar and prayed she could work her way to that level of expertise.

Now it was Wednesday, and she and Bryson had spent every evening together after he finished working on the three-story house next door.

Hadley and Izzy entered the small outbuilding and Hadley led the way to the plastic-draped painting corner. Once the table was in position, Hadley propped her hands on her hips and caught her breath. "Time for some lemonade?"

Isabel grinned and nodded, and the two talked about the upcoming Labor Day weekend two weeks away. Hadley was beyond excited because Max and Abby were coming to visit her for the long weekend.

"I can borrow Mom and Dad's Jeep and Everett could take us all out on the South end," Izzy said. "We could pack a cooler? Spend the day?"

"Oh, that sounds fun. They'd love that."

"You can invite Bryson, too."

Hadley inhaled, faltering at the thought. "I dunno. Is it too soon?"

"You tell me. How serious is it getting between the two of you?" Izzy asked.

Hadley poured them both a tall glass of lemonade, and Izzy rolled her eyes and moved to look beneath the sink for Nan's not-so-secret stash.

"Ah. Here we go," Izzy said, holding up the bottle of vodka in triumph.

"Isn't it a little early for that?" Hadley asked.

"Not when you're on island time. Besides, it's for you, not me."

Hadley laughed at her friend's grinning statement, grasped her glass, and held it out for Izzy to pour.

They carried their lemonades out onto the porch, and Hershey paced for a while before finally settling down, panting from the heat of the day despite her spot in the shade by the door.

"So?" Izzy said, bringing them back to the topic at hand. "Bryson? You? Fill me in."

Hadley couldn't stop the flush that raced up her neck and into her face.

"Ohhhh, girl! That look says it all!"

"It says *nothing*," Hadley countered. "Bryson and I are taking things slow and...getting to know each other."

"Uh-huh."

"I mean it."

"So you haven't...?"

"No!"

"Because?"

"Because I'm...I'm..."

"You're...?" Izzy prodded, waiting expectantly.

"*Old*," Hadley whispered, sliding her friend an embarrassed look.

"Oh, stop it."

"I'm serious. My last first date—first *time*—was almost thirty *years* ago. The whole concept of dating is weird to me now. I don't want to rush and...screw things up."

"Then why all the blushing?"

Heat flooded her once more when she thought of

the kissing and touching and, okay, a *little* heavy petting in the shed out back over the weekend.

"Ah. Because you're rethinking the going slow part."

"No. I'm not."

"You're totally falling for him."

"I am totally *intrigued*," Hadley corrected, smiling into her glass as she took a long sip of her spiked drink and stared out at the Atlantic to keep from looking at Izzy. "He's...so different from Kyle."

"That's a good thing, right?"

"Yes. On every level. I mean, Kyle wasn't always awful. He could be a class-A jerk but I'm sure I wasn't always easy to live with. That's just marriage, and things happen a little at a time. The fights and comments. But when you've got years between you, kids and bills and responsibilities... You don't end something because someone's a jerk."

"Hadley?"

"Hmm?"

"What does that have to do with Bryson?" Isabel asked.

What *did* it have to do with Bryson? "It's just... I haven't known Bryson long enough to know if I'm falling for him or merely infatuated or flattered by the attention. I haven't seen him angry or sad or...

There's a lot left to learn before I truly know *anything*."

"You're scared."

Hadley shifted her gaze to her friend and found Isabel had curled her legs up on the chair, looking every bit the beautiful, newlywedded, and now pregnant artist she was known to be. "Wouldn't you be? I mean, if I couldn't trust the man I've spent half my life with, how can I trust one I barely know?"

Izzy pointed a long, slender finger at her. "You focus on the fact Bryson hasn't given you any reason to doubt him. And until he does, you have to live in the moment."

Hadley shifted her gaze back toward the ocean and pondered Izzy's words, knowing it was true. Kyle and Bryson were two very different men and she couldn't compare them. Everyone had their own moral code and beliefs and boundaries they either crossed or kept.

"Mmm, here's your gorgeous hunk now," Izzy said in a low, sultry voice.

Hadley followed Izzy's stare to see Bryson moving between the hedges. Hershey apparently heard him coming, because she scrambled to her feet and ran to the edge of the porch barking, feet prancing up and down when she realized who came to visit.

Hershey glanced at Hadley as though for permission and Hadley waved her hand. "You can go."

The dog bolted at the word *go*, jumping over the stairs entirely and landing on the sidewalk, where she raced toward Bryson. Bryson laughed when he saw the dog coming and zigzagged, playing tag with Hershey and earning a gigantic doggie grin as Hershey spun around and came at him again.

Bryson played for several minutes and then raced for the porch, Hershey hot on his heels as Bryson made his way up the steps.

"Ladies," he greeted, breathing heavily.

"Bryson," Izzy said with a smile.

"Hi," Hadley said, eyes widening when Bryson didn't hesitate in lowering his head and brushing a kiss over her lips in front of Isabel.

"Man, that dog is fast," Bryson said when he released her.

Isabel raised an elegant eyebrow and grinned when Hadley glanced her way.

"Hmm. Someone started celebrating early. What's the occasion?" Bryson asked.

"A beautiful day on a beautiful island," Isabel said. "The sun is shining, the sky is blue, it's five o'clock somewhere and...I think I'm going to go for a walk and see what my gorgeous husband is into. Talk to you later," Izzy said to Hadley, winking.

Bryson murmured goodbye and dipped his head when Isabel walked past.

"Hm," he drawled, staring down at Hadley. "You're looking pleasantly muddled."

She laughed and shrugged. "Izzy pours with a heavy hand when she can't have some herself."

Bryson braced his arms on either side of her and kissed her again. "You taste delicious."

Hadley sighed against his lips, reminding herself of Isabel's words. "I'm glad you came over. I wanted to talk to you."

"Yeah?" Bryson lowered himself onto the couch beside her. "What's up?"

"Well, my kids are coming to visit next weekend and I didn't know if... I mean, how do you feel about... Is it too soon to, you know, meet?"

Bryson lifted his arm and wrapped it around her shoulders, tugging her close. "I think that's entirely up to you. Do you want us to meet?"

"I guess I just don't know the proper order of things. If they were younger, it would be different, I'm sure, but they're adults and we're...you're...you. Plus, we're sure to see you at some point, and I don't want to pretend you're just the guy next door."

"I appreciate that. Because you're definitely not just the girl next door."

She let her head roll back on his upper arm to see his face. His gaze lowered to the direction of her lips, and she waited, pulse picking up speed when his lips covered hers, this kiss slower and deeper and fantastically exploratory.

By the time he lifted his lips from hers, Hadley's head whirled from more than the alcohol.

"I should get back to work."

"Oh."

His lips curled at the corners and he smooched her again.

"Stop frowning. It's your call, sweetheart. Meet them, wait. You decide what's best for you and for them. I'm okay with your decision."

Hadley watched as Bryson stood and walked away, her mind slowly putting itself to rights again.

Bryson had left the decision up to her and yet... he'd made it the moment he'd put them first.

BRYSON TOOK Hadley to meet his father the following Friday evening. He could tell he'd surprised her in the doing, but he wanted her to truly know whatever she decided about him meeting her children, he was okay with it. He was in this for the long haul and wanted to see where things between them might go.

They picked his father up from the assisted living center and took him out to dinner and for a drive, then back to the center, where they sat in the common area and listened to stories of the island from the old days.

Hadley laughed and asked about people she thought his father might know, and his father told her what he could remember.

When he began talking about Bryson's mother, Hadley's eyes had teared along with his father's because of the depth of the man's mourning.

"She was a saint," his father said as he always did. "Best woman I've ever known. Beautiful. Sharp as a tack. It nearly killed her when we lost our baby."

Bryson had hoped his father wouldn't reminisce to the point of grief, but as they often did, the memories of that time emerged. "I'm adopted," Bryson said to Hadley, catching her low gasp of surprise at the news.

"Best thing that ever happened to us," his father said, nodding as his thick hand patted Bryson's shoulder. "Bryson brought my Clara back to life. I don't think she wouldn't have survived it otherwise."

Bryson could tell Hadley had questions, but she

steered the conversation toward stories of Bryson's antics as a boy and got his father smiling again.

"He pulled that stuffed toy around on a string everywhere we went until we finally agreed to let him get a dog."

"No wonder you're so good with Hershey," she said, smiling.

"Hadley has a beautiful dog," Bryson told his father. "We'll bring her to see you sometime soon, Pop."

The chime sounded that visiting hours were over, and Hadley hugged his dad an extra-long moment and kissed his father's cheek.

"Thank you for sharing those stories with me," she said. "I can't wait to visit again and hear more of them."

Bryson waited for Hadley to straighten before he bent and hugged his father. "I love you, old man. Don't be giving the nurses a hard time, you hear me?"

"Don't be giving that pretty girl a hard time," his father said, giving Bryson a hard look that was far too easy to read.

His father had urged Bryson to date in the years since Tish's death, but since Hadley was the first woman Bryson had brought to meet his father, his old man understood the significance Hadley held.

Bryson nodded and wrapped his arm around Hadley's shoulders, tugging her close and turning them to walk out the door with a final wave goodbye.

Hadley was silent all the way back to his truck, and once he climbed behind the wheel, he turned the key to get the AC going, waiting for her to speak.

"He's wonderful," she said softly. "And you're wonderful with him."

"He taught me everything I know. I wouldn't be who or where I am without him."

"You didn't tell me you were adopted."

He stared out at the darkened parking lot and shook his head. "Because I don't think of myself that way. Technically I am, but they were never anything but Mom and Dad. I had a great life. Great childhood. They'll always be my parents."

Hadley scooted to the edge of her seat and stretched her arms across the way, lightly tugging on his shirt to pull him close enough to kiss.

"Does it bother you?" he asked.

"That you're adopted? Not at all. Why would it?"

Staring into her beautiful blue-green gaze, he could tell she spoke true. "Just wondered. Sometimes Tish would worry about whatever genes might be running amok inside of me, but since we never got pregnant, it didn't matter."

Hadley brushed her lips over his again.

"All I see is a very handsome man who appreciates the life he was blessed to have."

Bryson grasped her around the waist and simultaneously lifted and tugged her over the console and onto his lap, trapping her between him and the steering wheel.

"Bryson!"

Her laughter filled the vehicle, and he captured the sound on her lips. "Let's see if we can fog up the windows some, hmm?"

"Other people are leaving. They'll see us."

"Do you care?" he asked, a knot in his gut that one day she'd wake up and have a change of heart when he'd already given her his.

Hadley nuzzled his mouth with hers before sliding her lips along his jawline to his ear.

"No. But we *would* have more privacy at my house."

Bryson groaned softly before lifting her once more, gently tossing her back on her side. "Well then, get off my lap, woman. We have somewhere to go."

MARY ELIZABETH SPENT several days overthinking every aspect related to the DNA results. The impact on her husband and marriage, her children.

Ever since Adam had walked out of the room that day, things had remained strained between them. They spoke about general everyday topics like the mail and his work schedule, ate silently at the table together, and went about their daily activities like before. But the tension was there, building with every unasked question and moment that slipped by.

She sometimes caught Adam staring at her with the saddest expression, and she hated that she'd hurt him. Hated that she'd hurt *all* of them, whether they knew it or not.

She debated how to tell their girls, what their response would be. When they were little, they'd talked about wanting a little brother. Would an older one at this late date traumatize them?

And Hadley. Hadley would understand, of that Mary Elizabeth had no doubt. But then Mary Elizabeth did wonder about the impact it would have on Hadley's relationship with Bryson, and on Bryson himself. He was nearing fifty. What man wanted to find his birth mother at fifty? Did he even know he was adopted?

She let out a small cry of frustration and turned to find Adam watching her from the doorway of the kitchen. She met his gaze and her heart pinched, emotions crumbling. "I'm *sorry*."

Adam dropped the newspaper he carried into the recycle bin.

"Does that mean you've made a decision?"

A decision? How could she possibly make a decision when... "Every time I think I have, doubts creep in. I don't know what to do." She wet her lips and took a fortifying breath to prepare herself for his response to her next question. "I know I should've talked to you before doing the test. You deserved that but I didn't, and it's too late to change that. So I'm asking you now...what do you think I should do?"

Adam moved toward her, and for the first time since that fateful, awful day, he wrapped her in his arms, cradled her against his chest, and kissed the top of her head like he had thousands of times in the past. She curled her arms up around his back and clutched him tight, breathing in the scent of him that brought such comfort and love.

After a long, long moment, he spoke.

"I guess the question boils down to whether you want him in your life as a son. If the answer is yes, you know what you have to do."

"But the girls..."

"They'll be fine."

"How can you be sure?"

"Because every time we had a baby, we learned to love more and so did they. We can all do it again."

She squeezed her eyes tight. "Bryson's hardly a baby."

"No. But that might make it easier for them. And me."

She lifted her head to stare up at him. "How so?"

"He's a grown man. And...since you told me, I've had some time to do some digging."

"Oh, Adam. You had him investigated?" She wasn't sure how she felt about that.

"If he's going to be around you and my girls, did you really think I wouldn't?"

She supposed not, but she felt she'd already invaded Bryson's privacy enough without adding a private investigation and background check to the mix. "I understand, it's just... What did you find out?"

Adam released a low chuckle and drew her close again, lips brushing her forehead as he said, "He was adopted within hours of birth by a family who had lost a baby the night before. The couple had the same doctor as you."

"Were they kind?"

"No history of domestic violence or police inter-action. The father was a carpenter Bryson apprenticed under during school, and he later took over the business."

She plucked at a button on Adam's polo shirt, afraid to ask about the woman she wanted to know the most about. "And...his adoptive mother?"

"A homemaker and seamstress. She died of a stroke when Bryson was thirty-four."

"And the father? Is he alive?"

"He's in an assisted care center in Wilmington after he took a fall last summer and broke both hips."

Oh, poor man. She was grateful to them for caring for her son but also angry that they'd been allowed to raise him whereas she... "Did Bryson marry? Does he have children? Was he... What?"

"Sweetheart, I understand your curiosity, but I think these are questions you need to find out for yourself."

Even though that meant asking Bryson? Revealing herself and her identity to him? Confess what she and Tessa had done in order to discern the truth?

And then what? "How do I tell him? *How* do I walk up to him and tell him I'm—" Her voice broke and she couldn't finish the sentence.

"I suppose you just have to set your mind and do it. Then wait for the consequences."

"And if he doesn't want anything to do with

me?" she asked, voicing her greatest fear. "What if he's angry because he thinks I didn't want him? What if he has no interest in knowing me and then I've told him and... It'll break my heart."

"Don't worry about something that might not happen," Adam said, his hands rubbing up and down her arms. "What you need to decide is who you're going to tell first. The girls? Or Bryson?"

CHAPTER FIFTEEN

Bryson touched up the paint in the kitchen when he heard a car drive up and gravel crunch. From his view on the ladder, he could see Hadley's empty driveway, so he bent down to get a gander at the house on the other side of the one he worked on and noted nothing unusual there. That meant...

"Hello? Bryson, are you here?" a familiar female voice asked.

"Up the steps," he called, dropping the mini roller into the pan and climbing down the ladder. He wiped his hands on a cloth as Mary Elizabeth topped the second-floor landing and entered the combination kitchen-living area. "Good morning. What's this?" he asked, seeing the plastic container in her hands.

"I-I've been baking and there's too much. I thought you might be working and h-heard Everett talked to you again about buying the house."

"He did. I haven't decided if I'm going to sell just yet, though."

"I thought I'd come see it. I hope you like German chocolate cake?"

"It's my favorite."

Joy washed over the older woman's features, and she glanced toward the kitchen island before heading that way.

"That's wonderful. I'm so glad. I b-brought plates and napkins, forks. Would you like a piece now? I'll cut you one."

He wasn't sure why the woman was there bringing cake but figured it had something to do with Hadley more so than the house. "Uh, sure. I'm due a break."

Bryson noted Mary Elizabeth's hands visibly trembled as she set about performing the task, confirming his thoughts that this wasn't just a cake drop-off. "Is something wrong?" he asked. "I'm guessing you're here because you want to talk to me about Hadley?"

Mary Elizabeth stared up at him, eyes wide.

"Did Mrs. Dummit ask you to come talk to me?" He wouldn't put it past the woman to pull her friends into the fray and gang up on Hadley, but wasn't this taking things a bit too far?

"Oh, no. No, that's not... I'm not here because of Hadley. I mean, she'll be surprised, I'm sure but... What I mean to say is she's not why I came to speak to you."

Bryson moved to the sink and used the soap he'd brought in to wash up as best he could. "Okay. Not to be rude but why are you here?"

"Because I'm your mother."

Bryson froze, sure he'd misheard the woman. He flipped off the tap and grabbed a fresh rag to dry his hands and give himself a few precious seconds to process the words before he turned to face her. He leaned his hips against the countertop, knees locked, and stared. "Pardon? Did Hadley tell you I was adopted?"

Mary Elizabeth shook like a leaf in a storm.

"No. No, not at all. I haven't talked to Hadley a-about any of this."

"Then how did you find out?"

"Bryson, th-the moment I saw you, I recognized you," she whispered, chin quivering. "You look so much like your father."

Bryson actually felt a little light-headed, and he gripped the edge of the countertop until his knuckles cracked. "You're saying that *you're*..."

She nodded repeatedly, like a puppet on a string held by a manic master.

"I thought... Bryson, I was told you died at b-birth. I had no idea... I swear to you, I didn't *know*."

Bryson shoved himself off the quartz countertop and stalked across the room, away from her. "How is that possible?"

"My parents," she said, voice quivering. "I was fifteen. Unwed. My p-parents sent me away to my aunt's for the summer."

She filled him in on the details of the birth, being knocked out and the like, and Bryson figured he caught every few words between the blood pulsing through his ears drowning out the others.

He'd always wondered about his birth mother but figured she was some version of what Mary Elizabeth described. A seventies flower child too young to parent. But this...

"Bryson, please, say something. Anything."

He blinked back into the present and realized he'd moved through the periscoping balcony door to stare out at the Atlantic while he gasped for air. "I don't know what to say."

"I wouldn't have given you up," she said, moving onto the balcony behind him. "I wanted you. *So much*. Especially after Dean—your father—was killed in Vietnam," she said.

Details. She disclosed a lot of details but... "How do you know for certain that I'm...the baby?"

"Your haircut. Tessa helped me g-get a sample for a DNA test but please, please don't be angry with her. This—all of this—is my doing and I take one-hundred-percent responsibility."

He turned to face her, shaking his head in disbelief.

"I'm sorry, Bryson. I was too afraid to ask you and stir up trouble if it wasn't true, b-but the results prove... I realize your adoptive parents will always be your parents, but if you could ever bring yourself to forgive me, I-I'd like to get to know you. And you me. If you want to, I mean."

And what would happen if he said no? "Does Hadley know about this?"

"No," Mary Elizabeth said with a shake of her head. "The only people who know are me, Tessa, m-my husband, and..."

"And?" He watched as she closed her eyes and fisted her hands.

"The, um, private investigator my husband hired to look into your history. *Please*, don't take offense. Adam just wanted to know that you were..."

"Someone worthy of you and your rich friends?" He watched as his comment struck a nerve and Mary Elizabeth flinched.

"That's not it at all. Adam is very protective of me and the girls—your sisters."

Sisters. He'd always wanted siblings, but since his adoptive mother was unable to conceive, that had never happened. Now suddenly he had sisters?

Talk about a lot to take in and process.

"Bryson, I know I've surprised you with this, but now that I know for sure, I had to talk to you. Tell you... I had to know about your life. Adam's report... Your company is quite successful," she said as though the compliment would make up for the invasion of privacy.

"My father's company, you mean," he corrected.

"Y-yes. He taught you well. He must be so proud."

"He was there for me. Always has been." He told himself to stop blaming someone who sounded as if she was as much a victim of circumstances as he was, but he couldn't help it. He was *angry* although he wasn't sure why.

He'd had a good life. A great life. But this news?

"I-I hope in time you'll want to talk. Perhaps get to know me as badly as I want to know everything there is to know about you."

"The investigator wasn't thorough enough?" he asked, crossing his arms over his chest.

She winced at the question, and he watched as

she worried her lower lip between her teeth. "What are you going to tell them? Your daughters?" he asked.

Mary Elizabeth lifted her hands as though that would give him an answer.

"The truth," she finally said, "though I wonder if I should wait and give you more time." She smiled weakly. "I know my girls. Once they know about you, they'll be here on your doorstep."

He inhaled and shook his head. No, he wasn't ready for that. "Don't tell them."

"Bryson...?"

"Not yet," he clarified.

Tears filled the older woman's eyes but she nodded.

"Of course. You need time. I understand. You'll let me know when you're ready?"

"Yeah. Sure."

"And Hadley? Will you tell her or...would you like for me to do it?"

Hadley... What would this mean to her? "I'll do it." Maybe.

Because he couldn't help but wonder... Would knowing he was Mary Elizabeth's son change things between them?

LABOR DAY WEEKEND Hadley rushed to the front door the moment she heard a car in the driveway, Hershey scrambling after her like the ever curious dog she was.

Hadley spotted Max's sporty Jeep outside the window and yanked the door open, heart bursting with happiness—until she saw Max, Abby, *and* Kyle getting out of the vehicle.

What on earth?

"Hey, Mom," Max called out the moment he spotted her.

Hadley saw him make a face and tilt his head in his father's direction, and she got the feeling Kyle's presence might have been Abby's idea.

Hadley shut Hershey inside the house and moved down the steps into the yard, her legs feeling as heavy as her heart now felt.

"Mom, wow, you look *awesome*," Abby said.

"That you do," Kyle added, giving her one of his charming, patented smiles.

She'd taken special care with her appearance today in her excitement for the kids to arrive and her planned dinner with Bry— Oh, nooo.

How was she going to deal with Bryson *and* Kyle? What was he even *doing* here?

Abby left the guys to get the bags and came running up to Hadley. Her daughter gave her a tight hug, whispering, "Please don't be mad. You invited us to come and it's our house, too, right?"

"*Abby*—"

"They broke up," Abby said quickly, ending the hug to give Hadley a sharp look. "It's over with them. And you always said you didn't want the divorce."

Her stomach knotted up and then knotted up some more. "Oh, *Abby*—"

"Dad's sorry, Mom. And Grandma told us about that guy who's after the house and money Nan left you and... Just give Dad a chance, please. It's going to be okay. You'll see."

Her insides threatened to revolt and revisit the breakfast she'd stuffed down knowing she needed to eat something, and anger filled her. Obviously she should've told the children about Bryson before now, because instead, her mother had filled them in on *her* version. "Abby, you shouldn't have done this. You should've *talked* to me."

"Grandma said Dad could come. That it would be good for both of you."

Yeah, well, Grandma needed to be smacked. "Abby, this is *not* okay. And your grandmother is dead wrong about Bryson."

Abby glanced over her shoulder toward Kyle and back again. "Mom, please? It's just a weekend. He can sleep in one of the spare rooms."

Well, he certainly wasn't sleeping with her!

"Hadley," Kyle said as he slowly approached them. "Thanks for letting me come along. I was relieved to hear you're okay with me being here."

Okay? No, it wasn't okay! It put her in such a difficult spot and even more unbelievable was the fact he'd deliberately ridden with the kids, which meant to leave he'd either have to take Max's Jeep—which no one drove but Max—or have the kids drive him back to Raleigh—angry with her for ruining their weekend at the beach.

Hadley fisted her hands and swallowed hard, reminding herself that words said in anger would come back to bite her. "I'm not sure who told you that but...I guess we'll have to work something out."

Since her mother was so fond of Kyle, maybe he could stay *there*.

"I can't believe Nan left the beach house to you," Abby said, cheerful and smiling like she hadn't just dropped the most epic emotional time bomb. "Is that Hershey barking?"

Blasted by emotions from every direction, all Hadley could do was nod. "Yeah, she's... Let's go in."

"Hey, Mom," Max said as he joined them, wrapping his impossibly muscled arm around her to give her a hug.

"Hey, you. I've missed you. Both of you," Hadley said.

"And Dad, too, right?" Abby asked, halfway up the steps to the door.

Hadley took one of the duffle bags from Max's shoulder. "Let's get inside, shall we?"

"Is that MeMe?" Abby asked, lifting a hand to cover her eyes as she gazed next door.

Hadley turned in that direction and frowned. It *was* Mary Elizabeth. But what was she doing next door?

Hadley paused on the porch and stared across the yard, noting Mary Elizabeth didn't so much as look over but hurried toward her car looking a bit upset?

The older woman climbed in and sped away in a matter of seconds.

Could this day get any weirder?

Max slid by her and joined Abby inside, their voices excited as they met Hershey for the first time. When Hadley moved to join them, Kyle blocked her way.

"Haddie," Kyle said softly, "I know Abby came on strong right out of the gate, but I'd like to talk. Really talk. I messed up big, and seeing you at the house the other day, packing up... It's like it all hit home and got real."

"Really? It took that long?" she asked. "I would've thought sitting in divorce court would've done that. Or when you went to bed with another woman instead of your wife."

"Haddie, *please*. I just want to talk and see if we can work this thing out."

Work this thing out? Now? Was he serious?

"Dad! Come look! Hershey is so cute," Abby said from inside the house.

Kyle stared at Hadley for a long moment and then stepped back to open the screen door for her to precede him.

"Just think about it," he murmured as she walked by, feet so heavy she felt they were encased in psychological concrete.

Hadley crossed the threshold and forced a smile at the kids, welcoming Hershey's immediate rush to her side as her number one person.

Hadley ran her fingers over the dog's soft, fuzzy head and met Hershey's eyes. The dog seemed to sense Hadley's unease and the doggie smile and wagging tail lessened. Especially when she spotted Kyle. A low growl emerged from Hershey, and Hadley immediately set about soothing the dog in a gentle voice, using the time to process the last few moments.

She'd begged Kyle to reconsider his desire for

divorce. Begged him to work things out. But he'd wanted nothing to do with her anymore. In his words, he was "done with" her because he'd found someone else. Just like that, she'd been set aside.

But *now* he wanted to work it out?

Why couldn't he have done that a year ago? Two years ago when she'd discovered his affair?

Why now—when she'd finally managed to let go and take the first steps to moving on?

IT TOOK NEARLY an hour to get everyone settled into the upstairs rooms and find the right linens for another bed. Hadley would've normally made it up herself, but she refused to play hostess to Kyle when she hadn't invited him as a guest.

In a childish act of defiance, she left the folded linens on the bed for Kyle to make up himself, knowing without a doubt he'd be irritated at the fact it hadn't been done for him.

As a surgeon, Kyle was catered to on every level. At his job, in the OR, at home. But this wasn't his home. And she wasn't his wife.

Abby had followed Hadley around like a puppy, no doubt out of wariness for what she'd instigated. But during her daughter's many apologies and whispered pleas, Abby managed to layer on the guilt by stating Kyle would always be involved with their lives, and if nothing else, her parents needed to find a way to get along for the years and events to come.

Hadley *really* wanted to send Kyle to her parents' house to stay, but she worried her mother would somehow make things worse than they already were.

When her mother set her mind to something, she was a force to be reckoned with, but for the first time in a long time, maybe the first time in her life, Hadley felt ready to take on the challenge. Enough was enough. Boundaries had formed whether her family knew it or not.

The moment she was able, Hadley escaped and hurried next door to see Bryson since he worked on the house. To warn him of the unexpected development in their plans. The house was locked, and no one answered her knock despite the fact Bryson's truck was in the driveway.

She pulled the phone from her rear pocket to text him, desperate to temper any further shocks.

Where are you? Kids arrived—with Kyle. I had no idea so please don't be upset. I'll explain later. XO

She hit send, but since Bryson's notifications

were turned off, she had no way of knowing if he'd read it right away or not.

Hadley returned home, walking around to the back where the kids played with Hershey in the fenced yard. Kyle stood, drink in his hand, looking every bit the handsome, well-to-do doctor while he watched the antics and laughed.

As a whole, the image devastated her. To anyone watching, they looked like the perfect, happy family, and it gutted her with its familiarity and comfort.

A comfort she no longer enjoyed.

She knew she had to forgive Kyle for her children's sake, for her own, but forgiveness was hard when the betrayal and hurt ran soul deep.

Vows weren't meant to be broken. When people married and joined together, they didn't just join homes and incomes but hearts. Lives. As weird as it sounded, she'd believed their souls were tied in that moment. Minute by minute, week by week, year after year built a lifetime and experiences that increased the bonds. To end a marriage meant ripping one away from the other, leaving only the raw, shredded wounds behind.

Hadley didn't speak as she entered the side gate and made her way to the back door of the house. She stumbled up the steps, blinded by tears of fury and frustration. She wanted to rant, to throw things. To not have to hold things together for anyone's sake but let herself *rage.*

But she couldn't. Not here. Not now. Not with her children as witnesses.

So she did what any good mom would do with kids playing fetch in the yard with Hershey. She grabbed a pitcher and ice and stood in the kitchen making lemonade, the irony not at all lost on her.

"Hey."

In her head-down focus and desperation to calm down while slicing and squeezing the devil out of the lemons, she'd missed Kyle's return to the house.

Hadley shot him a look that should've made it clear what the good southern girl in her had been raised not to say, but typical Kyle leaned his shoulder against the door frame and acted as though nothing was amiss.

"You want me to leave?"

"Yes," she said bluntly. "But I know it will hurt the kids—which you knew when you agreed to come with them and not drive separately."

Kyle inhaled and shoved off of the wood molding, moving toward her.

"Look, I know this is hard for you, but let's not spend the weekend glaring at each other, okay? Hadley, I meant what I said. I want to talk, reconnect. I'm ready. Okay? You tried to get me to go to counseling once. Let's try it now. Whatever you want."

"It's too late," she said, slicing the lemons with harder and harder force.

"Don't say that. It's not too late."

"Papers were signed. Decisions made. We're done, Kyle."

"Not if we choose each other. Hadley, if you'll just look at me, you'll see how sorry I am."

He moved closer, lifting his hand to gently push her long hair over her shoulder.

She stiffened, fingers tightening on the knife she held. Knife plus lemon juice? That could be painful.

"Let's spend the weekend together as a family. Remember all the good times. Then go from there, okay?"

"Ahem. Am I interrupting?" Bryson asked from the back porch.

BRYSON COULD'VE EASILY THROTTLED the man touching Hadley, regardless of the fact the scene looked mighty cozy and she didn't seem to be protesting her ex's proximity.

Hadley backed up several steps at the sound of Bryson's voice and rounded the island toward him.

Bryson waited for her to push open the door, even though he'd normally have walked in after greeting her. But then, he'd been welcome. He wasn't so sure right now.

"Bryson, I'm so glad you're here," she said. "Come in. Bryson James, this is Kyle Masterson, my ex-husband."

Okay, so she threw in the *ex*, he noted, but she also hadn't given him the title of boyfriend. Maybe they hadn't made things official, but he was an old-fashioned, one-woman man, and he considered them exclusive. Didn't she?

Bryson lifted his head in a nod toward the man and knew in a heartbeat that Hadley's ex was on a mission to be more again. If his body language hadn't clued Bryson in, the predatory glare shot Bryson's way was unmistakable.

And given the day he'd already had, the warning tipped Bryson's anger into fist-clenching eagerness.

"I'm making lemonade," Hadley said.

Bryson watched Kyle watching them but didn't feel the relief he probably should that Hadley's hand lightly tugged him deeper into the kitchen.

He'd always been okay with himself. His profession. His life. He had what he needed, more than he needed, and couldn't complain. But when it came to being with a woman like Hadley, with her background and upbringing and expectations of those around her, it didn't take a genius to figure out that *he* was the square peg trying to fit into the round. "I can't stay long," he said to Hadley. "Something's come up and I'm going to have to take a rain check on dinner this evening."

"Oh, Bryson, no, really?"

He could see Hadley's upset and fought the urge to change his newly changed plans. Normally he wouldn't have given the other man a foothold, but in this case, Bryson needed to know exactly where Hadley stood on her own, without him in the picture. If she went running back... "Problem on a jobsite. Can't be helped," he said, not really lying because there were always some sort of problems on every jobsite. It was an inevitable part of the construction business.

"Well, maybe we'll see you around sometime this weekend then," Kyle said. "I'd like to get to know Hadley's...friends."

"Yeah, maybe." Bryson bent and kissed Hadley on the cheek. "Enjoy your kids," he said, knowing she'd looked forward to the weekend like any loving mother would.

Hadley had talked about all the things they could do, places to go, what she'd cook for them. He'd found it sexy and endearing, knowing that if she ever came to love him, he'd get the same kind of special treatment. She was just that way.

Which meant now, if she had to choose...who would it be?

And as Mary Elizabeth's long-lost son...how much of Hadley's potential reconciliation was he going to have to watch?

CHAPTER SIXTEEN

Hadley stayed as far away from Kyle as possible, but he didn't make it easy. As a group, they went for a walk on the beach, played board games, and listened to Max play guitar while sitting on the front porch enjoying the ocean breeze.

It wrenched her heart when she thought of how much she'd dreamed of this moment, mourned times like these after Kyle had made his choices known and the divorce had been in motion. And all she could think of now was how utterly cruel it was. Like sharp pokes to a painful bruise that had finally started to heal.

She couldn't relax. At every turn, she felt Kyle staring at her, and despite his repeated attempts to get her alone, she'd made one excuse after another.

Even going so far as to grab Max as he'd passed by for a hug that lasted so long she'd made Max uncomfortable.

And today...*oh, today.*

Her mother had invited them for lunch and swimming, and Hadley found herself forced to go along. Oh, she could've stayed behind and let the three of them go without her, but she hated to think what outrageous plan they'd cook up regarding her marital state without her there to vehemently protest.

Especially considering what had already happened with the planned surprise visit.

"Hadley, you look lovely. So nice to see you looking more like yourself," her mother said as they entered the house.

Hadley looked down and realized she'd automatically worn what she and the cousins had long ago nicknamed "battle gear." A term that meant something expensive and far too fancy for hot days at the beach but appropriate in her mother's country club circles.

"She's always beautiful," Kyle said, his hand at her back and touch much too familiar.

Hadley stepped out of reach once more and noticed a flash of irritation in Kyle's gaze before he quickly banked it.

No doubt her charming ex wasn't used to being rebuffed. Before, she'd humiliated herself by begging him to stay, desperate to salvage her marriage. But now?

She felt like she stood on top of a high wire, with no balance beam to help guide her across the precipice. But even so, she was slowly moving forward.

"I thought we'd eat and chat and then change for swimming," her mother continued. "Sound good to you?"

Of course. Because it would've been too shocking to just wear coverups over their swim clothes to make things easy.

"Kyle," her father said, joining them.

Hadley watched as her father hesitated momentarily before accepting Kyle's outstretched hand.

So that was it? They discovered her ex-husband had cheated on her but now they simply shook hands? All his bad behavior forgiven because of Kyle's status, money, and a few sorrys made it so? "I need a drink."

"It's a little early for that, sweetheart," Kyle said.

"Not for this day," Hadley said without looking over her shoulder.

"I'll have Tia make you a mimosa," her mother said, walking with Hadley across the patio.

"I can make it myself. Don't bother Tia."

"That's her job, Hadley," her mother said as she followed Hadley into the kitchen.

Hadley turned and gave her mother a flat stare. "Really? It's not enough that she cooks and cleans and runs your errands; you're going to pull her from whatever duty she's performing for you just so she can wait on me even though I'm perfectly capable of making my own drink?"

Cheryl crossed her arms over her chest and all pretense faded from her expression.

"Well, I can tell you're in a mood."

"Ha! Why wouldn't I be? How *dare* you invite Kyle to what was going to be a fun, relaxing weekend with my children? One I've looked forward to for *weeks*?"

"He's their father and your husband."

"*Ex-husband*, which means he doesn't get to tag along, nor do *you* get to ruin my plans by overriding them with your own—which, by the way, you'd best end, because Kyle and I are not getting back together."

"Hush," Cheryl said, waving her hands at Hadley as though that alone would lower the volume at which she'd said the words. "Hadley, you have to hear him out. He's quite contrite."

"Mom, he *cheated* on me, and while at the time, I

was willing to try working things out, time's passed and that's no longer the case."

"Why? Because of that man?"

Hadley didn't need her mother to specify the man she meant. "Because *Kyle* broke my trust and he can't ever get that back."

"He can. You can get over this—if you stop pushing Kyle away and forgive him. Completely forgive him. It's possible, Hadley. Your father is the perfect example of that very thing."

Hadley sucked in a sharp breath, nearly choking in the process and a bit dizzy from the blast of the words. "What?" She blinked at her mother, thoughts racing. "Are you saying... Are you saying Dad *cheated* on you?"

Her mother grabbed hold of her hand and pulled Hadley to the breakfast room table, shoving her into a chair with a glance at the empty doorway and those gathered on the patio beyond.

"No. Hadley, I-I'm ashamed to say this, and I wouldn't if I didn't think it might help you understand, but...your father is the one who forgave me."

It was a good thing she was sitting down. That was all Hadley could think when the world tilted on its axis a bit before righting itself. Nothing could have surprised her more than that verbal bomb. "*You...?*"

Tears filled her mother's eyes, and for the first time—maybe the first time ever—Hadley saw her mother looking vulnerable and broken and completely exposed. Definitely not the Cheryl Dummit she presented to the world.

"Hadley, I was eighteen when I had you," Cheryl murmured. "Your father began working for my father, which was wonderful, but he felt the need to prove himself, and that meant long hours and taking every assignment he could. Traveling far and wide. He was away so much and I was home alone with you and..."

Cheryl glanced up at Hadley but Hadley couldn't speak. Didn't know what to say.

"I was immature. *Stupid.* With a baby to care for and an absent husband, and...more than a little postpartum depression, I think, though in those days they didn't know much about such things."

"Mom..."

"A hurricane came through while your father was out of town, and we had damage to the house and property. My father found and hired someone to fix things here and"—her mother paused, shaking her head—"I allowed that man to charm me. He was so different than your father, and he made me think your father was horrible for leaving me to handle everything alone."

"I...don't know what to say."

"Hadley, I take full responsibility for my actions, but I allowed a handsome face and a few compliments to overwhelm my common sense, and I regret what I allowed to happen every single day of my life."

"That's why you're so freaked out about Bryson," Hadley said.

"It is," her mother said softly. "I see you, Hadley. I see you making *my* mistakes."

"I'm not married," Hadley countered.

"No, but you have to open your eyes. If you were in my shoes, wouldn't you be concerned? If it were Abby running toward a fire rather than away?"

Hadley closed her eyes and ran her fingers through her loose hair, shoving it back from her face just to give herself time to collect her thoughts. "Mom...I get what you're saying but I'm not eighteen. And your situation isn't the same as mine."

"Isn't it? You are reeling from a divorce you readily admit you didn't want, and you've just inherited a home worth well over a million dollars, not to mention the money Nan left you. Hadley, for your own sake and that of your children, your future, I'm begging you to stop this nonsense with that man now. Give yourself time to regain clarity."

Hadley stared at her mother, the perfect hair and

makeup, the perfect clothes, home, life. Not a thing out of place. Except perhaps for Hadley and her rebellious ways. "I have clarity. Maybe for the first time ever in my adult life," she countered.

"You're kidding yourself then. Sweetheart, your father forgave me, and if he could do that, so can you. You can forgive Kyle and patch things up. You know it would be best for everyone."

Hadley drew back, shaking her head as the knot in her stomach grew at the thought. "No, it's not best for everyone. It's best for *you* and maybe Kyle but... why? Are you really that much of a snob that you think Bryson is somehow beneath me?"

"That man—"

"Has a name," Hadley said. "*Bryson*. You can say it."

Hadley glared at her mother before shoving herself to her feet. She paced across the room, unable to sit still and pretend her mother hadn't just rocked her world with her admission of an affair.

"Hadley, please, sit down."

"I can't. Do you have any idea of how badly you've hurt me? Angered me?"

"I'm sorry but I didn't know what else to do."

"No, Mom, you're not sorry. That's just it," she said as she whirled around to face her mother once more. "You still think you somehow have the right to rule my life and tell me what to do."

"Oh, Hadley, stop being so melodramatic."

"Stop being so *you!*"

Her mother stood and stepped into Hadley's pacing path. Hadley almost ran into her before managing to stop with a stumble.

"Just listen to me, please," Cheryl said. "Your children need their parents. Abby told me she cries herself to sleep every night because of the divorce, and anyone with eyes can see how devastated and uncomfortable Max is."

"They're coping. It's a process and it's *normal.*"

"But if you got back together, neither of them would suffer a moment more."

"Wouldn't they? It's not like they can't unlearn what they know about Kyle. Unsee the pain I failed to hide every time they mentioned the trips they took with Kyle and *his mistress.*"

"I know it's hard."

"Do you? Looks to me like if anyone should be having this conversation with me, it should be Dad."

Her mother flinched at the statement, and even though Hadley felt bad for inflicting pain, it couldn't be helped.

"You're right. I suppose this should have come from your father. So until you get a chance to speak to him privately, I'll leave you with this: It's possible to recover from adultery. Yes, we had several very rough, very intense years, but I swore to Jerry I'd never stray again and I *haven't*. It is my biggest, *worst* regret and shame, and I've spent my life trying to make up for it."

"By creating a picture-perfect life," Hadley mused, the insight opening her eyes to a lot of the pressures Hadley had felt over the years but hadn't understood.

"By doing the best I could do to honor your father in all the ways I hadn't during that awful time. Hadley...I've known so many women who've fallen for men like that contractor, and they've sorely regretted it for one reason or another."

Hadley blinked at the statement, at the expression on her mother's face. "What is that supposed to mean?"

"It means exactly what it sounds like. People talk. Tell stories. Do you think you—or I—are the first women to be approached by men looking for a little fun on the side? For a step up from what they're used to?"

"Oh, my— You *can't* be serious."

"It's a game to some of them, to see if they can score with someone normally out of reach. You're an adult. You know what I'm saying is true."

Hadley raced across the room once more, stood over the kitchen sink, and stared out the window, gaze drawn as it always was to the beautiful sea beyond. Yeah, she'd heard stories. Stories of mothers and pool boys, landscapers, and handymen. Rich, bored wives looking for attention because their husbands were elsewhere. But that wasn't Bryson. It couldn't be. "I honestly don't know what to say to you right now."

"Say you'll stop seeing that man. Say you'll give your marriage another chance. It worked for your father and me and it could work for you."

Their affair had happened over forty years ago, when she was a baby yet to be raised. Her mother and father had had more at stake. Lived in a different time.

"Hadley, I'm aware you think I'm too critical, too judgmental. I'm sure in some ways I am, but it comes from hard experience and a lesson learned through pain. I *see* you. In the short time you've been here, I've seen the struggle you're having to cope, and while I know Kyle's betrayal hurt you—"

"It didn't."

"What?"

"It didn't hurt me, Mom. It *broke* me," Hadley corrected, interjecting the words to try—*try*—to get her mother to understand the depths of the pain involved. "Hurt is a missed dinner and not remembering my birthday. This is walking in to see the mistress's ridiculously ugly shoes and underwear on our bed because I arrived home earlier than expected. Then again, I guess that's better than seeing *them* together in bed, but the imagery is all too easy to imagine."

"Hadley—"

"So knowing that he broke our vows willingly, *readily*," she continued, ignoring her mother, "and that he chose her over me *repeatedly* even though I loved him and trusted him? You can see why it's a wee bit more than *hurt*. We had twenty-five years together and he betrayed me, Mother. You and Dad had what? Two, from the sounds of it? Dad gambled and won. *If* what you're saying is the truth and you didn't cheat on him again."

Cheryl's face crumpled with tears and Hadley crossed her arms over her chest. Only her mother could pull off crying pretty at moment like this.

"Your father thought the same of me, Hadley, but he was wrong. It took time, years, but we made it. Don't you see? You could be wrong about Kyle. And if you are, you might miss out on the best years of your life. I know I would have if your father hadn't forgiven me."

She had to give her mother credit there. Her parents were still together. And seemingly happy?

Now that she'd had over a year of separation and time on her own, Hadley couldn't fathom the possibility. So much had happened between her and Kyle. She knew too many details about his time with the other woman, either from the kids or friends who'd wanted to fill her in as though every word wasn't a razor blade to her skin. Social media? Yeah, she'd seen it. Pictures of them together, them...and *her* children.

"Hadley, people make mistakes. Huge mistakes they regret and wish they could undo. I don't know what I would've done if your father hadn't forgiven me. I can't even explain why I did it, because I loved him."

"That's some way of showing it."

Cheryl wrung her hands in front of her, diamond wedding rings flashing in the sunlight streaming into the room.

"I know. There is nothing you can say to me that I haven't already said to myself, and I'm sure Kyle feels the same way."

Hadley wasn't so sure. When it came to egos, Kyle's was pretty far up there.

"But if you have any love left for him at all, just...

consider giving him another chance. Children have a hard enough time in life without being divided."

"My kids aren't toddlers, Mom. And it's not forty-plus years ago. It's not the same situation at all."

"Oh, Hadley... Isn't it? Can't you see how very much your children need you to be together? As a mother, how can you not do what's best for them?"

A LITTLE WHILE LATER, Hadley sat on the far side of the pool watching Max and Abby play volleyball against Kyle.

"Mind if I join you?" her father asked.

Hadley tilted her head back to better see him and nodded. "Of course."

Her father sat in the cushioned lounge chair, dressed in swim shorts and sunglasses. He looked every bit the fit, well-kept man in his sixties.

"So... I hear your mother told you."

Hadley huffed out a breath, not needing a clarification. "She did."

"Would you like to talk about it?"

"I'm not sure."

"Fair enough."

She pressed her head back against the chair and

rolled it side to side. "Dad...why? How could you forgive her for what she did?"

"It was the hardest thing I ever had to do. But like the saying goes, to hold a grudge is like drinking poison and expecting it to kill the other person."

Hadley adjusted the brim of her straw hat to better see her father. "Forgiving is one thing. Forgetting is another."

"A bit of advice I was given at the time was to say the words every day. Repeat them until you can say it without anger. Until you almost believe them. And then then keep doing it until you do."

"You stayed because of me, didn't you?" she asked.

"I stayed because I truly loved her. You were a bonus."

Hadley shook her head, angry for them both. "Dad, come on."

"I'm serious, sweetheart. I could've left and probably could've managed to get custody of you under the circumstances. Courts were different back then in how they looked at such things. But I didn't want that. I wanted my family."

"She betrayed you."

"Yes, she did."

"And you're okay with that?"

"Not by a long shot. But I made myself take a

step back and look at the whole picture. She was young, depressed, and alone. And some of that was on me because I didn't have to do all the traveling I was doing. I did it because it was easier than dealing with the stress of a new marriage, fatherhood, and the crying and complaints at home."

Hadley shifted her gaze to Kyle, and he turned his head toward her and smiled as though he sensed her stare. "I don't know that I could ever get past it."

"That's understandable. We're all made differently. I suppose the question is whether or not you actually want to?"

That was the question.

So what was the answer?

CHAPTER SEVENTEEN

Bryson entered his father's room at the care facility and managed to force a smile. "Hey, Dad. How you doing?"

"Bryson! Well, I'm happy to see you again so soon. You usually wait until Sunday."

Bryson made a show of turning. "I can come back then—"

"Get on in here," John ordered, chuckling. "But you can come back on Sunday, too."

"I'll do my best," Bryson said, leaning over his father's chair to hug him.

His father pounded Bryson on the back several times before releasing him.

"So? What's the special occasion? Is that pretty girl with you today?"

"No, she's not. It's just me—and some highly

illegal fried chicken from Bo's," Bryson added, pulling it out of the bag. "I only brought you two small pieces, though, so no complaining."

"Ah, better than nothing. You know how much I love it."

Bryson chuckled and got his father set up for the snack before settling into the chair opposite.

"Something bothering you?" his dad asked. "You look like you're chewing on something awfully hard over there and it ain't my chicken."

Bryson stretched his legs out in front of him and crossed his ankles, hands linked over his stomach. "I got quite a surprise this week."

"Oh?"

Bryson stared at his father, hoping the news wouldn't upset him. "I heard from my birth mother."

His father paused with the chicken leg halfway to his mouth before lowering it to the plate and fumbling for a napkin.

"Really? What'd she, uh, say when she called?"

"She didn't call. She's... She's actually a friend of Hadley's."

"What's that?"

Bryson could see his father's confusion and felt much the same himself. "A couple of weeks ago I walked into Hadley's house and the woman... She recognized me because she says I look like my biological father. She was so surprised she dropped a tray of dishes."

"Son, you can't base paternity on looks."

"I know. And so did she—that's why she managed to finagle a DNA test," he said, explaining how his free haircut had come about. "The results were conclusive."

John sat back in his chair, the forbidden chicken forgotten on his plate.

"I don't know what to say," his father said.

"I'm not sure either. Did you know the girl—my mother? Ma always said no, but—"

"No, no, we never met her. The doctor came in to talk to us the morning after we lost our baby. An older man was with him, but he didn't speak much. Just said he would pay for the lawyer to draw up the adoption papers, and if we agreed, it would all be taken care of. When we left the hospital, though, the man had also paid your mama's medical bills, and since the adoption was closed and we didn't know any names, we couldn't return the money."

"So you took me home, straight from the hospital? Just like that?"

His father nodded. "We were surprised, too, but once we signed the paperwork, the nurses brought you in and gave you to us. From that moment on, you were ours, and that's how they referred to you."

Bryson shook his head, unable to believe a person —a life—could be given away so easily. "She... The woman said she was fifteen. And that she was told her baby died at birth."

"Ah, poor girl. I don't know anything about that. The doctor said, if we weren't interested, that you'd go into an orphanage until someone could be found, but since they knew we'd lost a child, they thought we might want you. We were shocked that they thought they could just replace the baby we lost, but Clara couldn't bear the thought of you in some ward somewhere. Neither could I."

Bryson loved and appreciated the fact that they'd accepted him so readily. Made his life what it was, even though it obviously wasn't up to Cheryl Dummit's standards.

"Who is this woman? What does she want showing up after all of this time?"

Bryson pondered the questions for a long moment. "She doesn't seem to want anything except to get to know me. She has a family. I have some half sisters, I guess."

Bryson looked up in time to see his father smiling gently.

"That's good. Never sat well with me that you'd be alone after I go."

"Dad—"

"No, no, you know what I'm saying. I know you and Tish couldn't conceive, but after she died, I've often wondered how you'd fare alone."

"I'm not alone. You're going to be around for a long time," Bryson said to his father.

John smiled weakly but shook his head.

"We don't live forever, Bryson. And truth be told, I don't want to. I'm ready to see your mother again whenever the Good Lord says it's time."

Bryson pictured Hadley in his mind. Her smile, the way her hair curled over her shoulders in gentle waves. The fullness of her lips and how good she tasted, and the softness and kindness she'd shown his father and Hershey and everyone in her circle of friends.

"This got to you, didn't it?" his father asked. "What does Hadley think of it? Did she have something to say?"

"I haven't told her yet." He inhaled and sat forward, resting his elbows on his knees as he stared at his clasped hands. "Her kids and ex-husband are in town. They're staying with her."

"I see. They gettin' back together, her and the ex?"

Bryson drew back and shoved himself upright, stalking across the room toward the window. "She says she didn't know about it. That his appearance was a surprise to her."

"Maybe it was. Kids can be sneaky at times. And I'd say most any man would have some regrets letting one like her go."

"He's a doctor," Bryson said. "A plastic surgeon."

"So? I'll bet you can do a far sight more than he can when it comes to real life things. Don't let some letters behind his name get you down, son. Hadley's already chosen to get rid of him."

True. But he'd be crazy to think Hadley wasn't under a lot of pressure to stick to the status quo. Kyle, the kids. Her mother.

"How well does Hadley know you? Your financial state," his father clarified.

"If that's all that matters to her, I want no part of it."

"Well, then, you just answered your own question, didn't you? I don't think Hadley's like that, son, but obviously you need some convincing."

"It's not Hadley so much as her...upper-class family—her mother in particular."

"Ah. Well, son, it boils down to trust, just like it always does. If Hadley's the one for you, you have to trust that it'll happen. And if she's not, well, life goes on, as we both know."

Yeah, it did. Life moved on. He'd suffered a

horrific loss before, just like his father, but seeing as how his biological mother was one of Hadley's "aunts," he wondered if he'd ever recover if he lost Hadley to her ex yet had to see them together should he get to know his new family. If he let it be known he was Mary Elizabeth's son, he became part of that group, however unwelcome.

What would Hadley do when she found out?

THE FOLLOWING DAY, Hadley strolled the beach between the public access points when she spotted the point of a whelk in about three inches of water.

She splashed over and nudged the shell with her toe, and when it barely budged, she bent down to try again, uncaring of the waves.

The whelk was buried wide end up, and Hadley felt a surge of excitement as she continued to carefully dig out the treasure. Finally she got it free and pulled it from the water only to see that the almost-perfect shell had a hole where a point should be.

She checked it for occupants and, seeing it was free, bent and rinsed the sand from it.

She'd add it to Nan's collection back at the

house, the first of many to come during her time at the beach, Hadley mused.

"Nice find," a male voice said from behind her.

She turned to see Bryson standing just out of the surf, dressed in faded, well-worn jeans, bare feet, and a V-neck white T-shirt that showcased his tan, muscular chest and biceps to perfection. "Hey, stranger."

"Hey, yourself. Enjoying your company?"

A laugh huffed out of her and she rolled her eyes. "I'm on the beach alone. Does that tell you anything?"

The kids had been fighting nonstop since Friday about Abby flirting with one of Max's friends who was apparently quite the player. Hadley needed a break from the bickering—and Kyle's constant hovering and attempts to make up.

A wave broke and she stumbled when it barreled into her knees. She managed to stay upright, thanks in part to Bryson's quick reflexes.

He rushed forward and grabbed her elbows, the wave soaking the bottoms of his pant legs.

"Oh, no. Sorry about that."

"You live at the beach, you're gonna get wet. Should've put on shorts."

She looked up in time to catch his gaze shifting

from the direction of her mouth to her eyes. "Bryson, about Kyle—"

"Hadley, there's something I—"

They both broke off, and she loved the way the little lines around his eyes crinkled when he smiled at her. "You first," she said.

"Uh, well, I'd tell you to sit down but with the tide coming in—"

"That sounds ominous. Just tell me."

"Okay, but you should probably brace yourself. I'm Mary Elizabeth's son."

She choked on a gasp. "*What?*"

Bryson tugged her out of the surf and up to dry sand, and she let him lead the way, too stunned to do anything else.

"Apparently I'm her biological son. She came to the house a few days ago and told me."

"The same day the kids and Kyle arrived?" she asked.

"Yeah."

"We saw her there but... I don't understand. How? Who? *Really?*" She sounded like a bumbling idiot, but she couldn't seem to form the sentences required.

Bryson told Hadley the story, adding the information his father had provided, and when he finished, Hadley struggled to wrap her head around the news. "Wow."

"Yeah."

"And you had no idea?"

"Not until she showed up with the results of the DNA test."

"I wondered why Tessa insisted on giving you a free trim. It seemed a bit odd, but then I figured she just wanted to get you alone to grill you because of our friendship. That or she wanted to flirt with you herself. *Wow*," she said again, completely taken aback by the turn of events.

"It's crazy, right? I've always been curious as to who my birth parents were. Now I know."

Stunned. She was just stunned. First her mother's affair and now Mary Elizabeth had a secret baby? What other secrets were the Babes hiding? "Are you...angry with her?"

Bryson shook his head.

"It's hard to be angry with a fifteen-year-old kid. Her parents, on the other hand... But I wouldn't want to grow up where I wasn't wanted, and she would've been hard-pressed to raise me on her own. Plus, if what she says is true, and I have no reason to doubt it, she was told I died. No, it was better the way it went down. I couldn't have asked for better parents. It all worked out like it should've, I think."

Hadley's mind whirled and she stared down at the shell in her hand and then held it up for Bryson to see. "Did Nan ever tell you her philosophy on life?"

Bryson pursed his lips and shook his head again. "If she did, I don't recall. What is it?"

"Well, Nan always told us it was the broken shells that were the most beautiful."

"Why's that?"

"Because that's where the light gets in. Your adopted parents were your light, just like you were theirs."

Bryson lowered himself to the sand and looped his hands over his raised knees, staring out at the ocean. "They were definitely that."

Hadley dropped down beside him, the mix of sandalwood and spice from his cologne or soap teasing her senses. She liked it. A lot. "So what happens now? With you and Mary Elizabeth? I guess Adam knows, right?"

Adam, the keeper of secrets. Poor man. Yes, it was part of his job as an attorney, but Hadley wondered how he was dealing with this new revelation. It couldn't have been easy for him.

Had Mary Elizabeth told him about the baby she lost, or was that also a secret newly revealed? It boggled the mind.

"I think so. She mentioned not telling her daughters until I gave her the go-ahead, though. She said they'd track me down."

"Oh, they definitely would, especially Izzy. Bryson, you have three *sisters*. Isn't that wonderful?"

He gave her a wry smile and Hadley's heart pinched a bit. Yeah, she imagined Bryson was a bit overwhelmed at the prospect of an instant family, but since she knew them and loved them, Hadley felt confident he'd get used to the idea in time.

"Guess I have a lot of people I should get to know."

"The girls are great. They each have *very* different personalities, but they're smart and fun and... Oh, and you're an uncle, too. Allie has kids of her own. But there's plenty of time to meet them," she added hastily, sensing his growing unease.

Bryson turned his head toward her, his bright green eyes holding her gaze. "What?" she asked.

"Just wondering what's going on with you," he said, tilting his head toward the homes in the distance behind them. "You couldn't wait for them to get here; now you're down here alone. Is your ex giving you a hard time?"

Hadley faltered, unsure about everything. Especially what to say to him. "My mother wants me to give Kyle a second chance."

"That's hardly surprising."

"I suppose not," she said, running her fingertips over the knobs and ridges of the whelk, the smooth surface inside. "But the reason she wants me to give him another chance is because...my father gave *her* another chance many years ago, when I was a baby."

She felt Bryson's gaze sharpen on her but didn't lift her lashes from the shell. Round and round she swirled her fingertip over the shell, aged and colored by sand and saltwater and broken by the life it had lived.

"I see."

"Please don't repeat that to anyone," she said, her fingertip coasting over the jagged edge of the missing point. The break hadn't been easy, the shell's layers peeled back, with a hairline fracture that ran nearly the entire length of it.

Scarred for life.

"You have my word, Hadley."

She wet her lips and focused on the fact that the shell, while damaged, was still intact, beautiful, with its deep blue and gray coloring giving it a richness, not to mention being near perfect in every other way.

"I was shocked, needless to say," she murmured. "But it explains so many things. My mother has spent all of these years creating this picture-perfect life, but the reality is she's trying to make up for what she did, as though doing so would fix the past. For the first time, I saw her not as my mom so much as—"

"A broken shell?"

A huff left her and she nodded as she pulled her finger from the open point. "Exactly."

And her mother's light, Hadley realized with a heart-stopping jolt, was the forgiveness her father had offered. But did that mean *she* had to do the same? Try again with Kyle?

"So what are you going to do?"

She blinked, torn in two by her emotions and the confusion bombarding her. She'd resigned herself to the divorce over a year ago, had processed as much of the pain as she could in order to finally wake up one day ready to see what came next. Then Nan had passed. She'd found Hershey and Bryson and...

"That's why you're really down here, isn't it? To figure out if you want to reconcile?"

"You have to understand, Bryson. It's hard to let go of so many years."

"I do understand. But it's simple."

"*Nothing* about this is simple," she said.

"Hadley, at the end of the day, what do you want?" he asked.

His voice was so low she barely heard it because the wind threatened to carry away the words. She struggled to breathe, to focus and work through the emotional bombardment scattering her ability to concentrate. "At one point I would've done anything to make things work."

"And now?"

Her pulse pounded loudly in her ears. "I don't know. I really don't. And I realize how awful that sounds," she said, glancing at him quickly before looking away once more. "Kyle says he made a mistake, that it's over between him and her. He wants to go to counseling..."

Bryson didn't speak. She found his gaze on her, waiting.

"Again, not a surprise," he said softly. "Hadley, any man would be blessed to call you his. So I'll ask again—what do you want?"

"It's not that easy."

"It is. You make a choice and you pursue it until you see where it leads."

"Even if I don't know if it's the right one? I just want my children to be happy."

"Your children are grown and gone, Hadley. They have their own lives to live. This is about you. Your life. What do *you* want?"

"I want to be happy," she said softly.

"Good. But what does that mean?"

"I don't know. Why are you pressuring me?" she asked, her voice rising with the growing panic she felt.

"Because no man wants to be second choice and what you decide impacts me."

"Bryson—" She broke off, opened her mouth again only to close it. Tried and failed to find the words to defuse the conversation and give herself time to think. "I'm sorry. You're right but I need time to think about all of this. I can't even catch my breath because this entire weekend has been surreal."

"Sweetheart, look at me."

She lifted her gaze to his and wanted to cry at what she saw. Maybe she'd only known him a few weeks, but in that time, she'd come to truly care for Bryson. Strong feelings that were more than simple friendship.

"You are an amazing woman. But if you're having this much trouble making your decision, I'll make it for you."

"What do you mean?"

Hadley wiped a hand under her watery eyes as she waited for Bryson to clarify his words, her heart in her throat because she felt like she stood between the proverbial rock and hard place.

Pre-affair memories of love and security chipped away at her fear and doubts of an unknown future. But her time with Bryson had also made her realize what it felt like to be appreciated for being herself.

"I'm taking myself out of the equation."

Hadley gasped, but having once begged a man to stay only to watch him walk away, she'd sworn to herself she'd never beg again. If it was so easy for Bryson to leave, well, so be it, she thought, hurt and anger sliding through her.

"*Mom!* Mom?"

Max's timing couldn't have been worse. "I see. If...that's what you want to do, I understand."

"It's what I need to do," Bryson said, his gaze warm with feelings and emotions she didn't dare name. "I won't be the guy standing between a family getting back together, and this is a decision only you can make. Go after what you want, Hadley. Just be happy."

Max closed in on them with a too-wise expression on his handsome face.

"Bryson, please, just give me time to sort this out. It's so complicated. The history I have with Kyle..." Kyle had done what he'd done, and she could forgive, but she couldn't forget. The pain was too deep. The hurt unimaginable if one hadn't lived it in person.

But on the other hand...what if Kyle was sincere and this was her chance to have the marriage she'd always wanted? One that weathered the storms and emerged battered but whole? Stronger? Faithful? Was she going to turn her back on that?

The seconds lengthened as she struggled to find the words to express her convoluted emotions. She felt suffocated from all levels, Bryson, her kids, Kyle, her parents.

"Hadley?"

Her name on his lips drew her attention, and she struggled to contain her emotions at the somber expression on Bryson's face.

"Just remember that you deserve someone who loves you. Only you."

Her heart shattered and she sucked in a breath. "Bryson—"

"*Mom?*" Max said, now only a few feet away.

Hadley turned, spotting Kyle and Abby in the distance in the process of crossing the bridge over the dunes to descend the stairs leading to the sand. "Uh, hey," she said, turning her face toward the wind to dry her eyes and give her an excuse to wipe them again under the pretense of shoving her blowing hair off her face. "Max, h-have you met Bryson?"

Bryson stood in a fluid motion and shook her son's hand, greeting him like men do, his expression revealing nothing of their conversation.

"We've been looking everywhere for you," Max said to her. "Dad wants to go to the Oceanic for dinner."

"Oh, Max. It's a holiday weekend."

"He wanted it to be special for the four of us," Max said. "Plus Grandma and Grandpa."

Hadley glanced at Bryson and found him frowning at the comment.

"Sounds like a special occasion. You should get going," Bryson said. "Enjoy your dinner."

"Wait—what about visiting your father?" she asked, referring to their tentative plan to pay the man another visit. They'd discussed it last week, before chaos had arrived in Max's Jeep.

"I'll tell him you're with your family," Bryson said.

Hadley swallowed back the lump forming in her throat, accepting the comment as Bryson setting a boundary to prevent further pain. "I guess I'll...see you around then?"

It wasn't a breakup. They couldn't break up when they weren't technically together. But it felt like one because of his statement about removing himself from the situation. She wasn't sure what she wanted, but she didn't want him to do that, even though it probably wasn't fair to Bryson. Was it wrong to want someone who wouldn't walk away so easily?

Bryson looked like he wanted to say something, but he didn't. He gave her a short nod and murmured goodbye to Max, ignoring the duo now at the bottom of the stairs.

"Mom? Are you okay?" Max asked after Bryson turned to walk away.

"Yeah."

"Are you sure? That seemed...tense."

"I'm fine. Help me up." She lifted her hands and Max grasped them and tugged her to her feet with the ease of a strong young man.

"That guy..."

"Bryson," she gently corrected. "He's a friend, Max. And I've needed a good friend more than anything these days. Whatever you're about to say? Be kind."

Max seemed to accept her words at face value and nodded.

"I'm glad you had a friend," he said softly.

"Me, too." The words emerged thick and full of emotion.

"Is that yours?" Max asked, indicating the shell.

Glad to have something else to focus on, she swooped down and lifted it from the sand. "Yeah, isn't it beautiful?"

"It's broken."

Hadley laughed softly, tears flooding her eyes once more as she cradled the whelk in her hands. *Broken shells really were the most beautiful.* "No," she murmured huskily as she held it up. "See how the light gets in?"

THIRTY MINUTES LATER, Hadley stared at her reflection in the mirror.

Make a choice and see where it leads, she thought, paraphrasing Bryson's advice.

She'd taken extra care with her appearance, picking Kyle's favorite color on her, a light periwinkle-blue spaghetti-strapped dress that V-ed deep in the front and flowed all the way to the floor. She added wedges and a silver necklace Kyle had purchased for her many years ago for her birthday, the delicate sapphire catching the light from the window.

That done, she pinned her hair up and took another long look at her nearly perfect appearance.

Like her mother?

Hadley inhaled and pressed her hands to her stomach, her gaze locking on the rings she'd removed the day she'd told her parents the truth. They sat in a pretty dish atop the dresser, gathering dust like all the knickknacks remaining in the house.

Tonight would be a test of sorts. A trial run to see if she and Kyle could begin anew. Get through a dinner without thinking bad thoughts or experiencing the anger that often caught her by surprise when it appeared like a sucker punch to her stomach.

A soft knock sounded on her door and she murmured a distracted, "Come in."

She turned to find Kyle leaning against the doorframe. "Oh. I was expecting Abby."

"She and Max already left. You look beautiful, Hadley."

"Thanks...wait, what? They left?"

"They'll meet us at the restaurant."

She glanced at the clock and realized she'd taken longer than intended. "I see. I'm ready to go."

She crossed to the bed and plucked up the thin, gauzy scarf and a beaded purse of a sea scene with the ocean and palm trees and sand on one side.

"Haddie..."

Hadley turned so fast she almost plowed into Kyle. His soft hands gently gripped her bare shoulders as he steadied her, and she caught at the instant comparison to Bryson's deliciously calloused ones. "We sh-should be going. We don't want to be late."

Kyle lifted one hand and gently stroked his fingers over her jawline, stopping at her chin to nudge her face a bit higher. "Kyle..."

"Shhh," he said, lowering his head.

His lips brushed over hers and she froze, unable

to move, unable to respond. Memories bombarded her. Good and bad. But the familiarity was there, the comfort of time, the feel of her husband, the scent of his cologne.

By the time Kyle lifted his head, Hadley considered herself more confused than ever, though she supposed her response—or lack thereof—was understandable due to the trauma they'd endured. "We should g-go."

Kyle gave her a handsome grin and wrapped his arm around her shoulders before sliding his hand down to the small of her back.

Hershey raced down the stairs ahead of them, and Hadley gave Hershey a treat and said goodbye while Kyle waited impatiently.

"I still can't believe you got a dog. Can you give it back?" he asked as he used her key to lock up behind them.

"What?" she asked, aghast that he'd even ponder such a thing. "No, I can't give her back."

"Are you sure? Have you asked?"

"Kyle, Hershey is mine now. When I got her, I promised her I wouldn't abandon her."

"She's a dog, Haddie. And a messy one at that."

"I'm not giving her up."

"Fine. But I'm not walking her or picking up dog poop."

"No one has asked you to."

Kyle turned on his heel and headed down the steps, mouth twisted in a mulish line because she hadn't immediately acquiesced to his demand.

She slowly made her way across the porch and down, the doubts she'd quelled earlier turning into full-blown disbelief as she followed his long strides down the walkway.

As familiar as it was to be with Kyle, it wasn't the same at all. She'd lost her ability to ignore his childishness and overbearing demands, and the knot in her stomach grew to the size of a beach ball.

In fact, as she watched him walk ahead of her like some arrogant royal, Hadley couldn't help but be aware that something important was missing.

Was she being overly critical—or was her love for him truly gone?

CHAPTER EIGHTEEN

Mary Elizabeth gripped the chair back tightly and watched out the window as Bryson made his way up the walk.

He paused halfway, turned like he wanted to retreat, but then finally turned back again to continue toward the door.

She loosed the breath she hadn't realized she held and forced herself to wait until she heard Bryson's steps leading up to the main entrance.

He didn't knock.

She opened the door anyway. "Hello."

Her son—her son!—looked her in the eyes, his expression that of a love-hungry boy looking for answers. Her heart broke, and in that moment, she knew Hadley had made her decision and it hadn't been Bryson.

Cheryl had been all aflutter the entire weekend and revealed what she'd done in inviting Kyle to stay at Hadley's with the kids. Mary Elizabeth couldn't believe her friend's audacity—until she remembered Cheryl's own transgression early on in her marriage and the struggle to repair the damage.

She understood wanting her daughter's marriage to heal and her family to remain whole, but Mary Elizabeth didn't believe Kyle to be truly remorseful. To her he fell into the category of once a cheater always a cheater. He was only sorry because he'd been caught. "Bryson, come in."

Cheryl seemed not to notice Kyle's wandering eye whenever another female was around. Why, her own girls were often under Kyle's perusal, and it made her uncomfortable to think Hadley would put up with such behavior having already felt the consequences once—that she knew of.

"I don't know why I came here," Bryson said. "I just looked up and it was your house."

"I'm glad you did. Please, come inside. Would you like a drink? We can talk?"

Bryson ran a hand around his neck as though to ease the tension but then lowered the hand and crossed the threshold. Mary Elizabeth watched as he looked around with interest, his gaze taking in each of the family photos on the walls.

Mary Elizabeth moved to where he stood and pointed out each of her girls—his sisters. "You met them the other night at Izzy's gallery show. That's Izzy, of course, Allie, and Sophia.

"They're pretty. Hadley said one has kids?"

She tapped beneath Allie. "Yes. She has two children, and a third on the way. And Izzy is expecting now as well."

Bryson smiled and lifted his head when Adam's footfalls echoed down the hallway from the kitchen.

Mary Elizabeth took hold of Bryson's forearm as though that alone would keep him from bolting out the door and turned toward Adam, introducing them.

"Sir."

"Please, call me Adam."

"Yessir—Adam."

"Bryson, we were about to sit down for dinner. Won't you join us? There's plenty."

Color filled Bryson's face and Mary Elizabeth's heart pinched at his embarrassment. She remembered Dean coloring up the same way whenever he felt awkward or shy or embarrassed.

"I should've realized the time. I'm sorry. I'll go—"

"No, stay. Please?" Mary Elizabeth asked. "There's more than enough food and I'd love to...chat."

Bryson looked from her to Adam.

"You're welcome here, Bryson," Adam said. "I hope you'll join us."

"I suppose I can. If you don't mind."

Mary Elizabeth squeezed his arm and then released it to wrap both arms around his lean waist for a quick hug.

Bryson chuckled softly in surprise, as did Adam, and after a second, Bryson's arms surrounded her.

Mary Elizabeth couldn't hold back the tears and blinked hard.

Was there anything better than this?

LATE MONDAY EVENING, Mary Elizabeth sent out a text inviting everyone to a cookout the following weekend.

The kids and Kyle had gone back to Raleigh Tuesday morning, but all three said they'd return for the party.

Kyle had wanted Hadley to return to Raleigh as well, but she'd used the excuse about getting Nan's house sorted out.

She needed time to process this whiplash change in direction. Besides, as she'd pointed out, if she and Kyle were going to try again, they had to start from scratch. That meant dating and the whole shebang. Not moving into a house together and pretending their history didn't exist.

Kyle had grumbled about her being "difficult," but he'd agreed to her terms, and Wednesday morning, a gigantic bouquet of red roses was delivered to her door with a note about how he couldn't wait to see her again.

She put the flowers in a dusty vase she found in a cupboard, remembering a time when the gesture would've left her smiling instead of frowning as she was now, weighted down by the endless cycle of what-ifs blasting through her mind.

Hadley decided to work out in the paint shed and finally get around to painting that first piece of furniture, though when she entered the shed, all she could think about was how fun it had been working with Bryson on setting the shed up.

She crossed the yard and couldn't help but glance over at the house next door. The hammering and banging had stopped, and the delivery truck parked there early this morning was now gone.

While Hershey played in the yard and chased everything from bees to butterflies to birds, Hadley ran through her list and began painting a table she'd already sanded down with Bryson's help and instruction.

It didn't take long to get the first coat on, but it wasn't as smooth as she would've liked. Thankfully the paint dried fairly quickly despite the humidity, and after she'd sanded and coated a couple more pieces, she went back to the first to start over again. She lost herself in the tasks, working to the point of exhaustion just to try to keep her thoughts from over-whelming her.

The following day was more of the same, but Hadley was pleased with the results of her handi-work. She'd given an old dresser a coat of robin's-egg blue but accented the grooves and nicks and carvings with a chalky white, following the how-to videos she'd watched on YouTube.

Once she got the final protective coat sprayed on, she stood back to take a long look and then danced in place. The piece was simply stunning and perfect for the house and the look she wanted for it. Not only that, she'd done it herself. Well, mostly. She had to give credit to the video instructors as well as Bryson for getting her started.

She bit her lip and moved to the doorway of the shed, wiping the sweat off of her forehead as she squinted toward the house next door.

She found herself looking over there more than she liked. Wondering what he did. If he ever thought about her.

Bryson hadn't been back to share a morning cup of coffee, nor had she seen him coming and going due to the tall hedges. He arrived in the mornings with a bang of the truck door and left in the evenings without so much as a hello or goodbye.

She hated that. Hated that when all she desired was to drag him across the yard to show him her finished project, she couldn't because...well, because it was awkward now. And if she truly wanted things to work out with Kyle, she didn't need to confuse herself by throwing Bryson back into the mix after he'd made a point of removing himself from it.

It wasn't fair to Bryson—or herself. Or Kyle, for that matter.

Hadley worried her lower lip between her teeth and turned to go back inside the shed. Hershey appeared, and Hadley felt a wet doggy nose brush across her leg before Hershey leaned more of her weight against her, trusting Hadley would hold her.

She emptied her hands to pet the large dog, squatting down and pressing her forehead against Hershey's. The tears came out of nowhere, and she blamed the paint fumes and grit and the fuzzy Doodle hair tickling her lashes for the wetness. "Oh, Hershey. Am I doing the right thing?"

The dog lifted a paw and draped it over Hadley's forearm, nuzzling her head and nose into Hadley's chest. Hadley kissed the dog again and sniffled. "I have to give it a shot, don't I? For my kids?"

Hershey stared up at Hadley with her big brown eyes, but her gaze looked sad. Maybe because her human was crazy? Crying in a paint shed in the heat of the day instead of going inside where it was private and cool?

"Come on, you. Let's clean this up so we can go in," she said. "Maybe we'll invite the cousins over for dinner? How's that sound, huh? Would you like someone to play with who doesn't cry all over you?"

HADLEY'S INVITATION to the cousins wound up resulting in Michael coming by in his Jeep to pick Hadley and Hershey up for the trip out on the south end of the island.

Getting there was bumpy and bouncy, but the beautiful evening resulted in lots of laughter and Michael playing guitar while Hadley, Zoey, Lily, and Logan drank margaritas and beer and talked about the problems of life. Everett and Izzy came a bit later to join the fun.

Hadley stared at the group gathered around her and realized how very much she'd missed her tribe. Missed this.

Oh, she'd seen them often enough over the years during her visits, but it wasn't the same. It wasn't this fun, relaxing, supportive group away from the Babes and Kyle and responsibilities, just enjoying the beautiful day.

"Hey, you okay?" Izzy asked, taking a seat beside Hadley.

"Just reminiscing. I've missed this more than I realized."

"We've missed *you*. So many of us scattered like dice to get out of town, but thankfully we have you in our clutches again."

Hadley laughed but then made a face. "For now at least." It was something else she'd have to figure out. Because now that she was here, did she want to move back to Raleigh? If she and Kyle got back together, she would have to.

"What do you mean by that?" Izzy asked.

Realizing they didn't know about Kyle, she told them about the previous weekend and his desire to reconcile. Hadley was prepared for the conversation to come—what she wasn't prepared for was the silence. "Really? Come on, guys, no one has anything to say? You're just going to sit there and stare at me?"

Michael stopped strumming the guitar he'd brought along and glanced at Everett before meeting Hadley's gaze again.

"What do you want us to say?"

"The truth. Always."

"Okay... You're crazy if you do it. You deserve better," Michael said.

"Decisions were made that brought Kyle to that point," Izzy added. "Not a few decisions, either, but lots," she added, her gaze soft, wary, as she stared at Hadley. "And you just moved here. Are you really going to move back?"

Hadley shifted her attention, glancing into the many faces now staring at her, and shrugged. "I don't know. And I know there were decisions made over time that shouldn't have been but...I'd be lying if I said I hadn't let the kids' activities and schedules come between us. I traveled so much with Abby's lacrosse team, I was away every weekend."

"So what? Did you cheat on Kyle while you were staying in those hotels?" Izzy asked.

"Of course not."

"Exactly. Because you loved him and you respected your marriage vows. He didn't," Izzy said. "And there's no excuse for that."

"So you don't believe there's any chance that someone could stray and the marriage could still work?" she asked, knowing they obviously didn't know about her parents but curious as to their responses.

"There are always outliers," Michael said. "But it takes two."

"Three," Allie corrected. "God's gotta be in there, too."

"Speaking of which...what about forgiveness?" Hadley asked next. "After twenty-five years and two kids, what if I was too hasty in walking away?"

"Were you?" Michael set the guitar aside and reached into the cooler for a bottle of water. "From what I gathered, it wasn't a spur-of-the-moment decision. The reason you did it is because he walked out on you. He chose someone else."

"And what about all of that horrible stuff he said to you?" Izzy added. "Haddie, he was cruel, needlessly so. Are you going to let him do that again? What happens next time? We get what we allow."

It was a struggle to breathe normally. She'd asked for truth. And all that they'd said was painfully honest. Even if it came as tough love. "What if there's not a next time?" Hadley asked.

Michael cracked open the bottle but didn't lift it to his lips.

"Look, I hate to be the guy who rats out other guys but...cheaters cheat, sweetheart."

"I don't think he cheated before...her," Hadley said.

"Are you sure about that?" Michael asked.

Hadley squirmed in her seat, her mind flashing back to the times when Kyle would get a call and leave the room, when she'd picked up his phone to see who'd just texted him only to have him yank it out of her hand using privacy and HIPAA as his excuse.

But was that really why? Hadn't she *wondered* before but not wanted to face the truth? "You think he'll do it again," Hadley said, trying and failing to keep the tremble from her voice.

Michael tilted his head to one side as he regarded her, his dark gaze sparkling in the waning sunlight.

"Ah, sweetheart. The question is...do you?"

THE SEED of doubt had been well planted, and as Friday approached, Hadley began to stress over Kyle's return to Carolina Cove.

Mary Elizabeth's party sounded like an evening of torture. After her trip to the south end with the cousins, she knew they'd all be watching. As would the Babes and everyone else in attendance.

Maybe they shouldn't go? Maybe she could cry off with an excuse? Surely Kyle would be tired after a day of work and the drive?

Kyle arrived and got out of his car, tucking his

phone into his pocket as he grabbed a small bag from the trunk. He bounded up the porch steps, smiling as he dropped the suitcase and gathered her up, kissing her.

"I've missed you."

"We've talked every evening," she said.

"Yeah, but talking isn't the same," he said, his gaze lowering to her mouth. "Are you sure you want to take this thing slow?"

Hadley pressed her hands on his chest and pushed, insisting on being lowered to her feet. "I'm sure. Especially after...everything. In fact," she said, taking a deep breath, "I want you to be tested," she said, bringing up the very touchy subject Izzy had brought to her attention later that night on the beach.

"What?"

"I know, my timing is horrible—"

"You've got that right."

"But you're a doctor, so surely you see the importance of blood work?"

"You think I'd give you something?"

"By sleeping with her, you've slept with everyone she's been with, so is it possible? Yes."

Kyle ran his hand over his face and glared at her.

"I can't believe I drove all the way here, and before I can even get in the house, you're giving me orders to get tested."

"Not an order, a request. Besides, you're the one who wants to go straight to bed, so it's as good a time as any to discuss it," she countered. "You can't be angry with me for wanting to protect myself from harm."

The words hung in the air between them, and Hadley ignored Hershey's whine from behind the screen door. No doubt Hershey felt the tension and anger.

"You're not going to sleep with me unless I do your bidding, so fine."

"Thank you," she said, meaning it despite his anger at the thought. "Would you like to change before the party? Take a shower to freshen up?" she asked, leading the way into the house.

"Yeah. Guess a cold shower is all that's left for me."

She ignored the statement and led the way upstairs, showed him to the spare bedroom, while noting the mulish glare he sent her that they wouldn't be sharing a room, the shower, or sex.

He dropped the case onto the bed and Hadley watched, uncomfortable. The old Hadley would've jumped in and unpacked his clothes, hung them up, and organized things. The new Hadley expected him to do it himself like the adult he was. "Hershey and I will be downstairs."

"Does that dog have to go everywhere with you?"

"Dogs are pack animals," Hadley said. "I'm now her pack so yes. Enjoy the shower."

Hershey followed Hadley back downstairs when she remembered she'd forgotten to take up the load of freshly laundered towels. She went to the laundry room to collect them and then reluctantly told Hershey to stay in the kitchen while she took them back upstairs.

Kyle obviously needed time to get used to having a dog and to realize his every wish wasn't going to be met upon request. Hadley also didn't want him taking his anger with her out on Hershey.

She entered the bedroom and found the bathroom door slightly ajar, the shower running on the other side.

She left the towels on the bed and hurried out into the hallway, not wanting Kyle to catch her in there and try again to seduce her.

Men thought differently than women. She knew sex meant acceptance to men, but in this case, she couldn't take that step. Not until she felt safe and loved and—

And what?

She moved downstairs once more, her thoughts whirling like a spinning top filled with disorienting facts, fears, and unwanted images of Kyle with his twenty-something playmate.

Forty-five minutes later, they arrived at Mary Elizabeth and Adam's house a quarter after the designated time. Hadley carried the lemon cake she'd made for dessert, while Kyle carried a bottle of Mary Elizabeth's favorite wine.

Hadley smiled at the greetings and hellos, noting Michael's frowning face over in a corner with...Bryson?

They knew each other? Or had Mary Elizabeth just introduced them? Wait—did *they* know who Bryson was?

"What is he doing here?" Kyle asked, the low growl sounding in her ear.

"I'm not sure," she said, even though the lie sounded awkward to her own ears. She hadn't told Kyle about Bryson and Mary Elizabeth's connection because she knew Kyle wouldn't like it. Nor did she want to share information that might not be public as yet.

"I didn't realize we'd be slumming it with the hired help," Kyle muttered.

Hadley sucked in a gasp. "He's a guest, just like we are. Maybe you should focus on that."

"He wants what's mine," Kyle said.

Seriously? "You're being ridiculous."

"Am I?" Kyle asked, his gaze zeroing in on Hadley from behind his sunglasses. "Did you make him show you test results?"

Her pulse pounded in her throat and she shook her head at him. "I'm going to take the cake inside so the icing doesn't melt."

"Oh, Haddie, honey," Mary Elizabeth said as she approached, "I'm so glad you're here. Thank you for coming."

"Of course. I was just about to run this inside."

"I hate to say this but our AC went out this afternoon. It's hotter in there than it is out here. Just put the cake over in the shade."

"Why don't you ask the maintenance man to fix it," Kyle said.

"What?" Mary Elizabeth asked, not following Kyle's statement and the implied insult.

"Kyle," Hadley said warningly.

Kyle lifted his hand and pointed in Bryson's direction. "Isn't Bryson a janitor or something? Have him take a look."

Kyle's words echoed across the pool and concrete, and silence descended among those gathered.

Mary Elizabeth gasped and looked legitimately appalled whereas the others appeared extremely uncomfortable. "Kyle, that's *enough*," Hadley said.

"What? I know everyone here and what they do. I'm simply pointing out the obvious."

"Bryson is a *guest*," Mary Elizabeth said. "Actually, he's our special guest tonight and I want you to treat him as such."

Kyle smirked. "Special guest. Why's that?"

Mary Elizabeth lifted her chin and narrowed her gaze on Kyle.

"Because Bryson is my son."

CHAPTER NINETEEN

Bryson sat at a table with twin brothers Michael and Logan, and the moment Hadley had appeared with her ex, the two had commented on it. They didn't like the man any more than he did, and that crack about being the maintenance guy?

Yeah, he'd been called worse, but it still didn't keep him from wanting to plant his fist in the man's face.

"What an ass," Michael muttered. "Bet you my boat you've got more in the bank than he does."

Bryson lifted the bottle in his hand and took a long drink. He'd known Michael professionally for a while, having built several of the homes Michael had designed. Michael had been surprised by Bryson's appearance for what was a family gathering, but the man hadn't said anything. Unlike Hadley's ex. "That doesn't matter. I'm not who she wants."

"I think he's playing her. Again," Logan said. "Guilting her based on their history. I give him a month before he's cheating again."

"I think he still has his sugar baby on the side," Michael added.

Bryson's fingers tightened on the bottle to the point of pain. "What makes you say that?"

"Gut instinct."

Maybe. The problem was Bryson felt the same way. There was something about the man that just reeked of self-indulgence and deceit. Kyle was the epitome of wanting his cake and eating it, too. "Hadley has to figure things out for herself."

"Yeah, that's not going to be easy to watch. Not now that we know what happened already," Michael said.

Bryson eyed Kyle from behind his dark sunglasses, noting the way he grabbed Hadley's arm when she started to walk away with the cake.

The two shared hushed angry words Mary Elizabeth interrupted, but both managed to smile at their host before Kyle used his grip to tug Hadley into the house.

"Did I hear Mary Elizabeth say"—Logan looked at Bryson—"*son?*"

Michael looked equally surprised but Bryson's friend then grinned from ear to ear.

"Don't know how that came about, but man, welcome to the crazy."

"Uh, guys?" Logan said, tilting his head toward the couple entering the house. "You going in there or am I?" Logan asked.

"I will," Bryson answered, getting to his feet.

Bryson crossed the beautifully landscaped rear of the house as discreetly as possible but felt multiple gazes on him as he followed the couple inside.

Hadley was nowhere to be seen when Bryson entered, but Kyle stood in the kitchen glaring at the cake—now splattered across the tile floor.

"What happened?" Bryson asked. "Where's Hadley?"

Bryson watched as Kyle's hands fisted before he lifted one hand and pointed a finger at Bryson.

"You need to *back off*."

"Where's Hadley?"

The other man told Bryson what he could do to himself along with a few more expletives.

"Hadley may have had some fun slumming it with you but that's over now. Got it?"

"Where is she?" Bryson demanded for the last time.

"I'm here," she said in a small voice.

Bryson knew immediately she'd been crying though she'd tried to hide the damage to her mascara. She hugged her arms around her front, fingers covering the red marks her fair skin revealed that would no doubt show bruises soon. "Are you okay?"

"I'm fine."

"What is this?" Kyle asked Hadley. "You said it was over with him."

"Bryson and I are friends."

"Friends, huh?" Kyle released a derisive chuckle. "That's why you pushed me away. You're screwing him for payback?"

"*Kyle!*"

"Watch yourself," Bryson ordered, trying to play it cool but his fists ready to fly.

"I get it now. He finds out he's got some blue in his blood because Mary Elizabeth played the whore, and suddenly he's acceptable?"

"You're being ridiculous," Hadley said. "You know nothing of the situation. And how dare you call Mary Elizabeth that!"

"A spade is a spade," Kyle said. "That's why I'd barely made it out of the car before you started nagging me about getting tested."

"I didn't nag you. I made a request."

"And if I don't do your request, what then?"

"Kyle, calm down. Bryson and I are friends. Just because he's Mary Elizabeth's son doesn't mean—"

"That I'm going to have look at his ugly mug and know he wants my *wife*?"

Bryson grinned. He couldn't help it. Let the good doctor swim in his jealousy.

"He's part of the family now no matter what happens between us."

"You are coming back to Raleigh with me. This ends right now."

The patio door opened and Cheryl and Jerry walked inside.

"What is going on in here?" Cheryl asked. "We can hear you shouting outside."

Probably not well enough, Bryson mused, otherwise she wouldn't have had to come in to hear things firsthand.

"Now that Mary Elizabeth's secret baby news is out, he thinks he has a chance with Hadley," Kyle said.

Cheryl seemed to notice the cake on the floor for the first time.

As though sensing her mother's disapproval, Hadley dropped to her knees and began scooping the cake back into the container.

"I'll help you," Cheryl said, knowing the kitchen

well enough to know what cabinet the paper towels were in.

She knelt next to her daughter only to pause. *"Hadley..."*

The woman's shocked murmur drew Bryson's attention along with her father's. And even though he'd figured Hadley would sport bruises from her ex's tight grip earlier on her upper arm, he wasn't prepared for the dark marks to be quite so vivid so soon.

Bryson shifted his gaze from the bruises to Hadley's father to Kyle before stalking toward the man, grabbing him by his expensive shirt, and relishing the sound of seams ripping. "You like to hurt women?"

"Hey! I'm a surgeon! Jerry, stop him. I can't fight and ruin my hands."

The pitiful excuse was said in such a high-pitched, panicked voice that Bryson laughed. He shoved the man backwards so hard his head whacked the wall with a satisfying thud Bryson had a hard time not wanting to repeat. "Get out."

"What?"

"You heard me," Bryson said. "Get out."

"Who do you think you are? You can't kick me out," Kyle said.

"If he can't, I can," Jerry said, the man's face twisted with anger and grief.

"Hadley— *Cheryl.*"

"You need to leave," Cheryl said, glaring at the man.

"Fine. Fine, I'll go. Haddie... I'll see you at the house."

"No," Hadley said, lifting her head to face him. "Pack your things and go back to Raleigh. The attorneys can handle the sale of the house and distribution of funds."

"Hadley, baby, come on. You can't be serious. We're just... This is all getting blown out of proportion. Let's go get some air and talk about this."

Hadley slowly got to her feet, and Bryson watched as she clasped her trembling hands in front of her.

"It's not going to work, Kyle. It never was."

"You don't mean that. Don't let this—*them*—make you—"

"The only one *making me* do anything is you. But I thank you for it. Because of your behavior, I remember all the other times I found myself belittled and hurt by you. Mistress and cheating aside, you talk to me like...like you are some god and I am *nothing.*"

"Sweetheart... Fine, I have an ego and it gets the best of me at times, but you know I don't mean it."

"Do I? Because after being away from you, not having to *put up* with you, I've finally healed enough to know I don't deserve to be treated the way you treat me. No one does. I know who I am. What I'm capable of—without you."

"You inherited a beach house and cash. You think you're doing this on your own?"

"Maybe not in that sense," she admitted. "But I thank God for it because it allows me freedom, and it's freedom I didn't even realize I wanted or needed from your petty putdowns and lies and...*cheating*."

"You said you'd forgiven me for that."

"I did. But in the last hour, you've reverted to that same man. You *hurt me* and destroyed what should have been a wonderful evening with friends and...and it's all too familiar."

"What's that supposed to mean?" Kyle asked. "Couples argue. They get over it. You'll get over this."

"Because I'm the cause, right? I'm being overly dramatic? Making more out of it than there really is? Kyle, you've thrown bagged toilet paper on me in the middle of the night when I was sleeping because it wasn't the kind you liked. You *screamed* at me for thirty minutes once because you thought I'd bought 'cheap cheese' for a party and said I embarrassed you in front of your boss because of it. You...you put me down *day after day after day* in order to build yourself up and feed your ego, and all of those *years* I just kept making excuses for you! I told myself I couldn't walk away from a marriage over things like that. I told myself you did it because you were stressed and overwhelmed with your job, but the truth is you're just a self-centered, cheating, narcissistic jerk and my life will be—*is*—better off without you!"

Kyle's face turned blood red and he took two steps toward Hadley.

Cheryl gasped and Jerry quickly moved toward his daughter before Bryson cut Kyle off by stepping into his path. "Try to lay another finger on her. Please," he growled.

The man's eyes actually filled with tears, no doubt born of anger and frustration at his true self being outed, but tears all the same. His nostrils flared and he cursed at Hadley.

"You're done here. Get out before I take great pleasure in throwing you out," Bryson ordered, using his size to step forward and force Kyle back a step.

Kyle sent one last glare at Hadley before he turned on his heel and slammed out the patio door.

Bryson, Hadley, and Cheryl turned to watch him

go, and Bryson noted Michael and Logan followed the man to the rear exit.

The windows facing the patio were a sea of faces, all of them watching, listening?

When Kyle was out of sight, Bryson shifted his attention back to Hadley, noting that Cheryl had tears running down her face and Jerry had his arms wrapped around both of them.

"I'm so sorry, Hadley. I had no idea," Cheryl said in a choked voice. "I wouldn't have pushed you to reconcile with Kyle if I'd known. Oh, honey, I'm so sorry. Please forgive me."

"Bryson, would you mind giving us a moment alone?" Hadley's father asked.

The last thing Bryson wanted to do was leave Hadley after all of that, but he shoved his emotions down and nodded. "I'll be outside if you need me."

"Bryson?" her father said. "Thank you. I'm very glad my daughter has you as a friend."

Bryson nodded. "My pleasure."

<hr>

HADLEY DIDN'T REJOIN the party, Mary Elizabeth noticed. And even though Bryson had returned, he was anything but there.

She slowly made her way over to him and set a

glass down on the table in front of him. "You look like you could use this."

One side of his mouth curled up in a grim half grin that reminded her yet again of his late father. "May I join you?"

"It's your party."

Mary Elizabeth settled into the seat beside him. "What happened in there?"

"Nothing you'd care to know about."

"Is Hadley okay?"

"No. But she will be," Bryson said.

The way he said it was hardly a comfort, but she chose to accept it as such. "I want you to know that, no matter what, you are welcome here. I've talked to the girls, too, and they can't wait to see you. They should be here any moment."

Bryson inhaled and sighed.

"I'm not sure I'm at my most sociable right now."

"Just be you," Mary Elizabeth said, covering his broad calloused hand with her own. "You have no need to be anyone else."

She wasn't sure he accepted her words as truth but it was. If anyone spoke out against Bryson, they would have to deal with her. Kyle included. She was inordinately glad the man had left, though her curiosity regarding the reasons why after hearing the muffled argument through the bank of windows was thick enough to choke her.

"She's right, you know," Adam said from behind her.

Adam placed a hand on Mary Elizabeth's shoulder and gently squeezed, and she leaned her cheek atop his knuckles.

"You're family now," her husband said. "And always welcome."

It was no small consolation. Adam had needed time to adjust to the news of a surprise stepson, but in the days since revealing the test, he'd come around.

"I was shocked at first," Adam continued, "but Mary Elizabeth is as honest and forthcoming as they come. She wouldn't have let you go had she known you existed, and I haven't seen her this happy in ages."

"Thank you, sir." Bryson nodded at Adam's words. "I appreciate you saying that."

The patio door opened and everyone turned to see Hadley and her parents emerge. "Oh, poor Hadley. She looks wrecked."

"So do Cheryl and Jerry," Adam murmured.

It was true. Hadley's parents looked like someone had pulled the rug out from under them and then beat them with it as well.

Mary Elizabeth glanced at Bryson as she stood. "You see to Hadley. The Babes will comfort Cheryl while the men talk to Jerry. Divide and comfort," she ordered them.

Assignments given, Mary Elizabeth hurried over to the threesome and repeated her instructions, well aware of the moment Bryson appeared behind her.

Cheryl met Mary Elizabeth's gaze, her blue eyes filling with tears once more. Mary Elizabeth wrapped an arm around her, and the Babes prodded their friend toward the pool house while Adam led Jerry to the bar.

Inside the pool house, the Babes made a fuss over Cheryl, bringing her a cool cloth for her tear-swollen eyes and forehead and something cold and spiked to drink.

After another round of crying, Cheryl finally sat up and took the drink, eyes downcast.

"I owe you an apology," Cheryl whispered. "All of you."

Tessa leaned forward and poured Cheryl another glass while Rayna Jo dropped in a few ice cubes.

"What on earth happened in there?" Rayna Jo asked.

"Why do you feel like you owe us?" Mary Elizabeth softly questioned.

Cheryl downed—literally chugged—the drink and wiped her mouth in a most unladylike fashion.

"I've lived a lie," Cheryl said. "All of this time, I've kept a secret and pretended—and all I've done is hurt the people I love the most. Jerry and Hadley, all of you."

"What secret?" Adaline asked.

Mary Elizabeth glanced out the paned windows to see Hadley being led to a chair by Bryson, his thickly muscled arm wrapped protectively around her shoulders.

"I thought," Cheryl said softly, "if I tried hard enough, I could erase something horrible I did in the past. But all I did was make my daughter put up with a man who isn't worthy of her, all to keep up appearances."

Mary Elizabeth leaned forward, taking one of Cheryl's hands in her own. "You know my secret. Cheryl, what happened?"

HADLEY HAD THOUGHT nothing could embarrass her more than that day when she'd arrived for Nan's funeral alone. That just went to prove how silly someone's thoughts and beliefs could be.

But as Bryson steered her toward a swing in

Mary Elizabeth's beautiful backyard, all Hadley could think about was how the blinders she'd worn for far too long had been ripped away completely and the sun...it burned. "Can you ever forgive me?" she asked Bryson, voice thick. "I know I have no right to ask but I hope—"

"There's nothing to forgive, Hadley."

"There's *every*thing to forgive. All I can say is that for a very brief, very weird moment, I thought I was doing the right thing."

"I know."

"I was weak," she added.

"You were human."

"I was *stupid*. I let sentimentality and pressure from family override what I'd already learned the hard way. What I'd *lived* and didn't want to go through again. But I fell right back into that pattern because I-I felt I owed them. The kids and my parents and...even Kyle, because we'd been together so long." She shoved her fingers into her hair and clenched them, the pain clearing the fuzziness of tears and anxiety and regret. "I'm sorry, Bryson."

Bryson gently turned her and pushed her into the swing before he sat beside her.

She leaned her head against his shoulder and slowly slid her fingers into his palm, hoping he wouldn't reject her and yet fearing the possibility.

His calloused fingers curled around hers, and she blinked away the hot flood of relief mixed with gratitude.

"Hadley...one of the first things I learned about you is that you wear your heart on your sleeve. You look at people and see the best, no matter the issues in the past. I would be surprised if you didn't have misgivings about your ex. It's who you are. Because you're so sweet and loving."

"You are kind for saying that, but we both know I was seriously wrong. And just so we're clear, I didn't follow my heart." She lifted her head and stared into Bryson's steady green-eyed gaze. "Because if I'd actually done *that*"—she paused, heart racing—"I would've never allowed Kyle to worm his way between us."

Bryson's gaze flared a bit, his lips parting as he drew in a breath. "Go on."

Revealing her feelings took more courage than she'd imagined, mostly because of screwing up before this. "Bryson, you encouraged me to follow my dreams. You helped me to find...myself. The person I was—am—before everything got so mixed up."

"Hadley, emotional abuse doesn't happen overnight. Like you said, it builds over time, with little things you make excuses for because your mind is desperate to protect itself. All I did was treat you as you should be treated."

He drew back so he could reach out and gently cup her cheek, his thumb lightly brushing her skin with its raspy roughness.

"I wanted to kill him for hurting you."

She leaned toward him, her fingers wrapping around his wrist to steady herself as she pressed her lips to his and kissed the man who'd made her realize the difference between manipulation and love. Self-centeredness and care. Fake and real.

Bryson lifted his head, his gaze blazing hot.

It was then she realized she'd whispered the love words aloud. But she didn't regret it. And she wouldn't take them back. Not when she meant every word.

She didn't feel rushed in the saying, nor had she said she loved him on a whim in the aftermath of all that had happened. The words came from deep within her heart, her soul. The one he'd helped heal even though it had taken a dropped cake and Kyle's belligerence to see it. "I do, you know. I love you," she whispered again. "I don't know what I was thinking. Wait, that's a lie. I do. I was scared."

"Of me?"

"Of...falling in love and making a mistake again. Kyle was...familiar but you... I felt myself falling for you and it frightened me. It was so different than what I once *thought* was love. I don't expect you to say it back though. Not after all of this. Just know... Things wouldn't have gone any further between me and Kyle. I planned to end it before all of *that* happened in the kitchen. I think he sensed it, too."

"Should I ask why?"

"The things he said. And he was pressuring me to get rid of Hershey. He talked about it the whole way to the party."

Bryson's mouth curled into a smile as he kissed her, lifting her onto his lap, cradling her in his arms in the most protective, loving way.

"Good thing you love that dog."

"And you."

"And me," he said huskily. "Almost as much as I love you, Hadley."

After several long, heart-stopping kisses, Bryson lifted his head, and Hadley turned to find everyone at the party had reappeared and now stood watching them with amused looks. Including her parents. "Oh! Um...hi."

Michael chuckled and said, "Does this mean the pact we took to never date one of the cousins is void? Inquiring minds wanna know," he said, turning his head toward Logan much to his brother's annoyance. "What? Bryson *is* one of us now."

Michael grinned unabashedly at Bryson's scowl and Hadley tightened her arms around her hero. "I think it's safe to say the pact is over." Lowering her voice, she smiled at Bryson and said, "What do you think?"

Hadley opened the car door to get out and found Bryson's extended hand. "A year later and you're still being a gentleman. I like it," she said, straightening and lifting onto her tiptoes to kiss him. "Thank you for not making me come alone tonight."

"I wouldn't miss it for the world," he said, his gaze twinkling. "You have become quite the celebrity with your videos on furniture painting. It's only right that the paint companies treat you to a special dinner to celebrate your sponsorship."

She grinned gleefully as she wrapped her arm through his, her two-carat Montana sapphire engagement ring twinkling in the waning light of the day. The stone was breathtaking and, according to Bryson, the exact same color as her eyes.

In another month, she and Bryson would be married in a small ceremony on the beach, Hershey included as the ring bearer along with Allie's daughters as flower girls.

It had been a full, glorious, beautiful year of laughter and teasing and falling even deeper in love. The grown-up kind of love that included mutual interests, busy days, and falling asleep on the couch together because they were both too tired to do anything more than cuddle.

Bryson had sold the house to Everett and Izzy to stay in while their home was being built. Their baby boy had arrived right on time and now that their part-time island home was complete, the house next door would be used by Everett's father, the Babes, and their offspring for visits and fun. Bryson was slowly moving things from his small home in Wilmington to Nan's—their—home and had begun remodeling his old one for sale.

Max had recently graduated and was about to start a job as a cybersecurity specialist and had accepted a position working with Dara and Jack at Guardian Group.

Abby worked the summer at London's Lattes as a barista and would begin her sophomore year of college in the fall. Thankfully she had finally given up on trying to get her parents back together once she finally came to see how happy Hadley was with Bryson, not to mention how different—in a good way—their healthier relationship was.

Hershey had been an unbelievable comfort to Hadley as she went through counseling so she would be free of the past baggage and able to start her marriage fresh with Bryson, or at least more aware of triggers due to her marriage to Kyle.

Hershey's funny, sometimes bumbling, but always comforting presence as Hadley had worked through the painful reality of her first marriage made her realize how much comfort Hershey had to offer. Which was why Hershey was now a certified therapy dog.

Once a week, Hershey and Hadley went to nursing homes or schools or other venues to offer cuddles and love to those in need. They visited Bryson's father often, and John proved to be as charming and sweet as his adopted son.

Hershey and Bryson and all the cousins had played a huge role in carrying Hadley through the painful process of healing.

Them and her mother.

Gone was Cheryl Dummit, perfectionist incarnate, and in her place was a happier, less tense Cheryl who had finally found forgiveness for herself. A less critical and more content woman who loved the fact that her daughter had found happiness as well, no matter Bryson's profession as a blue-collar worker/business owner. Cheryl had finally opened her eyes and seen Bryson's amazingness, and she even introduced him now as her wonderful future son-in-law, recommending his business to anyone who'd listen.

While Hadley and Bryson dated and got to know one another, the other cousins had also started to find love. When Hadley looked at them, it never ceased to amaze her how quickly the group had grown in size in such a short amount of time, especially seeing as how many of them had included a plus-one for the wedding festivities.

"Sweetheart? What are you waiting for?" Bryson asked from behind her on the steps of the restaurant.

She'd paused halfway up, not because she dreaded going inside like that day of Nan's funeral but because she'd been so distracted by her thoughts and all she'd been blessed with she needed a moment to breathe. To take in the salt air and show her appreciation with a silent whisper of thanks for all the good in her life.

All the changes that had begun with a horrific divorce and Nan's funeral and ended with the man behind her and the love she'd found in people she'd hidden so much from.

Hadley turned and faced her fiancé. She looped her arms over his shoulders and, standing a step higher, stood eye to eye with him, smiling.

"What is it?" he asked in his sexy, husky voice. "What's gotten into you?"

She leaned forward and brushed her lips over his, holding his gaze and hoping he saw all the love she simply didn't have the capability to express. "Light."

*I hope you enjoyed **SEASHELLS AND WEDDING BELLS**. Keep reading for a peek at Devon and Oz's story in **SEA GLASS AND SECOND CHANCES!***

As a popular TV host, Devon Tieks has seen firsthand how lives can be ruined by scandal. Too bad her father didn't consider that before he and his mistress collided head on with it. While the paparazzi swarms and Devon fights to keep the salacious details of her father's death private, she can't help but question her politician boyfriend's poorly timed proposal.

Oscar "Oz" Roman has always been a close family friend even though Devon broke off their first-love engagement to pursue her dreams in New York. Ten years later, Oz has established his career as a thriller writer, but hasn't found a love like he had with Devon.

While Devon's life is crumbling around her, her fiance is busy protecting his image at all costs. Oz proves he's steadfast, salt of the earth, and irresistible... but can she find a way to move forward with him when she left him behind with her past?

"SO THERE YOU HAVE IT, New York. I'm Devon and that's *What's Hot.*" Devon Teeks held her smile until she received the all clear and then sank back into the uncomfortable chair on set. The splashy designer furniture might look fantastic on camera, but it was as comfortable as sitting on a rock.

"Devon, you said to remind you to leave *on time.*"

Devon blinked, her mind drawing blank.

"Your dinner with Mr. Up-and-Coming President?" her assistant, Tia, said. "Your anniversary?"

Devon stared at the twenty-something intern, fresh off the plane from Missouri and starry-eyed, just like Devon had been at the same age when she'd moved to New York City to intern at the station. "Of course. Thanks. I'm on my way."

She left the host's chair and moved off the dais toward the darkened area behind the cameras leading to the hallway and beyond. The greenroom was closest to the set, with her dressing room in a more private area toward the rear.

Halfway down the hallway, Devon paused to remove one of her ridiculously high heels and sighed when the cold floor tile seeped into her aching foot.

Had she really reached the age where she wanted comfort over looks? Didn't that make her *old*?

Giving in with a silent whimper, she removed the other heel and hurried along, reminding herself that it was the price to pay for going barefoot on Carolina Cove's sandy beaches the first twenty-five years of her life.

It wasn't until she moved to New York from the Wilmington, North Carolina, area that she realized just how casually she'd dressed. But in a tourist town, on an island no less, even newbie journalists couldn't fight the ninety-degree days and humidity of summer in the south.

She entered her dressing room and quickly showered off the heavy makeup, then redid her face and changed into the A-line bombshell dress Ted loved. The dress hugged every line and curve but was modest and sophisticated, with a zipper that ran full-length down her back that drew attention to her behind and all the squats she hated but did anyway.

Frowning at the shoes she'd chosen to go with the dress, she donned the ankle-strapped platform heels, grateful they lent a little more support to her achy feet. Finally ready, she grabbed her bag and belongings and headed out the door.

Ted had asked for her to clear her schedule tonight so they could spend some time together. They'd been working too many hours lately, and the stress they both carried from their jobs had started to intrude on their relationship. They got along great face-to-face, but when their schedules kept them apart, they wound up bickering over silly things.

But seeing as it was their one-year anniversary, tonight would be different. They'd block out the world, set all the stress and issues aside, relax, and be together.

Devon donned her oversized sunglasses as she left the building, smiling at her driver as he greeted her and opened the door of the black town car provided by the network to ensure their on-screen hosts arrived on time. "How are you today, Tony?"

"Ah, can't complain, Miss Devon. Things go well for you?"

"Perfectly." They had the same conversation every day, and today was no different—until John

Prescott came rushing out of the building calling her name and asking her to wait.

"Stay or go?" Tony asked quickly.

"Stay," she said with a glance at her watch.

She tossed her belongings into the back of the car and turned to see John skid to a halt a foot away.

"Devon, I'm glad I caught you. We need to talk," John said, breathing heavily from the rush.

"Whatever it is, it has to wait. I can't tonight."

"You said that last night."

"Because *you* insisted I go to that gala even though I had to get up at four a.m. to fill in on the morning show before taping my own."

"Your schedule is open this evening."

"No, it isn't," she said firmly. "I have plans."

"Well, this can't wait," John said. "I'm afraid I have bad news."

"Not now, John. Please."

"You know your ratings are down," he continued without pause, "and the network... they've decided to cancel the show. Today was the last taping."

The air left her lungs in a rush and she gaped at him. "*What?* How is that possible? They can't just... Can't we at least finish the season?"

John held up his hands. "I'm sorry. I'm not happy about it either. But they say we're done so... we're done. Don't bother coming in tomorrow unless it's to gather your stuff and take it to the morning show so it'll be there when you start."

She blinked at him, certain she'd misheard him. "I'm sorry, what?"

John's ruddy face broke out in a grin and he chuckled. "Congratulations. You got the fill-in position. Natalie officially goes on maternity leave next week, which means you get a week to make getting up before dawn a habit. It's been wonderful working with you. Congratulations."

John held out his hand and she shook it, a huff of a laugh leaving her chest before she stepped toward him and gave him a quick hug. Maybe she'd lost the gig she presented daily, but the morning host position would give her time to secure something else. "Thank you. It's been wonderful working with you. I've learned so much."

"Knock 'em dead, kid. And enjoy your week off."

A week off? What would she do with a whole week off?

She didn't remember having a week off since moving to the city ten years ago. After all, when you were trying to climb the network's ladder, time off didn't exist. She'd worked her job, filled in on others, volunteered, whatever it took, going above and beyond in order to move up the ranks. Her reputation as being reliable and there no matter what had given her ins with the network she didn't take for granted.

But a week... Maybe she and Ted could get away for a few days?

"Ms. Devon? Everything okay?" Tony asked.

A laugh rumbled out of her. "Yeah, it is. Surprisingly so. I just lost *and* landed a great position, and today is my anniversary."

"Well, now. Let's get you home so you can celebrate," Tony said.

From inside the car, Devon watched John's return to the building, her stomach fluttering with excitement.

The ride to her tiny apartment took a ridiculous amount of time considering the distance. She stared out the window at the crowded streets unseeing because her mind raced with ideas and plans and things to be done.

She had a feeling Ted was going to broach the subject of her moving in with him again tonight, but she'd promised herself from a very young age she would always have a place to go home to unless there was a wedding ring on her finger. Breakups happened. She'd watched it happen too many times to otherwise smart women who found themselves homeless and surfing friends' couches until they made other arrangements. She wouldn't be one of them.

They arrived at her building, and she flashed a smile at the doorman when he opened the car door.

"Good evening, ma'am. Mr. George arrived thirty minutes ago and is waiting upstairs."

"Thank you."

Devon said goodbye to Tony and made her way inside the building. The beautiful lobby was decorated in black-and-white checkerboard tile polished to a high gleam. The seating area on the right looked elegant yet sturdy, the red leather couch, matching chairs, and dark wood coffee table drawing the eye.

Devon bypassed the seating, greeted the ever-present and familiar security guard behind his shiny wooden desk, and punched the elevator button. The large doors opened in an instant.

The move to this building had taken place several years ago when she'd finally received a promotion, including a much-needed raise that allowed her to get her own place. While small, the apartment provided security and was more convenient to the network's location.

Once the elevator was in motion, she glanced at her reflection in the polished metal and sighed. Even that distorted image looked tired, but when she'd burned the candle at both ends for the last ten years, how could she not?

Maybe a vacation to somewhere tropical was just what she needed to celebrate? Could she convince Ted to leave his office for a few days and go?

Ratings for *What's Hot* had been down for a while. Those in the know didn't watch the show to find out the latest clubs or restaurants, plays. No, social media filled them in.

The generations that watched were the "oldies" and more apt to be retiring and moving out of the bustling city than clubbing the night away.

With any luck, maybe the host she temporarily replaced on the morning show would decide not to come back to work? Want to spend more time with her newborn?

The elevator doors opened, and she made her way down the hall, staring at the patterned carpet beneath her feet. The door was unlocked and she entered with a chipper hello.

She glanced around but didn't see him. "Ted? I have news!"

"Coming," he called.

Seconds later, Theodore Carlton George III appeared from the bathroom still straightening his tie. Ted smiled as he crossed the room and kissed her on her cheek.

"Look at you. My favorite dress."

"I thought you'd like it."

"You know I do. You look amazing, as always. What's this about news? Does this have anything to do with a certain morning news anchor position?"

"How did you know?" she asked, her excitement deflating a bit.

"I may have heard some rumblings about your show ending and... put in a good word for you."

Wait, what? So she hadn't gotten the position on her own but because of her relationship with Ted and his political future?

"Come on, don't look like that. All that's important is that you got the job, right?"

"Yes, but I thought I'd gotten it on my own."

"You did," Ted told her. "All I did was make a few calls. You can't be upset with me for that, now can you? Let's celebrate. I'll pop the champagne."

She watched as he moved toward the kitchen and forced herself to shrug off her upset.

She was very familiar with the red tape surrounding promotions within the network. And unlike others, she had no deep contacts or connections within the company, so she told herself to be grateful Ted had been willing to make the calls on her behalf. "You're right. Thank you for doing whatever you did."

"I just made it clear you'd be interested and that

it would be a personal favor if they gave you a chance. You did the work, Devon."

She had—though the way he'd stated it, he had not only pulled strings but tied them in a knot by connecting it with his political future. She didn't like it—but she also couldn't argue the doing since it was done.

"Come on. Don't be upset with me. If I was up for a job and you could say something to help me, wouldn't you do the same?"

She would. And when he put it like that... she felt petty being upset by what he'd done for her. "I would. Thank you," she said again.

"You're welcome. Now let's celebrate."

"Well, if you'd *really* like to celebrate, I have a few ideas."

"Is that right?"

"As of today, I have a week's vacation. I thought maybe we could take a trip? Just the two of us? Maybe go somewhere tropical?" she asked hopefully. With his schedule, it would be much more difficult for him to get away, but she hoped to convince him all the same. "Sugar-white sand? Umbrellas in our drinks? Steel drum music floating in the air?"

"That sounds fantastic, but you know I can't be away from the city right now. Not with an election coming up in a few months."

"I knew you'd say that," she said with a playful pout. "But I had to ask."

"One day, sweetheart. And until then, I know of a special way we can celebrate," he said.

"How?"

"Like this," he said, moving toward her and getting down on one knee. "Devon Teeks, will you do me the honor of marrying me?"

RAYNA JO TEEKS watched the online feed of Devon's *What's Hot* the moment she was able to and frowned at her daughter's image. Devon looked tired. And much too thin.

Like any mother, she worried about Devon's health and whether or not New York was actually good for her. She seemed to always be on the go, never resting, rarely calling.

"How's one of my favorite nieces?" Adaline asked.

Rayna Jo glanced at her twin, frown still in place. "She looks exhausted."

"Lots to do in that city," Adaline said in a distracted tone.

Her sixty-three-year-old sister put the finishing touches on a sample display board, noting the masculine colors and theme. "Who's that for?" Rayna Jo asked.

Adaline's face filled with color, and Rayna Jo felt her stomach clench in unease. "Is that for the man who came in last week? Dan or Dean—"

"As a matter of fact, it is. *Dale* has returned a time or two since and asked if I would handle his account personally."

"Oh, Adaline. Is that wise? He flirted awfully hard with you."

Adaline's color increased still more, and she lifted her perfectly manicured left hand and the wide gold band she wore. "He's well aware I'm married."

"That certainly didn't seem to stop him," Rayna Jo murmured, unable to keep the note of disapproval from her tone.

"Why should it? Flirting *means* nothing."

"Flirting eventually leads to more," Rayna Jo said. "Addy—"

"Don't Addy me. It's *fine*. You're overreacting and worrying about nothing. What's the harm in a few smiles and winks?"

"The harm is that you're a *married* woman, and he isn't your husband."

"So we've established. Ray-Ray, stop being so naive. It's totally innocent. Besides, I can't say as I mind getting a few compliments. Hugh's as flirtatious as a rock. *On the bottom of the ocean.* I don't know that he's even paid me a compliment these past *ten* years."

"Hugh is a gem," Rayna Jo argued. "Maybe he's not as outgoing and romantic as you'd like, but he's a good, solid man who worships the ground you walk on. Don't take that for granted."

Adaline pursed her lips and shot Rayna Jo a look from beneath her lashes. "I'm not."

"You *are*. You're playing with fire and think no one will get burned."

"I'm adding spice to a pot that hasn't simmered in a long, *long* time. Do you think Richard goes on all his business trips and *never* turns his head when a pretty woman walks by?"

No, she was sure her husband *did* turn his head. And a lot more. But it didn't make it right. Nor did it make the awareness of his actions and behavior hurt any less. "What's innocent to you might not be considered innocent to what's-his-name."

"*Dale*. And you worry entirely too much," Adaline said, pinning the last of the navy-and-white-striped fabric to the board. "There. What do you think?"

The board was as gorgeous as they always were when Adaline prepped them. She had a keen decorating eye and used fabrics and textures some might not think would work together.

The board she'd created made for a unique and fabulously understated nautical look well suited for a rich bachelor in a beach town. "When is his appointment?"

She'd hoped to get home early tonight because, unlike her sister, she *felt* her age. Plus, she liked to look her best when Richard returned from one of his trips, and if she could squeeze in a nap, the beauty sleep couldn't hurt.

"I'm meeting Dale at his house," Adaline said, avoiding Rayna Jo's gaze. "Speaking of which, I'd better get a move on or I'll be late."

"I'll come with you," Rayna Jo said. "We've been slow all day today. It wouldn't hurt to close up a bit early."

"No need," Adaline said, picking up the board after getting her purse from small storage area behind the cash register. "Go home. I'll see you tomorrow."

Rayna Jo watched as Adaline hurried out the door, heart heavy with the danger ahead for her sister. Maybe Addy could stay strong in the face of the client's flirting, but why take the risk? Why put herself in the position to teeter on a line that shouldn't be crossed? How would Hubert feel if he knew?

If Adaline was so unhappy with her marriage, why not go to counseling? Do whatever she could to get the spark back? Anything but seek attention elsewhere.

Rayna Jo left the check-out area and moved through the empty design and decor store, watching as Adaline loaded the board into the back of her Range Rover and shot out of the parking lot.

Adaline's comment about Richard's behavior on his business trips had struck a chord, and now she couldn't shake the dark thoughts or the pain Adaline had inadvertently caused.

She knew very well what took place while her husband was away. Every now and again, she'd see Richard's receipts. Dinner for two. Drinks. Charges from female clothing stores, lingerie stores that never ended up as gifts for her. Orders for flowers she didn't receive. Room service for two.

Funny how some men could be so charming and romantic before marriage, but afterwards, the only women they romanced were the ones who didn't wear their ring.

Her stomach knotted as it always did when she thought of her forty-two-year marriage.

By all accounts, she and Richard had it all. A big,

gorgeous house facing the Atlantic, two beautiful twin daughters, each successful in her own right. Nice cars. Great friends.

But peel back the layers, and for the last twenty years, it had all been a sham. She hated the deception of it. Hated that they played the part of the happy couple because... well, for her it was simply easier than facing the truth and starting over.

And for Richard, though they'd never truly discussed it, she believed he liked the convenience of having his cake and eating it, too. She was well aware that, for men like Richard, it was safer to have a wife. After all, it kept pesky mistresses in their place and the relationship between them exactly what it was —physical.

Still, it wasn't like she hadn't ever considered putting an end to the shenanigans. But then what? She was sixty-three. Her life almost over.

It was far too late to find her happily ever after.

Grab your copy of SEA GLASS AND SECOND CHANCES!

- BABY BE MINE
- SECOND CHANCE WEDDING
- THE GETAWAY GUY
- OFF-LIMITS LOVE
- FLIRTING WITH FOREVER

MAKE ME A MATCH SERIES:

- ROMANCE RESET
- RULES OF ENGAGEMENT
- THE MATCHMAKER'S SECRET
- PERFECTLY MISMATCHED
- BY THE BOOK

THE SEASIDE SISTERS SERIES:

- THE LAST GOODBYE
- LATTES AND LULLABYES
- MAP OF DREAMS
- WORTH THE RISK
- LOST LOVE FOUND

Want to read other books set in my fictional coastal town of Carolina Cove? Check out the excerpt of THE LAST GOODBYE:

Dominic Dunn hit his turn signal and waited for

a family of five to cross the sidewalk before he turned into the Carolina Cove Inn lot and parked, dread filling his stomach. Just the sight of the happy families and tourists wandering the sidewalks, lounging on restaurant patios, and enjoying the lively Saturday night left him angry. He should've ignored the letter. Ignored his next-door neighbor and best friend, ignored his boss and coworkers who said he had to honor Lisa's last request and come here.

"Mister? You gonna get out?"

The boy's voice startled Dominic and he turned to see a kid around eight years old watching him. The salt-air breeze blowing through the open windows of his car brought with it the smell of fried foods from the restaurants nearby, and seagulls squawked as they flew overhead.

"Mister?"

"Yeah," Dominic said, only then realizing he'd pulled into a parking place and was literally sitting there with his foot on the brake as he debated his choices of whether to throw the new car in reverse and floor it to get out of Carolina Cove as quickly as possible... or stay the prepaid two weeks Lisa had booked for him before her death.

"Doesn't look like it. Are you drunk?"

A rough-sounding chuckle left his chest. "Do you get a lot of drunk people here?"

"Sometimes."

"I see. Well, I'm not drunk. Just trying to decide if I want to stay here."

"Oh. You got a reservation?"

Did the kid ever stop asking questions? A memory formed, that of his son, Elijah, at the same age. "Yeah, I do."

"Then why don't you wanna stay?"

Dominic glanced at the clock and noted the time. If he left now, he'd add another six hours to his drive from Atlanta. Not how he wanted to spend what was left of the day. Maybe he should spend the night and head back to Atlanta first thing in the morning? "You've convinced me. I guess I will stay."

"I'll show you the way to the office."

"Do your parents know you're out here near the street? You're awfully young to be wandering about on your own."

The kid's shoulders squared and he lifted his chin to a defiant angle.

"I'm almost ten."

He looked younger, maybe because of his small stature. "Well, almost ten or not, there are a lot of strangers milling around, and it's not safe for kids these days. Are you visiting?" He sounded like an old man talking about "the good old days" but it was true. What kind of parent just let their kid wander the streets in a beach town full of people, some of whom probably waited on the opportunity to grab a kid and head out of town?

"No. I live here. You coming or not?"

The kid had spunk, Dominic had to give him that.

He rolled up the windows of the Porsche 911, killing the powerful engine with another press of a button. He felt a little conspicuous driving the flashy car, but he had to admit he loved the power. Just like Lisa knew he would.

He opened the door and climbed out of the low vehicle, yet another thing to get used to after driving a family-friendly SUV for so many years.

"Wow. You're tall. My mom is too. I hope I'm tall when I grow up."

Dominic locked the car and fell into step behind the boy. "I see the sign for the office. You can head home if you like."

"No. I need to check in anyway." The kid turned around and walked backward, rolling his eyes in classic kid fashion. "Or my mom will freak out and call the police again."

Again? "Does that happen a lot?"

"Her calling the police or freaking out?"

"Take your pick."

"Yeah."

Yeah to... both? Dom bit back another chuckle. Given the kid's intrepid personality, he probably kept his mom busy.

The kid flipped face-forward and Dom watched as the boy ran up the two steps leading to the office. He yanked open the door.

"Mom! Reservation!"

Dom noted the wide southern porch with its rocking chairs and a few chairs and tables before he followed the kid inside, well able to see why Lisa had liked the inn so much if the porch and office interior were anything by which to judge. It was her style of decorating. Beachy but understated.

The office walls were a soft gray with blue and sand-colored accents. There was a comfortable-looking couch and chair in the waiting area, a rope swing hanging from the ceiling in front of a painted mural of the beach and ocean behind, and on the opposite side, a coffee bar, popcorn machine, and snack area with a couple of parlor-type tables and chairs.

"Mom!"

"Samuel, how many times have I told you? No yelling. Inside voice," a woman stated as she appeared from a hallway behind the chest-high desk.

Dominic stilled, uncomfortable with the stomach-punching fact he found her beautiful. He'd guess her age to be early to mid-thirties, tall like her son said, at around five eight. Her auburn hair was scooped back and held at her nape, but curly tendrils framed her face and highlighted striking eyes that matched the blue of the ocean painting behind the check-in area.

"But, Mom, you have a reservation and sometimes don't hear me."

"A— Oh," she said, locking gazes with Dominic. "Sorry about that. Welcome to Carolina Cove Inn. I'm Ireland Cohen, the manager."

He forced himself to focus on her name rather than her beauty. "Ireland? Like the country?"

"Yes."

"Unusual name."

"Unusual family," she said by way of explanation. She flashed them both a smile. "I hope I didn't keep you waiting too long?"

"Not at all. Samuel kept me company."

"Mom, you should see his cool car! I'll bet it goes really fast. Does it?"

"It does."

"Maybe you'll take me for a ride sometime?"

"*Samuel.*"

"I'm leaving tomorrow."

"Oh."

"And even if he wasn't, Samuel, that's not something you ask our guests. We've talked about this, remember?" the boy's mother said while sliding her son a stern glare.

"Yes, ma'am."

Samuel glanced at Dominic and rolled his eyes, and yet again Dom found himself stifling a chuckle. And wondering at the last time he'd laughed so much in such a short span of time. "Tough break, kid."

"Let's get you checked in. Name?"

"Dominic Dunn."

"Domin—"

His name ended with a gasp and Ireland's eyes filled with tears. She blinked rapidly and managed to keep them from falling, but in that instant, he knew she recognized him—and knew his reason for being there.

CLICK THE LAST GOODBYE TO KEEP READING!

- SOMEONE TO TRUST

THE STONE RIVER SERIES:

- WORTH THE WAIT
- NOT BY SIGHT
- THROUGH THE VALLEY
- LEAD ME NOT
- CHRISTMAS AT HOLLY WOOD
- THEIR CHRISTMAS MIRACLE
- SECOND CHANCES

SMALL TOWN SCANDALS SERIES:

- BRODY'S REDEMPTION
- FALLING FOR HER BOSS
- WITH THIS MAN

SECRET SANTA SERIES:

- SECRET SANTA
- SECRET SANTA II: A CHRISTMAS
  TO REMEMBER

MAKE ME A MATCH SERIES:

- ROMANCE RESET

- RULES OF ENGAGEMENT
- THE MATCHMAKER'S SECRET
- PERFECTLY MISMATCHED
- BY THE BOOK

CAROLINA COVE SERIES:

- SEASCAPES AND VEGAS MISTAKES
- SEASHELLS AND WEDDING BELLS
- SEA GLASS AND SECOND CHANCES
- SEA BLUE AND LOVING YOU
- SEA VIEW AND SOMETHING NEW

COMING SOON: (LINKS WILL BE UPDATED ASAP)

THE BLACKWELL BROTHERS SERIES:

- BABY BE MINE
- SECOND CHANCE WEDDING
- THE GETAWAY GUY
- OFF-LIMITS LOVE
- FLIRTING WITH FOREVER

ABOUT THE AUTHOR

Kay Lyons always wanted to be a writer, ever since the age of seven or eight when she copied the pictures out of a Charlie Brown book and rewrote the story because she didn't like the plot. Through the years her stories have changed but one characteristic stayed true— they were all romances. Each and every one of her manuscripts included a love story.

Published in 2005 with Harlequin Enterprises, Kay's first release was a national bestseller. Kay has also been a HOLT Medallion, Book Buyers Best and RITA Award nominee. Look for her most recent novels with Kindred Spirits Publishing.

For more information regarding her work, please visit Kay at the following:

www.kaylyonsauthor.com

@KayLyonsAuthor (Twitter)

Kay Lyons Author (Facebook)

Author_Kay_Lyons (Instagram)

Kay Lyons, Author (Pinterest)

Romance Author Kay (TikTok)

FAQ ABOUT CAROLINA COVE:

Is Carolina Cove a real place?

Carolina Cove is purely fictional; however, it is **loosely** based on one of my favorite places—Kure Beach, North Carolina. Kure Beach is home to a wonderful pier, a pavilion for special events like weddings and birthdays, swings facing the Atlantic, pelicans Pete and George, coffee shops, restaurants, and more. It's also close to the North Carolina Aquarium, Carolina Beach, and Wilmington.

Can I stay at the Carolina Cove Inn?

While Carolina Cove and the Carolina Cove Inn are purely fictional, there are plenty of motels and rentals in the area to enjoy. One of my favorites is the Admirals Quarters. If you go, tell them Kay sent you! :)

The pier is real?

Yes! And it has quite a history. Be sure to check

out the Kure Beach Pier Cam for a view of Kure Beach and the Atlantic.

What about the restaurants and coffee shops and places you've mentioned in the series?

London's Lattes is based on two of my favorite local coffee shops in Kure Beach and Carolina Beach. Are there more? Yes, plenty. But those two shops I know well because I've visited fairly often while writing these stories. Neither of them on their own was perfect for what I had in mind for London's, however, so I basically combined the two and ta-da! London's Lattes was born. But, no, if you go into either of them, you won't find London's exact business. Isn't fiction wonderful?

Why make up a city? Why not use Kure Beach?

One of the best things about writing fiction is that when a story appears a certain way, you can write it just that way. Carolina Cove and the characters appeared to me in story form and while Kure Beach IS one of my favorite places, I had to change some things to better fit the series as well as steer far away from any real-life persons/families for obvious reasons. Doing so, that meant also changing the name of the city, etc. But, that said, you will find a slew of similarities in the fictional city and the real one. :)

Where is the dream catcher mailbox?

Unfortunately the dream catcher mailbox is pure fiction and an idea taken from a "beach mailbox" I visited once many years ago. The dream catcher mailbox first appeared in the SEASIDE SISTERS SERIES.

Update: I have been told a mailbox has been placed at the southern end of Ft. Fisher but I cannot confirm this.

How did you research the matchmaking aspect?

Oh, the answer to this was fun! Wilmington actually has a professional matchmaker. I interviewed her to get my details straight and learned a lot about a very fascinating business!

CAROLINA COVE SERIES:

- SEASCAPES AND VEGAS MISTAKES
- SEASHELLS AND WEDDING BELLS

- SEA GLASS AND SECOND CHANCES
- SEA BLUE AND LOVING YOU
- SEA VIEW AND SOMETHING NEW

COMING SOON: (LINKS WILL BE UPDATED ASAP)

THE BLACKWELL BROTHERS SERIES:

- BABY BE MINE
- SECOND CHANCE WEDDING
- THE GETAWAY GUY
- OFF-LIMITS LOVE
- FLIRTING WITH FOREVER

MAKE ME A MATCH SERIES:

- ROMANCE RESET
- RULES OF ENGAGEMENT
- THE MATCHMAKER'S SECRET
- PERFECTLY MISMATCHED
- BY THE BOOK

THE SEASIDE SISTERS SERIES:

- THE LAST GOODBYE
- LATTES AND LULLABYES
- MAP OF DREAMS
- WORTH THE RISK
- LOST LOVE FOUND